PENGUIN BOOKS

OTHER HALVES

Sue McCauley is well known in New Zealand as a writer and jounalist. She lives at Okaihau in Northland and writes a regular column for the *New Zealand Listener*. *Other Halves*, her first novel is autobiographical. She is at work on a second novel.

OTHER HALVES

Sue McCauley

PENGUIN BOOKS

PENGUIN BOOKS

Viking Penguin Inc., 40 West 23rd Street,
New York, New York 10010, U.S.A.
Penguin Books Ltd, Harmondsworth,
Middlesex, England
Penguin Books Australia Ltd, Ringwood,
Victoria, Australia
Penguin Books Canada Limited, 2801 John Street,
Markham, Ontario, Canada L3R 1B4
Penguin Books (N.Z.) Ltd, 182–190 Wairau Road,
Auckland 10, New Zealand

First published in New Zealand by Hodder and Stoughton Ltd 1982
Published in Penguin Books 1985

LIBRARY OF CONGRESS CATALOGING IN PUBLICATION DATA
McCauley, Sue.
Other halves.
I. Title.
PR9639.3.M34O8   1985   823   84-26625
ISBN 0 14 00.7686 7

The author wishes to thank the New Zealand Literary Fund for the grant that
assisted her in writing this novel.

Printed in the United States of America by
R. R. Donnelley & Sons Company, Harrisonburg, Virginia
Set in Times Roman

To Pat

OTHER HALVES

ONE

THE PHONE RANG for a long time. She had that chance to reconsider but she continued to stand there with the receiver pressed against her ear. In the kitchen Michael was kneeling on a chair, head bent over a comic book. She could see him through the open door, the hunch of his back, the fingers of one hand twisted in his brown hair. It was eight-thirty. The electric clock in the living room gave a loud and nervous jump, as it always did, over the half-hour. The miniature pink roses in the vase on the TV set were haggard and wilting. Two petals fell away together but landed apart on the floral carpet. The ringing stopped.

'Valleyview.' A man's voice, slightly short of breath. 'Are you there?'

'Yes,' said Liz, trying to shape the voice into a person and seeing, for no apparent reason, the local chemist. 'Yes. I'm ringing to find out...' It seemed almost too hard to explain. The words were knotted together with no loose end to begin to unravel from.

'To find out...?' The man prompted.

'I wondered,' Liz said in a rush, 'how people get to you. I mean... if someone wanted to....'

'To visit?'

'No. I meant....'

'You would like to be admitted?' The word had a frightening ring of finality.

'I just wondered... if the situation....'

1

'Do you drive?'

'I don't often have access to a vehicle.'

'You could just take a taxi,' he said. 'Put it this way — if you get yourself here you won't be turned away.'

'Oh.' But she felt strengthened. Her voice took on a crisp, discriminating-consumer tone. 'Well thank you. Thank you very much.'

She heard his voice saying something else as she put down the receiver. Such a kindly, concerned voice. She preferred him to the Lifeline people, but did not know why. She had never talked to the Lifeline people, she just rang them sometimes at night when the waiting got unendurable. She would let them answer and say their piece, then hang up quietly, reassured to know they were still there.

She went back to the kitchen. The Beagle Boys peered back at her over Michael's shoulder. Their colour was out of register. Liz remembered having a 3D comic that looked the same, unless you used the spectacles with red and green lenses.

'Like a cup of milo?'

'All right.' He didn't look up.

She poured milk into a saucepan and set it on the stove. If they had gas it would be so much quicker. If they had gas....

I can last till ten-thirty, she thought. Ten-thirty isn't really late. If I can sleep tonight, have one night's proper sleep, things will seem different. If I could just go to bed and sleep and get up and make breakfast and carry on as if this were a real life.

A tear slid down her cheek, she waited for it to reach the edge. Sometimes they dripped off and sometimes they negotiated the slope down her neck. She supposed it was a matter of volume. This one stayed with the skin. She didn't bother to wipe her eyes. Brimming had become their normal condition; Michael no longer appeared to notice. She thought some day he would remember her as a woman with wet red eyes.

'Can I stay up to watch *Mannix*? It was real good last time. They were shooting at him out of this helicopter.'

'It's on so late,' she protested half-heartedly.

'You said I could. You promised.'

'Did I?' Perhaps she had? In any case she knew she would agree, she felt too fragile for a battle. She told herself that his presence was at least a diversion.

'Can I?'

'I suppose so.' She set their drinks on the table.

'They were machine-gunning him and he was on this beach so he couldn't get cover. Looked like he'd had it. They were going Brrratatatatatatatata....'

'All right!' she screamed. 'That's enough!'

She couldn't endure him AND *Mannix,* it was asking too much. She felt the terrible rage that seemed to have settled within her just below the surface. Michael had gone very still, his face was expressionless, just watching, his eyes slightly squinted as if he were gazing from a long distance. The anger subsided and she felt abject with contrition. She got up and needlessly wiped the bench.

'How would you like to stay at Jamie's tonight?' she asked in a bright careful voice, watching Michael's reflection in the window glass.

'Why?' Instant suspicion.

'I just thought I might go out.'

'What for?'

'To see someone.'

'Who?'

'No one you know. Shall I ring and see if it's all right for you to stay there?'

'Will I be allowed to watch *Mannix*?'

'I don't know. You can tell Jamie all about the helicopter last time.'

'I've already told him that.'

'*Please,*' she begged, looking at him now and seeing that the desperation in her voice frightened him. He nodded, his eyes anxious.

She dialled the number thinking, even if I just go for a walk — yes, that's probably all I'll do.

Glenda answered and Liz put on her wry motherhood voice. 'Look, I feel really bad to spring this on you at this time of night, but do you think you could possibly have Michael for the night? Something a bit urgent's come up and Ken's out on a call somewhere, so I thought maybe....'

3

There was just the slightest hesitation. 'Of course,' said Glenda.

'I don't think you will be able to watch *Mannix*,' she told him, stuffing his pyjamas into a plastic shopping bag. 'They send their kids to bed early. They were probably in bed long ago.'

'I don't really want to go,' he said.

'Please?' She dropped to her knees in front of him and wrapped her arms round his waist. 'Please, love, for me?' The tears were coming again. Michael looked down at her in silence, his arms stuck out awkwardly, and did not return her embrace. She thought she saw in his face — in his embarrassed, reproachful glance — a reflection of Ken.

Walking up the street past the three neat street-lit gardens, the curtained windows, the concrete paths and tidy carports that separated the Harvey household from the Woollam household, Liz invented reasons and destinations. They were sure to ask. The Woollam household was not the kind that suffered unforeseen circumstances.

Glenda opened the door when they had barely reached the steps. 'That was quick,' she said. 'Hello Michael.'

Michael mumbled and headed for the living room.

'Hello Liz,' called Walter. 'How's things?'

She went to stand at the doorway and smile at him and nod. She found the exchanging of greetings an awkward and rather absurd business.

Jamie and Neville, scrubbed pink and wearing pyjamas and dressing gowns, were playing Battleships over the coffee table. Walter Woollam lay back in an easy chair, feet propped up, drink in hand. Diffuse wall lighting, and the harsh glare of the television. Liz watched wistfully; it looked so cosy, so normal, so enviable.

'I hope you don't mind,' she apologised in Glenda's direction.

'The boys are delighted,' said Glenda. 'It was an excuse to delay bed a little longer.' Glenda wore lipstick, freshly applied, and shoes with heels.

Walter heaved himself out of his chair and came through to the kitchen. 'You'll have a drink, Liz?'

'No thanks. I'm sort of in a hurry.'

4

'Where are you off to, then?'

She had it ready. 'The airport. A friend just called. She's been overseas for years. On her way to Auckland. Apparently there was some delay. She's waiting for the flight, so I thought I'd really like to go out and see her.'

'I didn't know there were flights this late. Where's she come from?'

'I'm not sure. She travels all around.'

'And Ken's out? Suppose he'll be sorry he missed her.'

'Oh, he didn't know her very well.'

'But how will you get there?' Glenda hovered above them. In her heels she was taller than her husband. Liz came only to her shoulder.

'I've ordered a cab from our place.'

'But Walter could take you, couldn't you dear?'

'It's all right. Really. The taxi'll be coming.'

'You can cancel it,' said Walter. 'That's easy.'

'No,' she said. 'Truly. I've bothered you enough, and I have to get tidied up and everything.' She edged for the door. 'I shouldn't be late.' From the steps she called, 'Goodnight, Michael,' and knew it would be drowned out by the television.

'Enjoy yourself,' said Walter.

'Yes. Goodnight, and thank you.' She felt the relief of escape, restraining an urge to run. Her invention took shape in her mind; she imagined it was Kathy at the airport, elegant and bored. Kathy shaking her head in exaggerated amazement, 'It's really you. After all these years!' The picture seemed entirely plausible.

'Hundred and fifty Maling,' said the operator. 'Right. And where are you going to, love?'

'The airport,' said Liz.

'What time's your flight?'

'It isn't. I'm just going to see someone.'

'Be about ten minutes then love.'

'Thank you.'

Sometimes she could sound just as capable as Glenda.

It didn't come. Ten minutes, twenty-five minutes and it still hadn't come. She watched from her windows in the dark,

5

afraid Ken would arrive before the cab, afraid she would change her mind, and afraid she wouldn't. She tried to picture the hospital waiting-room. She was standing in a queue and up ahead a woman in nurse's uniform was examining tickets and putting labels on luggage. Luggage. Should she take things? What things? A nightdress?

But they were bound to turn her away. They would see at once that she was a fraud, that she was the wrong kind and that her problems were insubstantial. She had no ticket.

She made her way in the dark to the bathroom and there flooded the room with the dazzling glow of electric light. From the medicine cupboard she took and unwrapped a fresh razor blade. Part of her mind was sardonic, whispering 'melodrama'. She grasped the blade tightly, extended her left wrist and slashed at it.

She wasn't prepared for the pain. Yet when she examined her wrist she saw the cut went barely below the surface. As she watched a trickle of blood began to flow, but only a trickle. I'd die of boredom, she thought, before I'd die of loss of blood.

Outside the taxi tooted. Efficiently Liz selected two large band-aids from the cupboard, switched off the light and gathered her shoulder bag from the floor.

'Where to, love?' he asked.

'Valleyview hospital,' she said, wondering if the operator had told him otherwise. In the privacy of the back seat she pulled the band-aids from their wrapping and carefully affixed one to each of her wrists. Then she licked along her left arm, above the wrist. It had the bland warm flavour of blood.

The driver made conversation about the weather. Yes, Liz agreed politely. Yes the nights had got much cooler.

She wanted him to feel reassured that she wasn't dangerous.

But perhaps he thought she was a nurse. Or a cleaner. He would probably think she was a nurse. She watched the parade of suburban houses and thought, I can ask him to wait and just pretend to go in.

'Which section is it you want?'

They were turning into a driveway. Liz peered ahead over

his shoulder. There was a long low building, modern, all glass and insubstantial.

'I'm not sure,' she said.

'Better ask here then.' He pulled up beside the concrete steps. 'Just ring the bell on your right.'

'Thank you.' She gave him a five dollar note and he counted out the change.

'Cheerio,' he said.

She wished she had asked him to wait.

A man let her in. He was wearing day clothes and slippers. 'You can wait in there,' he said, pointing. 'Someone'll be along soon.' He scratched his chest and kept looking at her.

'Thank you,' she said and went into the room and sat away from the door out of his sight.

The chairs had seats of sponge rubber covered with a knobbly synthetic material in a colour called Old Gold. At home Liz had Old Gold curtains in the living room. Old Gold in a Regency stripe. She could remember going into the shop and choosing them, the pleasure of planning and sewing and hanging. Making a home, she had thought.

After a long time a man came in. He looked younger than Liz, like a student or something.

'Can I help you? he said, like the people on Lifeline.

'I rang up before,' she told him, 'and someone said if I came in....'

He pulled a chair out and sat down facing her.

'What's the problem?'

There was nowhere to begin. She felt the pressure of tears ready to flow.

'What's your name?' He was very kind.

'Elizabeth,' she said. 'Elizabeth Nicholson.'

'How old are you Elizabeth?'

'Thirty-three.'

'And you're married? You have a family?'

He was going to send her home. 'I live alone,' she told him, looking past him. 'They said when I rang that I wouldn't be sent away.'

'All right,' he said. 'We'll find you a bed. We can talk some more in the morning.'

Ken would be home by now and she hadn't left a note. He

would think she had taken Michael and run away.

They found her out of course.

'Elizabeth Harvey? You are Elizabeth Harvey?'

Liz lay looking up at this woman with the white coat.

'Well, Elizabeth, I thought we might have a talk.'

She waited. 'I'm Judith Morehouse. Sister Morehouse.'

Anything you say may be taken down and used against you.

Liz said nothing.

Judith Morehouse propped her bottom nonchalantly against the smooth cover of the other bed and sighed. 'Your husband will be coming in,' she said. 'We had to contact him of course. Your clothes are in the locker, but we've handed your purse and Post Office book and so forth in at the office for safe keeping. All right?'

Liz nodded. Her silence was beginning to feel safe and not a wilfully wicked act. In the night she had dreamt a familiar dream and fragments of it were still in her head. Souvenirs. In the dream she was kneeling on the living-room carpet cutting out a child's dress — yellow cotton and white chains of daisies. And he was beside her. She knew him from other dreams, though the features always escaped her. Yet dreaming she thought — she seemed to remember thinking — yes, this is the one I know from those other dreams. And she had looked up slowly from the yellow daisies, feeling fluid and full of longing, delaying the moment when their eyes would meet, yet knowing from past dreams that his eyes would be reflections of her own. Longings and promises.

She struggled to recall more. Nursing the fragments. Fondling them. Knowing the comfort it would give her to return to them. Thinking, he will come back, there will be other nights.

Judith Morehouse looked at her watch.

'Perhaps you'd like to get up,' she said. 'Do you know it's nearly lunchtime? We like everyone up for lunch.'

8

TWO

THERE HAD BEEN introductions, names had been fumbled and dropped, two hands had been proffered — one dry and rough as bark, one soft and limp. Liz had returned nods and vague smiles. She was just a visitor. Later they would give her a growling at, then Ken would come and take her home.

In the night someone must have removed the band-aids and exposed one scratched left wrist and one unscathed right wrist. And thought, imposter.

She was third in the queue at the cafeteria. Salad and luncheon sausage, bread and butter. She didn't feel hungry, but she would try. Occasionally she had taken the children to lunch on the third floor of Farmers and bought them cream horns and raspberry soft drink. She would look at the other mothers admonishing, pleading, grabbing the chance of a fag and a feet-up, and wonder if they too felt sullen inside their smiles.

She chose an empty table in the corner and watched the room fill. Funny how many of them you wouldn't have thought.... Some of them of course it was obvious. They seemed to flow — a slow dance. That was the pills, surely. She too flowed, having swallowed, dutifully, the two white buttons shaken out for her by the nurse in the corridor with the trolley that clattered and tinkled its approach. A Mr Whippy of the ward, measuring out ice-creams for the mind.

'She's taken your chair, Harold.'

The woman held her tray well out in front of her and looked upset. Her mouth furrowed in the middle, matching her eyebrows.

'I shall relinquish it,' said her companion, setting his tray on Liz's table, bobbing his head and smiling and pulling out the chair nearest to Liz. The woman seated herself across from them, watching the man.

'Your first ride on the merry-go-round?' He was looking at Liz. She smiled cautiously and nodded. He was a small man, dapper; his mouth ajar now in expectation.

'Is it? Your first ride on this merry-go-round?'

Liz looked down at her plate and sliced off a neat triangle of sausage.

The woman leaned towards her.

'Cat got your tongue? Cat got your tongue?'

Liz opened her mouth and stretched out her tongue. She curled the tip upwards, then down. The woman laughed and clapped. The man laughed too, patting Liz's shoulder. Liz began to grin, she felt at ease, and light-headed. She looked around the room still with a smile. Against the far wall a boy sat with his hands gripped on the edges of his plate. He was looking at Liz and for a few seconds their eyes met, then she saw his mouth curl into a sneer and he looked away.

She felt so foolish. Resentful, too. Unwarranted, she thought, it had been so entirely unwarranted. But then she kept furtively glancing back at him feeling there was some puzzle there — a difference. Because he was brown-skinned? But there was — yes — one other brown-skinned patient at a centre table. Another standing beside the door. The boy was eating now with fierce concentration, his head close to the plate, face curtained by heavy black hair.

He was young. That was the difference. He was young and all the others, herself included, were varying degrees of old. Time had tarnished them, but this one was little more than a child. Imagine Michael....

Ken felt her silence to be an act of provocation. 'I can't imagine what you think you'll achieve by it,' he lectured. 'I suppose you want me on the defensive. Well, I don't really know what I'm supposed to think. Frankly I don't see a great deal of point in coming out here to talk to myself.'

Liz sat on the end of her bed picking loose threads from the bed cover, puckering then smoothing the fabric. Ken leant against the window sill. She conducted a conversation of her own. Isn't the garden nice? Yes. Look at that silver beet. Exactly. I don't know how he does it. All the work I put into mine when you're out seeing patients. Patients? Isn't it a laugh the way we pretend? But did you notice the spinach? That rich sunset-hour green? I grew spinach last year, do you remember? Maybe you noticed it that time when we had the barbecue in the back garden and that American couple you knew.... That young woman with the bangles on her leg — you know the one — she walked all over my carrots. Of course it was dark, but. But growing things seems to be the only thing I do that's real any more.

'I told Michael you were in hospital — that you'd had a little accident. I do think you could have *prepared* him for something. Glenda's been great about it all. You really don't have anything to worry about. I don't know about bringing him here, though. We'll just wait and see how things go, I suppose. Anyway when you get around to talking again.... I brought you some clothes — I don't know how long you expect to stay here.... I'll come out again on Saturday.'

She wondered when Saturday would be, and what day it was now. How long had she been in hospital? Her mind was listless and opaque, it baulked at calculations.

They brought her Audrey as a room-mate. Audrey arrived in bare feet and a cotton dress torn under the arm. She smelt of patchouli oil and incense and the dress she wore was the kind of washed-out anonymous garment that might be worn, woefully, by a retarded girl in a sheltered workshop or, magnificently, by Sophia Loren posing as a poor Sicilian peasant. Audrey wore it the Sophia Loren way. She had tanned skin and a full, firm body. She was nineteen years old and her face, beneath the tan, was pitted with acne scars but Liz watched her with envy and thought her exotic and beautiful.

Audrey carried her possessions in a pillow case over her shoulder, and when the nurse had left she tipped the contents onto the floor. A jersey, a pair of jeans, a large stretch of unhemmed material, a few toiletries, a couple of magazines and a pair of black, strappy high heeled shoes.

'Don't mind me,' Audrey said to Liz. 'We're all out of our trees here anyway.' She began to shove her things into the locker. 'They told me you're not into talking. Well, that's okay, I can take it or leave it. I tend to talk quite a bit myself so I hope you don't mind if I sometimes do the talking for both of us.'

She rummaged in the new confusion of the locker for a bottle of baby oil and bounced herself onto the bed. 'I dunno how the fuck I'm gonna manage here. It's not really what you'd call my chosen environment.' She lay back on the pillow and hitched her dress up around her thighs. She wore no knickers. Liz looked away in embarrassment.

Audrey sat up and squirted oil onto her feet, massaging affectionately around her toes. 'I hope they put me on something strong 'cos I'm on withdrawal. These bastards never understand withdrawal.' She progressed to her calves. 'I haven't shaved my legs for two years but I reckon I might start again. When I get somewhere civilised where they have razors. I've been in one of these places before so I know what to expect more or less. My mother put me in one when I was fourteen 'cos I was screwing her husband. Like he wasn't my father or anything sordid like that, but she couldn't hack it, so she had me put away. Hey, you gotta husband or anything?'

Liz nodded. Changed her mind. 'I had one,' she said. Her voice sounded strange and raspy.

'There you are,' said Audrey, as if they had just, together, proved some profound theory. She oiled right up to her groin, lay back and began to massage between her legs. Her eyes were closed. 'What's group therapy like here?'

Liz, having looked back, returned to studying the ceiling. There was a stain like five long taloned fingers; a witch's hand. 'I haven't been yet,' she said in her husky voice.

'No point if you weren't talking. Hope they send me. I really get off on group therapy.'

At Ken's suggestion they sat outside on the wooden bench by

the oak trees. The sky was heavy with threats of a thunderstorm.

'I don't know if you want me to visit,' he complained. 'It seemed rather odd to come all this way just to talk to myself.'

Liz twisted her hands in her lap and wondered at the wrinkles. When had her hands grown so old? How had she never noticed?

'I didn't bring Michael,' said Ken. 'I don't really think he could handle this place. Unless, of course, it's really important to you that he comes. Glenda's being great about having him when I'm not home. I tell you this in case you worry about him, but how am I to know? I've talked to the doctor. He thinks it's all tied up with Nessa — which wouldn't take too much figuring. If you remember, I said at the time you should go for therapy.'

'I don't know how the doctor would know,' said Liz. 'He hasn't even seen me yet.'

'They didn't tell me you were talking,' he accused. 'So what was the silence for?'

'Perhaps I usually talk too much. I thought, maybe, if we could sit together and just hold hands....' She heard herself sounding silly and plaintive. Ken grimaced slightly but reached for her hand, her wrinkled hand, and held it. Limply.

'I'm trying to understand,' he said after a time. 'But you have to accept, Liz, that it's something that's been coming on for years.'

'Ought we get divorced then?'

'A separation? If that's what you want....' He tightened his hand around hers with something like tenderness, or relief.

That night Liz wept convulsively, rocking in her bed. After a time Audrey came to her and attempted to comfort her but Liz writhed and shuddered out of Audrey's arms. Finally Audrey went for a nurse and watched as a needle was plunged into Liz's arm.

'Lucky cow,' said Audrey.

'He still hasn't told us why he's in here.' The woman was staring at the Maori boy, staring and smiling a little.

The group turned its attention, nodding and murmuring.

13

Liz could imagine them in scarlet hunting jackets, blowing horns, pointing, redirecting their horses.

'Yes, Tug. Come on. You just sit there, doesn't he?'

'I don't have to tell yous,' said Tug. He smiled contemptuously. 'I'm just here for a holiday.'

'Come on,' said a fat young man. 'You can't get away with that.'

Tug hunched further into his chair. His dark eyes flickered around the faces. Liz had seen the same look on mice she had unwittingly disturbed in kitchen cupboards.

'He never tells us anything,' said the woman. 'How many groups has he been to and he hasn't told us anything.'

Tug clenched his fists and pushed them together. 'I been listening, though,' he said finally. 'I been listening and yous all make me sick the way you go on and on 'bout your problems. Problems? You don't know what you're on about, none of yous.'

'Tell us, then. Tell us yours.'

'What makes you think you're so different?'

'You youngsters, you think....'

'Go on, Tug.'

He stood up, pushing the chair so it toppled backwards, blazing with anger. 'Fuck yous. Fuck the lot of yous.' And he walked away from them in great swaggering strides.

That evening as Liz played patience in the otherwise deserted sun-room Tug wandered past, still sneering, and paused in the doorway. She felt him watching.

'Would you like a game of something?'

He shrugged and continued to stand there. She went back to her game, aware of him still.

'Seven on the eight,' he said finally. Liz moved the cards and tried again.

'Sure you don't want a game?'

'What? Poker?'

'If you like. But you'll have to show me. I haven't played poker for years.'

It was the first of a great number of poker games. And two-handed five hundred, and two-handed patience and, later, when they discovered the games cupboard, monopoly, checkers, draughts and chess. Sometimes Liz would suggest they invite others to join their games, but Tug objected, and on occasions when other patients asked to join them in a way that was difficult to refuse, Tug would abandon the game and go off on his own, glowering.

At first they didn't talk much, but all the time Liz would be aware of him watching her from beneath his long, half-lowered lashes. At meal times too she would notice him watching her from across the room, furtively. It warmed her, such attention.

When their talking began it was with Tug's questions. What was her home like? Had she travelled overseas? Had she ever taken acid? Dope? Speed? What was it like to have a baby? Could she knit? Play pool? Read music? Stand on her head?

And the other questions which Liz found both sad and endearing. Is he the Prime Minister? Is he a good man or a bad man? Who was Rumpelstiltskin? Tell me the story about him.

How come, Liz wanted to know, he'd never learnt such things? He shrugged. 'I'm dumb.'

But at school, she persisted. What had they taught him at school?

'I sat at the back of the dummies' class. I guess they tried to teach me but I was just real dumb. Mostly I just sat and looked at the teachers' legs. The young ones anyway. They kept me back. I was so dumb. I was fourteen and still in standard five with all the little kids.'

She imagined him sitting there, large, withdrawn and conspicuously brown in the far corner of the classroom cultivating contempt. 'How old are you now?'

'Sixteen.'

'Can you speak Maori?'

'Of course.'

'Teach me some.'

'Okay.' His eyes laughing at her. 'Ay boy, you want some kai, ay fulla? Plenty pork 'n' puha, and pipis and toheroas ay.'

Liz laughed. It was the first time in weeks she had laughed. 'Not that kind.'

'Mimi.'

'What's that then?'

'Piss.'

'Okay. What else?'

'That's all. Don't know any more. Used to, but I forget.'

His questions, once they began, were endless. Over poker hands and chessboards Liz, prompted by the questions, told him the things she couldn't tell the therapy group. About the hours after midnight spent waiting, sleepless, by the bedroom window, chainsmoking, switching the transistor from station to station, drinking when there was anything left to drink. Waiting. Compiling again in her head the details of her departure, inventing brave new starts, ultimate retorts and justifications.

She described for him her parents, the horse she had owned, her dog (long dead), Ken, Michael, and even Nessa. My daughter, she said. A little plump girl, always happy. She was three years old. At three o'clock in the afternoon in the parking lot of our local supermarket a car ran over her. She ran out from behind another car and fell in front of a back wheel. The driver didn't even see her. When I picked her up I thought at first she was all right. Her eyes were open, looking at me. Then blood began to run out of the corner of her mouth.

Tug reached across the chessboard and held Liz's hand.

'Is Tug your real name?'

'Thomas.' Pulling a face.

'Why are you called Tug?'

'It's better than boy.'

'That's not a reason.'

'Don't think there was a reason. We all got names like that, not our real ones. I got a sister called Tiny and one called Missy. A brother called Blacky.'

'Is that all of you?'

'How d'you mean, all of us?'

'All your brothers and sisters?'

'Hell no. Well, I don't think so.'

'You must know.'

'I do and I don't. There was a lot of coming and going.'

'Do they know you're in here?'

'Who?'

'Jesus, Tug! Your family. Your brothers and sisters.'

'Don't suppose so. They got their own troubles anyway. Why go visit your brother in a nut-house?'

'There's a girl comes to visit you.'

'You seen her? That's Karen. She's my missus. You reckon she's spunky? She's got a motorbike. Three-sixty. Dhrooom.' He revved up and turned a corner. She let him go. Although she tried to return his questions, his answers only confused. He had lived in that house with those cousins, then another house with some other cousins — well, maybe they were cousins — and for a while with his half-brother and his wife — at least he thought Eruera was his half-brother, but he could have been....

'Do you remember your mother?'

'Sometimes I do. Sometimes I think I do.'

'What was she like?'

'I don't remember.'

'And your father?'

'He went away. Overseas. They said he died. Maybe he didn't. Do you think he could be still alive?'

'Tug. How would I know? Do you ever go and see them?'

'Who?'

'The aunts and uncles and things you lived with.'

'Why should I?'

Sometimes he'd relate to her incidents from his past. The time he set fire to a hay barn while having a surreptitious cigarette. The Children's Home where he went with Tiny. They had corned beef for dinner often. It was near a beach. They had those wooden jigsaw puzzles. And at bath-time two of the nurses argued over who would bath Tug, though he was big enough to bath himself.

'How old were you then?' she wanted to build stepping stones, orderly and chronological, into the disorder of his past.

'Dunno. Seven maybe? Coulda been ten even.'

'Why were you sent there? Who were you living with then?'

'Hell, I dunno.'

'How old were you when your mother died?'

'I can't remember. Five, coulda been. Or four. I think she was a bit like you.'

'How?'

'I don't remember her much. It's just a feeling.'

'Why are you in here, Tug?'

''Cos I'm nuts of course. I pull these spastic faces and at night when you don't see me I dribble at the mouth and rip up the sheets.'

'The people in the group have all sorts of theories.'

'What's theories?'

'Ideas — on why you're here.'

'They would. They're a lot of boring old farts. Bet they think I done something real filthy. Bet they think that?'

'That's why I want to know. I think you've done something filthy and exciting.'

'I was sent here, that's all. By the judge. There mighta been other reasons too but I'll tell you those some time when I work them out. Reckon the main thing is to get you sorted out. Find you a man, eh? How about that funky old Jimmy with the warts and the dribbledy nose?'

'I see you've got yourself a new child?' Judith Morehouse tipped the evening pills, one round yellow, one long white, into Liz's palm.

'Is that against the rules, then?'

'Not at all. It's called self-help. You're looking for a child-substitute, he's looking for a mother-substitute. That's fine, except....'

'Yes?'

'You must remember this is just play school. Things are a lot different in the real world.'

THREE

AUDREY HAD FOUND herself a man in the alcoholics' wing, but he was about to be discharged and go home to his wife and four children.

'I couldn't hack it much longer anyway,' she told Liz. 'He's always scared we're gonna be seen, so we don't get to do much more than just feeling each other up. We've been waiting for the bloody weather to clear up so we could go in under those big trees by the old building.'

Ken brought Michael to visit. Michael gave Liz a drawing of a 'plane with pencil lines shooting from the wings. It had 'To Mum' written on the top right-hand corner.

'It's a fighter bomber,' he said. He seemed nervous and stood behind Ken's chair chewing on a piece of knotted rope he'd brought in his pocket. When she talked to him he answered politely as if she were a stranger, glancing at Ken from time to time for support.

Ken gave Liz a bag of oranges and wondered if she felt up to discussing the details of their separation. Michael being, of course, the crucial detail. Ken hoped that things would never reach the sorry situation where the two of them were battling to prove who was the most fitted for the parental role, but in such an event he felt he might have some slight advantage. He was of the opinion that Michael was old enough to choose, and should do so. What did Liz think?

Liz felt the kind of dimly disappointing inevitability that came with picking up a lousy hand of cards. She supposed...

if Ken thought so....

Ken recalled Michael's attention which was fixed on a patient in the far corner of the Day Room who was sitting, eyes closed, and spasmodically jerking his whole body.

'We want you to take your time,' Ken said. 'And if you really don't feel you *can* choose just tell us. It's up to you mate.'

Michael stood, looking at each of them in turn, pulling at a lock of hair and smiling unhappily. 'I guess, Daddy,' he said finally.

'I would've chosen you,' Tug consoled her later. 'How could he be so dumb? I seen you all sitting there together. I thought your husband looked a bit dicky if you ask me.'

'Why would I ask you?' she said, handing him an orange.

Tug's girlfriend, Karen, had dropped him. She used to come and visit him two or three times a week on her big Kawasaki motorbike that she'd bought with money her grandmother left her. When she hadn't come for a few days Tug had rung her home and talked to Karen's friend, Suzanne. Suzanne told Tug that Karen was finished with him and was now going around with Donny Walker.

'Never mind,' offered Liz. 'Donny Walker's probably dicky too.'

'Fuck, no,' said Tug. 'He's one of them Grim Reapers.' He threw the orange, unpeeled, at the fluorescent light tube above them, but missed. 'Cunt's got a bike of his own already.'

'Maybe it's Karen he wants.'

'Spare us,' he said. 'Have you seen her?'

Glenda came to visit Liz on a drizzling afternoon. 'I would've come before but I didn't want to, you know, intrude or anything.'

She was wearing red trousers with creases down the front and a red and white sweater. Her hair was smooth and shiny. She looked like the cover photo of a knitting pattern or a soap packet.

'Your garden's looking good,' she said. 'Much better than mine. You seem to have a knack. Everything's under control, you know; you've got nothing to worry about. Ken's managing really well with the house and Michael and all. Michael was a bit, well, quiet at first, but he's his old self now. He and Jamie have been building this tree hut in our big oak tree. Looks more like a bird's nest so far but it keeps them out of mischief.' Looking down at her hands, the nails painted red too, but not quite the same shade as the trousers. 'You're looking pretty good, actually, Liz. All things considered. Guess they'll be sending you home soon?'

'Home? Didn't he tell you he's getting a divorce?'

'Well....' Meaning yes, but.

'Glenda, he hasn't got that Valerie staying in our house, has he?'

'Well, not that I know of.' Cautious.

'Glenda, I thought you were my friend.'

'Of course I am. But it's difficult. Well, you know.... I feel I'm Ken's friend too. I want to stay friends with you both.'

'Don't tell me he's into you too. What would Walter say?' Liz wasn't sure for a second whether she had said it out loud. It wasn't the kind of thing she was used to saying. Glenda's lips snapped together in a tight line, but she gave a small forgiving laugh through her nose.

'I brought you some scented soap,' she said. 'It's difficult to know what your needs are in here, but soap you can always use.'

When Glenda had gone Liz went upstairs to her room feeling a weariness that began in her bones and stumbled along her arteries. The door was closed. She pushed it open and was inside the room before she saw that Audrey and Tug were together in Audrey's bed. She began to back out of the room.

'It's okay,' said Audrey in a honey-smooth voice. 'We've finished now. You don't have to run off.'

Liz went back into the room. Tug lay on the far side, his head turned towards the wall. She lay down on her own bed, not looking at them. None of her business. But she felt stirrings of resentment. I thought he was *my* friend. And astonishment.

'What if someone had come in?' she asked the ceiling.

'They would have caught us at it.' Audrey lit a cigarette. Smoking in bedrooms was forbidden. Smoking in bed was a mortal sin. Audrey's temerity was boundless. Tug, arched under the bedclothes was pulling on his jeans; Liz knew it in the corner of her eye. He climbed down over the end of the bed and swaggered to the door, his self-conscious swagger.

'See y'later,' he said in Liz's direction, but not looking.

'Okay.' Her voice was unnaturally cheery, positively Brown Owl jolly. So he's still my friend she thought with a kind of triumph.

'Chuck me that towel, will you?' said Audrey. 'I'm dribbling everywhere.'

Liz was now having regular sessions with Dr Wray. He was an over-weight, sad-faced man with a ginger beard. An outdoor man trapped in an office and a viyella shirt. He had a mistress in occupational therapy. The whole world knew because Mrs Wray had one day arrived shouting, accusing and blowing her nose. That had been months before but the grapevine swayed and nudged and chattered, keeping the past alive. Liz had a feeling that Dr Wray adapted to his own circumstances all that she told him. Looking for explanations; or perhaps absolution.

'I would have got over Nessa's dying,' she told him. 'It had happened. It was over. Nothing could be changed. But Ken — that was different. That went on and on and when I tried to talk to him it was like talking at a sponge.'

A pause. Waiting for encouragement, approval, something. Dr Wray sitting there sadly engrossed in his blotter. His head moves. It could be a nod.

'I thought it was a deliberate campaign to drive me mad. I suppose that seems silly and melodramatic but sometimes that's how it seemed. I thought even when he was at work he was getting at me by telepathy or something. He would say he couldn't have an honest discussion with me because I'd react in an over-emotional way. He said silence was his way of protecting me, but I was desperate to know the truth. Sometimes when Michael was at school I'd go and spy on Ken. I'd hang around the doorway of the commercial stationery shop and watch who went into his office and how long they stayed. But it didn't prove anything because how could I know if the women who came often and stayed longer didn't just have chronic bad looks. Or the men.'

Dr Wray's eyebrows raise, but wearily. 'The men?'

'Well, I don't know. It seemed possible. Ken said that sex was the only honest form of communication. He thought talk was irrelevant and misleading. I talked all the time. He said sex should be an accepted alternative to the handshake and monogamy was only for the emotionally undeveloped.'

Dr Wray shifts in his chair. 'About your daughter....'

In the evening Tug, setting out the chess pieces, muttered, 'Sorry. 'Bout today.'

'Why? What for?' Seeing his black head on the pillow beside Audrey's even as she feigned incomprehension.

'You know. When you walked in.'

'None of my business. But next time you ought to find somewhere a bit more private.'

'Won't be a next time. Slack screw.' Watching her now, wanting a reaction. Liz, the Jolly Brown Owl, not reacting. Until, three moves later, curiosity born of limited experience had to be satisfied.

'I'd have thought Audrey was a very sexy lady?'

'Huckery moll. Was her idea. I went up there looking for you and she.... I wouldn't've, only because of that bitch Karen and all. And, well, I did sort of fancy her a bit I guess.' Putting Liz's black queen in jeopardy. 'Where was yous, anyway?'

'I had a visitor. Glenda from down the street.'

'Bring you anything?'

'Soap.'

Four moves later, the black queen having escaped only to be firmly recaptured, he said, 'I might have to go with her a couple more times.'

'Audrey?'

'Yeah. Kind of a deal. She's a junkie y'know. Used to be.'

'She told me.'

'Well she's gonna give me a bit of her methadone. But I s'pose she expects something in return. So I might have to.'

'How very kind you are!'

Tug laughed, pleased at her sarcasm. 'Y'wanna know why I'm in here?

'Not especially.'

23

'Y'wanted to know before.'

'I was just making conversation. It's no big deal to me.'

'I'll tell yous anyway.'

It had been on a Monday. Tug and Brent had spent the night at the City Mission, despite the Missioner's displeasure. 'You guys have to get a place for yourself. This is an emergency shelter. You can't keep coming back here.'

'Oh come on Reverend, how are *we* gonna get a place?'

'And what about them old codgers?' said Tug. 'They keep coming here.'

'That's different,' said the Missioner.

Another problem with the Mission was you had to be out of the place so early, as if you were a worker or something. By the time the rest of the boys got into town the Mission boys felt just about ready for bed again. Hours to fill in. Tug wanted to go and see Karen at the biscuit factory but Brent wouldn't go with him.

'C'mon, she'll loan us a few bucks.'

'Nah. They won't let us in. Remember last time?'

'We'll say we've come to tell her her father's croaked.'

'Sure- Your old man's died, so give us ten bucks. Fuck *off*!'

So they sat around watching the aliens rushing to take up guard in shops, and then in offices. Looking at the faces; wanting some sign of recognition, a snort, a tightening of the lips — something to hang the hatred on.

By afternoon they'd met up with some of the boys and were hanging out in the Amusement Parlour. It was one of those days when discontent is contagious. The air smelt sour with boredom. No one had money — or no one was letting on he had money. Sometimes one of them would be asked to partner someone in a game of pool. And after school they bludged coins for the slot machines off the younger kids; if the attendant wasn't looking they backed their requests up with a little force.

They were hungry. All except Joe and Fat Boy who lived with their families and had access to refrigerators and kitchen cupboards.

'I once had a quadruple eggburger,' said Brent, watering in

24

fond memory.

'You wanna try a triple one,' said Tug.

'Quadruple's four, you dumb bastard.'

'I knew that. Only I forget things when I'm hungry.'

Making them laugh, but in empathy.

'What's happening,' said Luke after the laughter, 'is that you babies aren't pulling your weight.' Luke always spoke softly but everyone always heard what he said.

'This ain't kindergarten. You have to contribute, you know.'

He was looking at Fat Boy and Brent, not at Tug because Tug was his favourite.

'We done a damn sight more than Tug,' protested Fat Boy. 'What about that sauna place?'

'But Tug's different,' said Brent, his voice carefully expressionless so he could claim he meant it this way or that, depending.

'I got five dollars on Friday and yous all had your hands out.' Tug edged into an empty space, in case. A head bounced off a coin machine could split in two like a rotten orange.

'Bludging!' sneered Fat Boy. 'Five fuckin' dollars!'

'More than you'd get.'

Which was true. Fat Boy was a luckless bludger while Tug was the best among them, a master craftsman. It came to him easy, a natural talent. He would stand, carefully sweet-faced on a busy stretch of pavement, picking out the possibilities as they came towards him. 'Scuse me, but don't s'pose yous could spare twenty cents for my bus fare home?' Amazing how many of them would oblige, sometimes with more than just a twenty. He'd learned to concentrate on the office girls, eyeing them up and down as they came towards him, with a smile that could be construed as shy appreciation. They'd rifle their shoulder bags for him almost eagerly. Once a girl with slanting eyes and cropped hair gave him four dollars and invited him to meet her outside the Regent Arcade at five o'clock. But by five o'clock he was at Luke's place, stoned into immobility.

'Hah!' said Fat Boy. 'Bludging's for girls anyway.'

'There was the tape recorder,' reminded Tug. 'Twenty bucks worth.' He glanced hopefully at Luke but Luke was watching them all, looking at none of them. Fat Boy was encouraged by Luke's silence.

'We're talkin about *real* money. You never done a snatch or till or nothing.'

Tug twisted his upper lip and narrowed his eyes. He'd practised the look in front of mirrors and shop windows but he lacked confidence in it as the ultimate deterrent. Fat Boy sneered back then looked to Luke. Luke drummed his fingers against the Space Race machine with its purple astronauts and round green space creatures. He looked around the boys, one by one, drawing it out, taking his time.

'Yeah,' he said finally. 'Time Tug saw some action.'

He could smell his own sweat above the stench of the Grand Hotel urinals, and his hands were shaking. His hands had shaken to a rhythm all their own ever since he could remember, but now the shaking went right up his arms. He was leaning back against the concrete wall behind the toilet in the alley that ran between the hotel and the big government office building, giving a quick access between the main street and parallel High Street for those prepared to negotiate the rubbish tins and endure the dank piss smell.

A woman turned into the alley. She wore a long faded dress and Roman sandals and had a small child dawdling behind her. Tug bent over and held his hand above his mouth, pretending he was about to puke, waiting for them to pass. 'Take a good look at them first,' Luke had warned, 'We want a fat cat.'

He let three others go past, not sure — a young couple and an elderly man. He didn't feel able to wait much longer; sweat was breaking out on his face and his hands were going crazy. And yet he felt stretched-out, exhilarated — thinking, this is how the big cats feel before they jump on some poor dumb zebra.

She came thumping along in high heels, leaning forward a little in that ugly projecting way that some women walk in heels. The black leather coat made her seem, at first, quite youthful, but her face was old. She carried her handbag waist high and limp-wristed, like a drag queen. He let her pass him, sagging against the concrete wall like a drunk. He gave her a

26

couple of yards then caught up with her quietly on his bare feet. With one hand he wrenched the handbag, with the other he pushed her. She tottered but kept hold of the bag, trying to drag it from him. Game old girl, but no dignity. Panic flooded through him. He swung at her with his free hand, punching her in the face. This time she went over, letting go of the bag, screaming.

His legs were way ahead of his thoughts. It seemed only seconds later he was far away from the alley, nearing the top of High Street, dodging people, pushing others aside. Trying to shove the handbag up under his jersey as he ran. Thinking he could still hear the old girl screaming, and maybe he could.

He turned down a side street, his head working now, telling him slow down, for fucksake. Walk. Look ordinary. Someone shouting behind but don't look. Outside the library he ducked into the toilet. A women's toilet, but empty. He locked the cubicle door and opened the bag. Inside was a white lambswool purse containing eight dollars. *Eight fucking dollars.* Rummaging through the rest of the contents — lipstick, keys, assorted rubbish, and a bottle of pills three-quarters full. Little white pills; mandies, maybe, or something like that.

He put the money in his pocket, removed the pill bottle and, standing on the toilet, wedged the handbag behind a ledge near the ceiling. Then, leaning against the door, he unscrewed the cap of the bottle. It took him a long time because his hands were shaking again badly. He spilled the contents onto the palm of one hand, thinking if they were any good at all four or maybe six pills would have him cruising off down that street untouchable, away laughing, a traveller from another space. Back to face the boys still laughing away up inside. Letting them rubbish him about the pissy eight bucks, then producing the pills. 'A couple of these, boys, and you'll be away.' Seeing them look at each other with a kind of grudging admiration. 'Fucking Tug, ay. Sly cunt!'

He flushed the toilet and cupped his free hand to catch a little of the gushing water. Over the noise of the cistern he heard a man's voice, loud, close-by. He had one hand cupped with water and the other full of pills and there was no time to readjust. He poured the pills into his mouth and choked and

27

spluttered them down on that little bit of water and another fistful from the toilet. When the roaring of the cistern had subsided he waited, listening, but the sounds outside seemed insignificant — everyday footfalls and murmurs of conversation. He dismissed the wary, prickling feeling between his shoulders as foolishness.

When he walked out of the toilet a cop was standing at the door. It was the same young fair-headed cop who had taken Tug in two weeks before for obscene language. A squad car was parked across the street with another constable at the wheel. The fair-headed cop shouted to another who appeared from behind the toilet. These two each gripped Tug by an arm and propelled him across the road.

'Fucking Morton,' said the fair-headed constable to the driver.

'Just shove the black bastard in and let's get going,' said the driver.

Before they even got to Central Tug's mind began to have a private carnival. It was as if he was inside the Space Race machine and parts of it were metal with steep rivets and parts of it were coloured lights and little signs shooting up and down telling you things, and the lights were glaring and dimming and changing colours and the signs were flashing faster and faster. And there was very little air in the machine, he had to breathe in short gasps to avoid suffocation.

As they dragged him up the steps to Central Tug vomited on the trousers of the blond constable, causing the two of them to notice the peculiar shade of his face beneath the brown skin.

After they'd taken him to hospital and his stomach had been pumped out they took him back to Central. Tug knew from experience that if you refused to talk at the police station you were liable to be knocked around a bit — they'd take you for a ride in the lift and when it stopped between floors they'd hit you about, almost as if it was some ritual game. So he told them he had a habit, which was why he'd needed the money and swallowed the pills.

In court the next day he was remanded and put back in the cells, and when the probation officer came to see him Tug told the same story. It wasn't entirely his own idea. Luke had told him that he used to claim he was an addict long before he really became one. 'The thing is,' Luke had explained, 'if you tell them you did it 'cos you're hungry they'll reckon you're just a heap of shit, but if you say you've got a habit they'll think you're interesting, maybe even feel sorry for you. Reason is that some of these judges and even the older cops probably have sons or nieces or whatever that's junkies, but they don't have sons or anything that's *hungry*.'

So Tug told the probation officer that he'd been on smack for a year, and pointed to the remains of school-sores on his arm as evidence of needle marks. And the pro seemed quite impressed. And it was thanks to his strong plea for treatment rather than punishment that the magistrate duly had Tug admitted to Valleyview.

'But surely,' said Liz, 'they knew here that you weren't an addict?'

'They reckoned I wasn't a physical addict but a... thingee one.'

'Psychological,'

'Yeah.'

Liz thought for a while. 'What I don't understand is why? I mean why did you live like that? And the others? Who are these *boys*?'

'Boy, you're thick. You should be on television. You're like all the rest. You're not real, hardly.'

In occupational therapy they folded streamers together so the paper came out three-dimensional and multi-coloured, and made sad imitations of Chinese lanterns. There was to be a dance Saturday night.

Tug, left-handed and ham-fisted, worried away at a piece of crepe paper, stretching and folding. Finally holding it out for inspection.

'Whadda you reckon of that?'

Liz looking at it and beginning to giggle, 'I reckon it's a bit of scrunched up crepe paper.'

And Tug scowling, offended, 'It's a rose.'

So that Liz straightened her mouth and tried to make amends, saying, as she would to Michael, 'Of course. When I

29

look closer it does look like a rose.' Then looked up from the scrunched paper to find Tug silently laughing at her, shaking his head from side to side.

He began tearing the paper into little pieces and scattering them about the floor. 'The nutter's ball ay? Skipping around like a bunch of idiots. Grinning and dribbling and falling out of their slippers. Who you gonna be dancing with? Ol' droopy drawers? Or toothless Neddy? Reckon he fancies you. Watches you at the table. Dying to get his gums into you.'

'You could dance with me.'

'Stuff that. They're not getting me there.'

And they didn't. On the Friday night the nurse who gave out the evening pills said to Liz. 'You're going to miss your young pal.'

Liz felt something that resembled panic. 'Tug? He's being discharged?'

She went along the corridor and through the fire-doors into the adjoining wing. His door was ajar and he was lying on the bed. Until she saw the shuddering of his shoulders she thought he was sleeping. She sat on the bed beside him and eventually he turned his head towards her. His face was swollen and distorted, she was awed by the evidence of such unrestrained misery. She touched his shoulder. 'Where will you go?'

'Who gives a fuck?'

She waited.

'Guess I'll move back with the boys.'

'Do you want to?'

'I do and I don't'.

'What'll happen to you then?'

He shrugged. 'The same. Cops, pills, booze, the Mission.'

'Can't have to be like that.'

'What would you know?' He turned away from her. 'I'll be glad to get out of this slack hole.'

She waited, helpless. Eventually he asked the wall, 'Will you miss me?'

'Of course I'll miss you.'

'Who'll be your friend when I'm gone?'

'Guess I won't be here much longer.'

'But who'll be your friend?'

'Toothless Neddy.'

He laughed and took her hand in his, weaving their fingers together. 'Shall I come an' visit yous?'

'I'd like that.'

'Wouldn't bring you a present or anything.'

'Don't want a present.'

He removed his hand and got up, walking round the room with his calculated swagger. 'Back on the old streets again, ay.' He shoved his thumbs into the tabs of his jeans and slouched against the wall, head back, letting the old sneer take up guard.

'That's how you used to look when I first saw you,' Liz said.

He studied his fingernails. 'It's the real me, baby. Guess you may as well piss off now.'

'As you like.' She got up, wishing she could make some easy crack that would deflate his theatricals. When she reached the door he said, 'I might come and see yous.'

She smiled at him, and at the fragility of his act.

'Then again I might not,' he said.

FOUR

AUDREY LEFT A few days later. She said she was planning to go to Australia at the expense of a film-maker she knew who was about to make a rock musical. She expected to be cast as a Joplin character. Liz disbelieved the story but admired its flair and optimism so her expressions of envy were not entirely faked.

She lay on her bed and imagined Audrey in her strappy black shoes singing for a man with a clap-board saying Take 3, and she wondered about the poverty of her own dreams, her inability to imagine a future beyond Valleyview. Since the Saturday dance Liz had been suffering from a kind of exhaustion. It lay upon her like a damp and lumpy mattress. She suspected the staff of having changed her medication but this they denied. It was just a small relapse, they told her in those professionally reassuring voices. A little set-back because, one way and another, she'd been overdoing things.

What things? But she hadn't the energy to pursue the subject.

'Relapse my arse,' said Audrey. 'You've OD'ed on self-pity. You need to get out of here and do some real living.'

Somewhere Audrey had come by a duffel bag. She packed her things into it, including her pillow case, and her hospital pillow case to keep it company. 'If I run into your cobber,' she said, half-Australian already, 'I'll tell him you're getting crazier by the day. Wouldn't mind running into him, either. What the world needs is more horny boys. Always did like my

steak well browned.' She laughed and peered at Liz. 'You
don't think that's funny?'

'I was thinking,' said Liz slowly, 'that you remind me of
Ken. Only you're more honest.'

Ken had come to visit her twice in the past week. He had a
new approach.

'I want us to maintain a relationship,' he'd said, patting
her hand. 'I still have a lot of feeling for you. With you away
I've had time to think things through. I realise now that our
main problem was your loss of individuality. That may sound
hard, but it's true. There came a point where I couldn't
respect you any more. While I was growing in myself you
were regressing. It seems to me we could have a really
workable relationship if we lived apart but still saw each
other — not exclusively of course.'

Ken always sounded so clear-headed and convincing. Liz
had felt the old familiar sensation of being trapped by
reasons. One by one Ken would produce his arguments and
hammer them in around her like a picket fence. They would
appear so strong and flawless; monuments to reason that
could only be demolished by reason, and though she knew
the reasons were there in her head she could never quite
crystallise them, give them a sharp outline with a cutting
edge.

'Has Valerie dipped out on you then?' The best she could
manage. Admission of immaturity. Ken had sighed. The sigh
slid smoothly into the ground cutting off the last small escape
route. She was trapped and meekly apologetic.

'No, really, I guess you're right. I'd become really neurotic
and possessive. It's quite true.'

He patted her leg. 'Exactly. Look I think I can fix up a flat
for when you leave here. Not too far from me and Michael.
Okay?'

Yes. Yes please. Look after me. We'll be friends. We'll
have dinners together sometimes over bottles of wine. He'll
see me as a challenge, someone separate and exciting, the way
it once was. And then maybe. But of course he would. Want
to start again together. Everything as it was, only different.
They could turn back the clock.

When he had said goodbye with a look that was almost

tender and she had forced her weary body back up the stairs, she lay contemplating the stains on the ceiling and fashioned a sketchy witch to go with the pointed hand.

She thought of Ken winding back the clock, and of herself inside it trapped in an oiled spring which tightened around her until she could not cry out, even if there had been someone to cry out to.

On his second visit Ken had brought an aerogramme letter from her mother. Liz didn't read it until the following day, knowing how it would be; as her mother's letters always were — a recital of activities and events strewn with names of acquaintances. All the intimacy of a holiday brochure. It was difficult to equate the writer of these social jottings with the pinched and disapproving mother she remembered or to envisage the step-father she had never met.

During the thirteen years since her mother had flown 'home' to Britain — ostensibly on a visit but they had both known it was an escape — Liz had tried to introduce some thread of communion into their obligatory correspondence. *What kind of books do you read now?* ('We've had the chaise longue covered in muted blue brocade which I picked up in a little shop in Brussels.') *Are you happy with your life, Mum?* ('We stayed with Owen and Cynthia Hughes — he's *very* well thought of in diplomatic circles.') *Is it true, as our papers say, that unemployment is high over there?* ('We spent the weekend at the Langford's country house — fourteen bedrooms and the garden a dream.')

The garden at Valleyview was a comforting reality. Liz was spending a lot of time sitting at her window contemplating the vegetables in their tidy rows. She admired the gardener for his orderly miracles of early winter growth and could lose herself in the puckered green luxury of the silver beet. She was watching the silver beet when Judith Morehouse came to tell her that her buddy was waiting for her in the Day Room.

He was standing beside the door as if poised to leave, smiling a private and humourless smile. Watching him from the stairs Liz thought, if he's going to play those kind of games I'll walk away. I've got my own problems. But when he saw her the smile faded, left him looking simply young and ill at ease.

They sat in chairs facing each other, near the door and away from the other patients who were scattered among the chairs holding the drugged and desultory conversations that passed for communication. Tug's eyes darted about nervously as if he was trapped. Above his left eye was a cut, barely beginning to heal.

'What happened?'

'A fight.' Not looking at her. 'Some bikies did us over. Fat Boy's in hospital.' He made that sound like an achievement.

'You were lucky then.'

'I's quick,' he corrected her. 'I ran.'

'Am I going to have to worry about you as well as me?'

'Only if you want to.' But he was pleased.

'I don't want to, but looks like I'm going to.' Give him that much at least. It was so little to give, yet for a minute she felt he glowed. 'Where are you living?'

'With some of the boys.'

'Okay?'

He grimaced and hunched down in his chair. They sat in silence until Liz found it unendurable.

'Have you seen Audrey?'

'No.' A sly glance. 'Why?'

'Just she left a couple of days after you. Said she was going to Australia to be in a movie.'

But Tug wasn't listening. His eyes were on the move again, checking the exits, and his hands were playing an invisible guitar, just jamming around at first but then getting right into it, body moving, eyes narrowed in concentration. Liz felt inclined to slap him, to accuse him of rudeness or childishness, but she simply sat there watching the wall behind him with its angular and cluttered reproduction of small boats and motionless water. And she yawned, almost unintentionally. Tug observed the yawn but he played on to the last plaintive note, closing his eyes to savour its perfection. Then he watched Liz watching the painting for some time before he said, 'One of the boys's got some smack. Gonna gimme a hit tonight.'

'Then you're plain stupid.'

'What would you know?'

'Enough to scare me. Doesn't it scare you?'

'A bit. But what else is there?'

'There's... lots of things. People, children, doing things, loving someone....'

'For *me* what is there?'

She had no answer. She took it to be an accusation of a kind and felt resentful. What did he want of her, anyway?

'I gotta go now.'

'Well,' she said, both relieved and disappointed, 'thanks for coming. And take care.'

'You too.'

From the window she watched him walking up the driveway and had an urge to call him back. But for what? It's the aloneness we share, she said in her mind to him, but that sharing can't help either of us. I can call you back and say, I know how it is, I'm sorry for you; I can see that it must be worse for you because you're really only a child and you seem to belong to no one. I can say all that, but what good would it do?

Back in her room she thought about Tug coming all that way in the bus to sit before her playing his invisible guitar. Then she thought of the visits from Ken and Glenda and the polite business of exchanging words, lopping them back and forth like a tennis ball — an obligatory exercise in which there was a winner and a loser but rarely any pleasure. Tug's soundless recital began to seem an act of purity. I'll try it on Ken, she thought; a concerto on an unseen piano while he enumerates my failings!

That evening Liz began a letter to her mother. Her home address at the top: *Dear Mother. Our life must sound so very dull and domestic to you. I think I'll have to invent some excitement because really the three of us just toddle along uneventfully from day to day.*

She was interrupted from this chore of protective fantasy (not really a deception because how could she burden her mother with messy reality?) by a call for the 'phone beneath the stairs.

Reaching it short of breath because it was her first 'phone call at Valleyview and she was afraid whoever it was wouldn't have waited, 'Hello?'

There was breathing and the hollow sound of a fingernail tapping against the receiver.

'Hello?'

The tapping stopped. 'That you Liz?'

'Yes.'

'It's me.'

'Tug?'

'Who'd you think it was?'

'Marlon Brando.'

'What?'

'Never mind. Nothing.' It had been unfair, a generation game.

The taps began again, and the breathing.

'Well,' she said, 'you got me all the way down here so talk to me.'

'I dunno what to say on 'phones.' Liz sighed. Waited. 'Didn't talk much this afternoon either, did I?'

'No. Not much.'

'Don't like that place now. Makes me feel creepy.' Pause. 'What are you doing then?'

'Standing at the 'phone.'

'Oh. Yeah.'

'Tug,' she said, exasperated, 'Did you ring me for some reason?'

'Well... thought maybe you could come 'n' see me. If you liked. For the weekend maybe. You could ask them. I stay at twenty-seven Castle Street. You remember that?'

'Twenty-seven. But Tug I mightn't be able to.'

'You don't wanna?'

'It's not that. It's... well, they might not agree.'

'Say you're going somewhere else. Come Saturday morning. I'll be here.'

'But if I can't? Can I ring you?'

'I'm in a 'phone box. Just come or don't come. Doesn't matter to me.'

'I'll try. If I don't come would you ring me next week?'

'I might.' Pause, then he whistled a few notes. 'You know that song?'

'No.'

'Gotta go now. Someone's waiting. See you Saturday.'

'Tug, I'm not sure....' But he'd hung up.

A friend, she told them. An old school friend who now lived in America and was just back for a few days. She was surprised how easily the lie came. And they were pleased for her. If there were more friends we wouldn't have all these patients, said the Sister.

She caught the bus on Saturday morning. She'd packed a nightdress, a change of clothes, toothbrush, hairbrush, face flannel in a borrowed over-night bag and now she fretted over whether such accessories would be appropriate for her destination. She tried to imagine Tug's home ground. Would a toothbrush, in such surroundings, be an object of ridicule? Would a nightdress (a flannelette one at that) invite contempt in its comfy proclamation of age and respectability?

And she chewed over her deception. Would a weekend with the mythical school friend (blooming with Overseas Experience, tossing crumbs to Liz over her edge of acquired sophistication) have done more for Liz's mental health than a weekend in company of Tug and associates? Highly unlikely. And yet she had felt obliged to lie.

She considered the alternative. 'And just what is your relationship with this youngster, Mrs Harvey?' *We're friends.* 'Friends? I see.'

I see. the sharpest icicle of a sentence in the English language. *I see,* Liz's mother would say, lips compressing. *I see.* And you could tell by her face that what she saw was private and vile and not necessarily related to the facts presented. Why had Liz not learnt to lie more readily as a child?

It was exhilarating to have left the hospital, to be out on an adventure. Liz was a new person, frail in her newness but prickling with possibilities. By the time the bus reached the central city she was the only passenger. She thanked the driver as she got out.

'You're more than welcome, luv.' Beaming down at her.

She grinned back and waved, walking to the Post Office high on his good humour, the simple warmth of their exchange. The streets were almost deserted and shining from the early morning's rain, and the sky was beginning to clear.

She felt light-headed and wanted to draw out the morning like elastic. At the Post Office she checked out Castle Street on the big directory map. She was pleased to find it was walking distance, only a few blocks.

But walking along between the wreckers' yards, the empty workshops, her mood ran out on her. She thought of Michael. In the fogged and orderly world of the hospital she had scarcely missed him and had not dwelt on the implications of his choosing. But on this street she was real, and his leaving was forever.

She thought of his earnest face and the eyes which had always seemed older, more knowing, than her own. When he was born she had imagined she saw in those eyes a shadow of accusation. As if he had known. He had chosen Ken, but he should not have had to choose. If she had tried harder... been stronger....

I'll have him in the weekends, she thought, pacing the words to her footsteps. I'll have him in the weekends. And I'll try to make amends.

Castle Street was a street of tenants. Nice old houses gone to seed, gardens over-run, the odd piece of cardboard sellotaped over broken windows. It wasn't too late to drop her toothbrush surreptitiously down the grating of the gutter drain! In fact twenty-seven was neater than many of its neighbours. It had a small verandah in front, the railings entwined with wisteria. No sign of life in the house or on the wisteria's grey winter branches.

Liz went round to the back door and knocked. The door was opened by a slim young man, dark-skinned, narrow-featured. He regarded her with something like suspicion.

'Is Tug home?'

He looked her up and down as if considering. 'Yeah. Just a minute.'

He went back inside, pushing the door almost closed behind him. His voice carried back to her, even the laughter behind it; 'Hey, Tug. Your mother's come to see y'.' She heard a mumble of response, Tug's voice and a girl's, the words indistinguishable. The comedian returned, politeness itself.

'Sorry. Still in bed but he won't be long. I's just gonna

make some coffee, if you'd like some.'

'Thanks.'

He led her through an ominously barren kitchen and into the living room. It smelt of stale beer and feet. A mop of fair hair spilled out of a grimy sleeping-bag set on the floor beneath the window. It moved and the owner looked up at Liz then returned his face to the wall.

'I'm Tony,' the other said, playing gracious host. 'I'm afraid it's a bit of a mess, but do sit down. I'll make some coffee. Tug's been expecting you.'

The sleeping-bag began to shake then to give out little snorts of laughter. She saw the grin which began on Tony's face before he turned away. Well, what had she expected?

She sat at a table littered with comic books. The sleeping-bag turned a barely concealed eye in her direction. She took up the nearest comic book. *Mick hurled into the water and clawed his way through the reedy shallows.*

Tug stumbled his way through the yellow kitchen as Tony brought in coffee.

'You're early.'

'It's after eleven.'

He pulled up a chair at the table. 'Giz a coffee.'

'Sure, Tug, sure.' Tony's voice mocked, but he went back to pour another cup.

'Well?' said Tug to Liz.

'Well? said Liz.

Tony returned with Tug's coffee and took his own up the passage and out onto the verandah. Two girls came into the living room, sidling in, staying close to the wall. They were both around fifteen, skinny and pale with wide dark eyes. One had tattoos up her arms, the other had only freckles. They scuttled through the living room, skirting the table and staring. In the safety of the kitchen they giggled together. The freckled one peeked round the door at Tug.

'Jilly an' me's going out. See yous guys later.'

As they walked up the path their giggles drifted back, snufflings and helpless little squeaks. Tug was staring into his cup.

'Am I that funny?'

He shrugged.

'Your friends think so.'

'Them two? They're not *my* friends.' He was uneasy. 'What d'you wanna do then?'

'I don't know. Anything.'

'Let's go then.'

Where? 'All right.'

'Take your bag or someone'll nick your stuff.'

They walked in silence back the way she had come earlier. Liz set up words in her mind then let them drift away unsaid. Talking had always seemed a social obligation. Even with Ken, who was surely too familiar to provoke a sense of polite duty, long silences had made her uneasy. In fact with Ken she had, at least towards the end, become a compulsive talker, driven by some ill-defined feeling that if only she could come up with the right combination of words their marital malaise would disperse and everything would be clear and fine and happy.

But Tug had no regard for the serve-and-return rules of polite conversation. It takes two to chat, and if one party consistently fails to return the shots — doesn't even bother to watch where they land — and then makes a wild lop over the nets of propriety.... Silence was less bothersome and after a time Liz found their silence companionable and abandoned the typesetter in her mind.

'What d'you think then?' asked Tug.

'About what?'

'Them lot?'

'What am I supposed to think? It's quite a good house.'

'Bit poggy inside.'

'Better than I expected actually.'

'Might be out on our arses soon. Rent hasn't been paid for a few weeks.'

'Who are the girls? Are they sisters?'

'Nah. They run away from the Girl's Home. Billy — that guy on the floor — bring them home last night. Silly molls. They'll be picked up soon.'

'Tell me about Billy and Tony?'

'What about them?'

'Well, about their families?'

'I dunno. We don't talk about them things.'

41

They walked on.

'Dunno where you're gonna sleep tonight.'

'Doesn't matter. Anywhere. I could go back to the hospital even.'

'You wanta go back tonight?'

'Just if it makes things easier.'

'Nah. We'll sort something out.'

In the city centre they window-shopped. I like that....
Yeauck.... I'll have that and that and that. For Liz it was a
game, but Tug's claims were laid lustfully.

'You know,' she said, surprised. 'You've got good taste.'

'Waddya mean, good taste?'

'You like the same things as me.' It was the first time the
arrogance of the criteria had occurred to her.

He gave her a sideways look. 'You thought I'd like cheap
plastic junk, didn' yous?'

'Yes,' she admitted. 'I thought you'd be a bit of a peasant.'

'You don't know me,' he said. 'We don't know each other
at all.' He began to cross the empty Saturday street. 'C'mon,
I'll show you something.'

It was a second-hand shop. Not the selective, high-priced
variety but the cluttered, lucky-dip type that proclaims
everything has a use and a possibility. Tug pointed, finger
against the window.

'See that push-bike, the red one? And the tape recorder
over there? I sold them.'

'Where did you get them then?'

'Where'd y' think?'

'You stole them? Where from?'

'Just places. Got twenty dollars for the tape deck and
fifteen for the bike.'

'You were robbed.' She grinned at the irony of it.

He shrugged. 'Can't expect much when it's hot gear.'

'Do they know it's hot when they buy it then?'

'Must. I mean what d'*you* think? Where would somebody
like me get a tape deck like that, ay?'

She began to walk along the street. He caught up with her.

'Shouldn'ta told yous. Now you're pissed off.'

'It's just... don't you ever feel bad about the people who
owned the things? I mean maybe that bike belonged to some

kid who'd saved up for ages.'

'Never thought about that.' He thought about it. 'Why should I feel bad about them? Do they feel bad about me?'

She had no answer. They walked slowly down towards the park and the river and sat on the grass in the watery sunlight.

'What if Ken goes to visit you?'

'He won't. They've gone to Wellington this weekend to see his parents.'

'But what if he hasn't. What if he changed his mind and came walking past here now?'

'I'd say hello Ken.'

'Then what?'

'Then nothing. It's a stupid conversation. He's in Wellington.'

They sat in silence. She wondered if she had offended him. His face was impassive. He watched the ducks at the edge of the river. A motorbike roared along the street behind them, Tug swung round to watch it.

'Six-fifty. Someday I'll get one of those. Cruisie.'

'You'd kill yourself.'

'So? Who wants to grow old anyway?'

'Growing old's not so bad.'

'Hasn't made you very happy, has it?'

She laughed because again she had no answer.

'You're quite pretty when you laugh. Bet you was pretty once.'

'Yes,' she said. 'I was once. Think it was on a Friday in December 1955.'

'Then I missed it,' he said. 'I wasn't even born.'

She calculated. She would have been fifteen. Her father had still lived with them when she was fifteen. A big quiet man, a garage mechanic with grease smears on his face. Her father was the cause of her mother's migraines, the perpetual accused. The alleged crime was lack of ambition and social standing. Her mother's prosecution evidence rambled on for sixteen years, growing shriller with time and repetition. Liz, an only child, was a reluctant and cowardly juror, wanting to find in favour of her father but afraid of her mother's displeasure. Supporting her mother by silences and small acquiescent gestures, ashamed of her cowardice but unable to rebel because her mother had terrible powers.

When Liz was sixteen her father left home to live with a plump, dark-haired widow in the State Housing area of town. From clues and hints Liz deducted that the widow had featured in his life for some years before his departure. She felt he had abandoned her. She joined her mother in a chorus of vilification and her fear of her mother transmuted itself into something closer to pity. Nevertheless in the back of her mind there was a belief that her father would soon invite her to join this new and cosy family he was establishing for himself and Liz.

Six months after he moved in with the widow, Liz's father, the widow and her eight-year-old son died in a car crash on the main south highway. 'There's some justice, after all,' said Liz's mother when the young policeman broke the tragic news.

'Are you bored?' asked Tug into the silence.

'No. I'm glad I came. It's good to be away from there. I feel really positive, you know? I'll get a flat and a job. It'll be okay.'

'You'll be lonely.'

'You'll come and visit me.'

That pleased him. At times he was so transparent she felt frightened for him. 'I'll probably be inside by then,' he said. Fishing further for commitment. 'Or else you'll have a fulla and yous won't want me hanging around.'

'No fulla. I just want to be on my own for a while. Get myself sorted out. I'll enjoy being on my own.' She believed it.

His face had closed up again. He was alone. So she said, 'You're good to be with. I missed you when you left.'

'Why am I good to be with?' Testing her.

'I don't know.... Because you make me laugh. Because I think you're a bit like me. Because you haven't got too many hidden corners.'

He was pleased but looked away from her, watching the river, the ducks. 'You could adopt me,' he said to a weeping willow.

'What?'

He looked at her. 'He's taken your son away. Well I could

be....'

Her mind balked at the idea. 'They wouldn't let me. I'm not old enough, Tug.' Relieved to have such a definite and objective excuse.

'Yes you are. Lots of people have babies at sixteen.'

'But not adopt them, women on their own. I wouldn't be able to.'

'I's only joking anyway,' he said. 'You'd believe anything.' He stood up. 'It's slack here, let's go to the pub.'

Worn lino on the floor and yellow painted walls. A smell of disinfectant, ripped vinyl on the bar stools and not a single concession to comfort. She liked these kind of pubs, at least on a day-tripper basis. They made no demands and there was no danger of encountering people who resembled her mother. Above the bar a plump infant in a leopard skin held aloft bar bells. A poster that must have, at one time or another, adorned every pub in the country. It made Liz nostalgic for the days before her marriage when they'd all drive up the coast for a Saturday country pub crawl.

'They know me here,' said Tug, 'so we won't get hassled.'

They played pool, a pastime her education had never catered for. Netball had been obligatory and tennis a social necessity, but pool? In her pub-crawling days they'd been too enthralled by their own company to consider hitting balls around a table. But it pleased him to teach her, to be patient and encouraging and to give dazzling displays of his own prowess.

A drinker plonked a coin down on their table. 'Give you and your missus a game.' Tug grinned across at Liz. They played, and despite the handicap of Liz's sheltered youth Tug won the game for them.

The bar room began to fill as the afternoon wore on. Tony and sleeping-bag Billy arrived. Tony acted as if he and Liz had a tacit understanding by virtue of mature years. Tony was twenty-three and had been around. He was very attentive, buying Liz drinks, asking her not-too-personal questions with studied sophistication. Tug, circling the pool table in match and rematch with Billy, glowered across at them. Finally he said he was leaving, tossing his cue on the table and striding out. She went after him.

'Y' don't *need* to come.'

'I want to.'

In fact she didn't care one way or another. The day had begun to seem easy and endless. She was happy to stay or go. But he was her friend.

The fresh air assaulted her stomach, she directed her feet with some difficulty. 'Let's get something to eat.'

'Got no money left.'

Tug and then Tony had paid for her drinks. She had not thought to wonder about the limits or source of his finance. In her world everyone had access to an income of some kind. 'I've got money,' she said.

They ate at the Hong Kong. Tug ate his meal and most of Liz's. Her stomach rejected the theoretic need for food.

'You can have my bed,' he said between chips. 'I'll sleep on the sofa.'

'I can sleep on the sofa.'

'Nah. Them lot'll be coming home staggering and falling all over yous.''

But when they got home they found the two pale girls entwined together on the sofa under army blankets, asleep.

'Where did they sleep last night then?'

He looked embarrassed.

'Your room? Both of them?'

'Well?'

'Why were they giggling about me?'

'Because they thought you an' me....' His voice faded off. It was unthinkable. Ludicrous. Neither of them laughed.

They made coffee in the kitchen and carried it into Tug's room. The room was little bigger than an extended cupboard. It had a small curtainless window and one unmade bed. Tug went off and returned with an armful of blankets. 'Them lot'll be too drunk to know if they're cold.' He spread the blankets on the wooden floor then began to pull his own bed into order.

'There aren't any sheets. D'you mind?'

'That's okay.' She had to ask. 'Where did the girls sleep then? In there? All three of you?'

He nodded, a trace of a grin. 'They were both skinny.'

She was torn between vicarious excitement and maternal

disapproval. They were all of them only children.

'Am I spoiling your sex life then?' She made it casual.

'Nah.'

'You sure?'

'Course I'm sure. It's there if I want it.' Still in his clothes he rolled himself in the blankets on the floor. Liz looked down at her over-night bag and decided against the nightdress and the toothbrush. She removed her jersey and jeans and climbed into bed in shirt and knickers. Tug pulled at the light cord. 'G'night,' he said from the floor.

'Night Tug.'

She lay there wide awake. The bed had a sour body smell and the touch of the blankets discomforted her. Not so much a matter of not knowing where they had been, as knowing almost too well. She thought about being fourteen and giggly and having the kind of girlfriend you wanted to share *everything* with. She thought about it with a kind of envy for experiences by-passed and opportunities lost. She reminded herself that she had been a privileged youngster; at fourteen she was top in Latin and had a poem about nuclear warfare in the school magazine. She had never even been kissed. She wondered now whether those who breezed through Latin declensions were inevitably unable to enjoy casual and experimental tumbles in bed, and vice versa.

She listened to the sounds that daylight muffles: cars on the street, Tug's breathing, television in a neighbouring house and the papery scuffle of a mouse behind the wall lining, and when she finally gave up the effort of sleep and opened her eyes she could see the walls of the room palely in the reflected streetlight. She looked at Tug. His eyes were wide open, staring at the ceiling.

'I can't sleep,' she said.

'Me neither. Let's have a smoke.'

He found the packet and lit two.

'I feel mean having your bed. We could both fit in this one. I mean, you'd be more comfortable.'

'I'm okay.'

They lay and smoked in silence.

'You're different,' she said, 'away from the hospital.'

'So are you.'

47

Silence again.

'It's not really us that's different,' he said. 'It's things.'

'I suppose it is.'

They finished their cigarettes and dropped the butts in an empty cup. They heard the others returning from the pub — loud voices and banging doors, more than two voices.

'Fuckin' Tug!' roared one of them. 'He's swiped the blankets.'

Tony tramped up the passage and into their room. He dragged the blankets from Tug, glanced from Tug to Liz, laughed and left.

'Bloody hell,' Tug sat up.

Down the passage Tony said something that prompted guffaws of laughter.

Liz moved close to the wall and held back the blankets. He hesitated then climbed in beside her, turning his back to her.

She lay beside him feeling his warmth but trying to keep unobtrusively to her side of the bed. His back looked like an invitation, she felt longing for a body to snuggle against but she was afraid he would be shocked — maybe repelled by her aging embrace.

When his breathing told her he was surely asleep she moved against him, sliding an arm round his waist, and felt comforted if not relaxed. Wanting a second opinion, closing her eyes and inviting Ken in to observe her. Predictably, despite his professedly liberal views he is shocked. 'My God, Liz!' He's not displeased; his expression comes somewhere between scorn and triumph.

Glenda? But Glenda won't even enter the front door. So Liz composes a letter to her mother. *Had a jolly weekend at the boys' place in Castle Street — the boys are awfully well thought of in criminal circles around here. Played pool at the Occidental and wound up in bed with promiscuous sixteen-year-old I met at the nut-house.*

A laugh began in her stomach but aborted. She was disconcertingly aware of the body next to hers. She remembered him saying on the river bank 'You could adopt me,' and knew it was never a joke.

'What is your relationship with this youngster Mrs Harvey?'

'There is no name for it, Sister. It's fragile. If you name it you'll destroy it.'

'I'll ask you again, Mrs Harvey?'

Falling asleep, unable to answer.

FIVE

KEN TOOK HER, the following weekend, to look at the house. She liked it on sight. It was old and solid and the garden was lush, overgrown to the edge of enchantment.

Ken took the key from under a brick beside the back door. The owner was away for the day. He was a patient of Ken's and was leaving for Kenya in a week's time. There were packing crates in the living room and the house already had a vacated air. The owner would be leaving most of the furniture behind, said Ken, as he would only be in Kenya in an advisory capacity for about a year. Ken was international; he constantly rubbed shoulders with people who went to Kenya in advisory capacities. Liz looked at the crates and thought of ebony and voodoo and mystery. She had not learned to be nonchalant about the jet age.

'I think it's ideal,' Ken enthused. He turned on the kitchen taps to see how they ran. 'And very reasonable. It's a good area, and you're not too far from us.'

'It's quite a long way from town if I'm going to be working there,' Liz said. She felt a need to raise objections. 'Since you're keeping the car.'

'There's a good bus service. And once the house is sold you can get a car.'

Ken had decided that he and Michael would move to Wellington. A fresh start, he said, and he'd be nearer his parents. He hadn't set a date yet. We'll see how our new relationship develops, he had said. Liz had made no

50

comment.

'I might not stick around long,' she said now. 'I might go overseas or something.' She liked the sound of it after it was said and began to believe it, though it had just been words to impress Ken with her potential for exciting living.

Michael, who had been exploring the tangled little garden, came to the kitchen door and stood silently watching them.

'What do you think?' Ken asked him. 'This is going to be your mother's new home.'

Michael looked at each of them in turn then ran back to his private jungle. Ken gave Liz a wry shared-parenthood smile and she smiled back out of habit though a small voice told her that such exchanges could be treacherous.

'Doctor Wray'll be pleased you've found a decent place,' said Ken as he locked the door behind them. As if Ken and Dr Wray were her guardians and all they asked was that she be a good girl.

'Ken's being very considerate really,' said Glenda, who had persisted with occasional visits for reasons Liz assumed were to do with Glenda's private sense of virtue. For her final visit she wore a long checked skirt and a yellow body shirt with long sleeves. Even her perfume was intimidating.

And Dr Wray did seem at least relieved. 'Everything under control then,' he said with an air of cautious surprise.

She left the following weekend, pleased to find the leaving was easy, there was only that slightly pleasurable guilt of being more fortunate than her fellow patients. She resolved to visit those she had grown more fond of, then thought of Glenda sweeping in like the good ship sanity and resolved not to visit.

Ken had already moved her clothes and personal belongings into the house. The clothes were in the closet on hangers, her assorted junk shop treasures were set out on top of the bookcase. A new thoughtful Ken, or Valerie's feminine touch?

'If there are things I've forgotten,' Ken said, 'just come round and get them. Since the place was furnished I just brought what I thought you'd need.'

'I'd like the stereo,' she said. 'Well, it *was* mine.'

He sighed. 'Okay. I'll drop it by sometime.' His fingers rested on her shoulder. 'We'll leave you to get settled in.'

Alone. A house to herself. A cautious excitement flowing into her veins. She walked through the house, imagining she was showing it off to a visitor. My room, the spare room, the little sun porch. But why only one visitor? She filled the house with people, talking, laughing, refilling glasses, passing a joint.

Friends! She'd had them before she got married, now she could have them again. The married years would be just an aberrant bubble; shake it loose, blow it away and she could be twenty again. At twenty, every day had been full of possibilities. She had a bed-sitter, her very own. She was independent, energetic, free; released from the burden of being a daughter, joyfully motherless. She belonged to herself, to her friends. Her friends were witty and talented and kind. Liz wore green nail varnish and stiletto heels and permanently rose-coloured glasses. She was in love with shop windows and pavements and student parties and liquid lunches and weekend pub crawls up the coast and office morning teas.

Kath, Geoff, Martyn, and Carol — they were her special friends, her inner circle, her family. Why had she made no real efforts to keep in touch? Friends, how have your lives treated you since then?

Kath, she knew, had gone overseas shortly after Liz got married. Carol, she'd heard, had spent time in Hamner trying to kick her drink problem. Geoff had married a continuity announcer from TV, Liz had seen their photo in the Sunday paper. No word of Martyn.

And what of Liz? Remember Liz? I wonder what became of her?

Standing before the bedroom mirror she decided she would grow her hair long the way it used to be and her eyebrows and buy some extravagant shoes. Some false eyelashes even, why not?

She went outside and considered the garden. If she cleared a space by the back door she could transplant some of her herbs there. But tugging at weeds made her restless.

In the kitchen she considered the matter of food. She sat at the table and made a list of things she would need, pleased to have found such a necessary activity. Then she took the list to the dairy a couple of blocks down the street. She knew it would be open, they'd bought ice-creams there sometimes after listless family Sunday drives.

She hoped the shopkeeper would chat to her, she wanted to establish her position as a new resident in his neighbourhood, but the shop was full of Sunday families buying ice-creams and chocolate bars. The shopkeeper showed no appreciation of her more substantial purchases.

Ken had given her money that morning with the pale fortitude of a blood donor. She was no longer a wife but a remittance woman.

She walked home the long way then made herself a meal of scrambled eggs, enjoying the novelty of cooking her own meal and cooking it for her alone. She ate it slowly while reading an old copy of *Newsweek* she'd found in the wash-house, then she cleaned up the kitchen more fastidiously than she'd ever cleaned up a kitchen in her wifely role.

She could feel the panic nudging at her even as she swept up the last few crumbs and gave up pretending she was twenty again, and complete. At twenty, at eighteen, at twenty-two even, she had no knowledge of the panic. In those days she had been confident. In control.

The panic had begun after Michael was born; it was the possibility that his baby breathing would suddenly stop, it was the sound of the clock, it was waiting for the sound of their car turning into the drive, it was the walls of the house closing in. It came and it went, like a thunderstorm and beyond her control. She had learned that it could be subdued by a sufficient intake of sherry or by the night air. Telephone conversations could also help if you had someone to ring. There had been the nights when she'd dialled Lifeline, waited to hear the voice on the other end then quietly replaced the receiver. Checking the liferafts; it helped.

She hadn't expected the panic to seek her out in this house where no child or children slept to be maybe invaded by nightmares and call out to her or go stumbling from room to room to seek her. (And what if the house should be empty? How terrible to be a child in a dark house searching and searching and finding no one. Elizabeth Nicholson, only child, had never been left alone at night yet she knew how it felt. She knew exactly how it felt.)

In this house, free to go, she went. Walking up the street in her old duffel coat and feeling better immediately. Walking for an hour or two, peering through lit windows at people eating dinner, people watching television, people opening wardrobes. Reassured by such ordinariness and the neon-lit respectability of the suburban streets she turned for home.

And at first the house seemed welcoming. She made a cup of coffee and switched on her transistor radio. Two men were discussing inflation as if it was of consequence and she willed herself to listen but it was all words words words. People were dying, people were giving birth, people were going mad quietly or spectacularly and two men sat in a studio talking about inflation. She could feel the panic moving in on her again.

She considered going to look for Tug. The Castle Street house came into her mind as a refuge. Two Sundays before she had woken to find Tug was up already, in the kitchen with Billy exchanging insults. It was raining. Billy, excessively polite that morning, made Liz toast and coffee. Tug was carefully casual, as if she were a stranger. The girls roused themselves from the sofa, whispered to each other then sat in fidgeting silence. Liz crunched the toast and felt adult and alien. She had decided to return to Valleyview that morning when Tony joined them with a pack of cards and a half-bottle of whisky.

They played poker for matches and after a time she was no longer an alien but an audience. Tony talked of the year he'd spent in prison, the girls aired grievances about the Girls' Home, Billy raged about his stepfather. Liz listened and asked questions, sometimes in disbelief. She wanted to disbelieve and when she could not she wanted to silence them.

Tug said very little. In the late afternoon he walked with Liz to the bus stop.

'Thank you,' she said. 'I had a good time.' They stood together formal and awkward. She sensed that he was relieved that she was going.

'I might ring you,' he said.

He rang on the Friday. She knew him by his breathy silence.

'Tug? How's things?'

'All right.' Pause. 'Got picked up yesterday.'

'Picked up? By the police? What for?'

'Charged me with assault. On a cop.'

'How come?'

'Cunt was hassling me. I just pushed him outa the way.'

'So what happens now?'

'Nothing. Spent last night in the cells, came up this morning. Judge fined me seventy dollars.'

'Seventy dollars! How will you pay that?'

'Won't.'

'What happens then?'

'You don't pay they put you inside to work it off.'

'That won't be much fun.'

'*That won't be much fun.*' Imitating her in a prissy voice, angry.

She thought of hanging up on him but stood there waiting. 'Well?' she said finally.

'Them girls was picked up. Fuckin' serve them right.' He waited for her to comment. She said nothing. 'Got to be outa the house by Monday landlord said.'

'How much rent do you owe?'

'Dunno. Five, six weeks, maybe more.'

'If I had that kind of money I'd lend it to you,' she said, words being cheap.

'You'd never see it again. None of us's got money.' Silence, then, 'Liz?'

'Yes?'

'Nothing. Just wondered if you were still there.'

'Well I am.'

'Gotta go now.'

And she hadn't heard from him since. If he needed her he wouldn't know where to find her. The hospital could give him her address but it wouldn't occur to him to ask. She told herself to be glad, she could do without his problems.

She went to the 'phone and dialled her own number — Ken's number. Hating to do it. Having to do it. Dialling slowly while her mind searched for a plausible pretext. The 'phone rang three times and a woman answered. That possibility hadn't occurred to Liz. She hesitated, confused.

'May I speak to Mr Harvey please?' Not Ken or my husband, she was a coward avoiding confrontation. The woman placed the receiver on the table. Liz had done the same thing so often. It was as if she were spying through the mouthpiece as the woman walked into the living room — or was it the bedroom? — to fetch Ken.

'Ken Harvey speaking.' In his careful work voice.

'It's me Ken.'

'Oh.' Then he spread civility over his irritation. 'And what can I do for you?'

'I just thought I'd like to have Mitzi. For the company.'

He thought about it. 'Well, if you really want her. But it'll upset Michael. He's pretty fond of her, you know.'

'I hadn't thought of that.' Guilty again. How easily he could make her apologetic! 'She better stay with you then.' The cat had just been a pretext but now she felt deprived. It was her cat and it would have been company. 'I'm sorry,' she said falsely, 'to have disturbed you then.'

'Oh you didn't disturb me.' She thought he was smiling to himself. 'Good night Liz.'

Still, absurdly, she felt better. The panic had subsided and she felt able to read a little, even to sleep.

And in the morning the world was all in order. She got up early, breakfasted, and caught the workers' bus into town, pleased to be one of those fresh commuter faces. Part of the world again. She rehearsed her hiring in her head. Yes, I worked for Lawrence and McArthur as a copywriter. For five years. They wanted me to stay on but I'd got married and my husband wanted us to move. I handled the Jolly Jelly account — you remember that jingle? *Jolly jelly instant setter, Jolly jelly serves you better*. Yes, that one. That was one of mine. Television? No, well television was only in its infancy at that time. We handled radio and newspapers, but I'm quite confident I would find television no problem.

In the city she bought a morning paper and took it to a coffee bar, turning to the Work Wanted section, setting her cup down on Entertainment. By the time she had read to the bottom of the second column her hopes had turned sour. Everything in there seemed to require certificates, degrees, references. Where were the openings for a Jolly jelly jingle writer, eleven years out of practice. Eleven, or was it twelve? Doesn't time fly when you're having fun!

She dragged the cup of coffee out as long as possible, wondering what else she could do with the day. She stayed until she was the only customer, then because the man behind the servery was watching her and, she imagined, was resenting her prolonged stay for the price of one coffee, she folded up the paper and walked out onto the street. Looking back through the plate glass to see if he was still watching her she saw a board propped beside the door. It said, waitress wanted.

'I figured you were looking for a job,' he told her. 'You had experience?'

'Yes.' And it was true. For four months she had moon-lighted in a restaurant. Before she met Ken. When her options were open.

'We open eight-thirty to five-thirty, what about your family?'

'I live alone.'

A quick glance of pity, or maybe interest, then he shrugged. 'Wish to hell I did.' He spoke with an accent she guessed to be Middle European. 'When could you start?'

'Whenever you like.'

'Suppose you give me a hand with the lunchtime crowd today. A couple of hours? See how you go?'

She had a job.

It wasn't an office with jokes and friends and morning tea shouts for birthdays and engagements, and tense executives and dizzy typists, but it was a job. The boss was called Irwin, born in Estonia. A fair man, she decided, tolerant of her nervous mistakes on the first couple of days, generous in praise as she grew more efficient. She smiled at the customers and most of them smiled back. At night she ached with exhaustion. At night she slept, too tired for the panic.

She grew to know the regular customers. There was one, a male, who watched her with more than a passing curiosity. She liked the look of him. He was tall and thin with a beard and brown hair, receding. In his thirties. He wore a carved ivory ring on his right hand. No wedding ring. All these things she noticed coincidently.

At the end of the first week he said, as she cleared his table, 'You don't look like a waitress.'

'Oh? I thought I did it rather well.'

'You know what I mean.'

As he was leaving he stopped her mid-tables.

'Are you married?'

'Separated.'

'Could I see you some time?'

'If you like. When?'

'Saturday? Evening?'

He was so suitable. She could scarcely believe it. She had been on her own less than a week and here was this man, personable, interested and entirely *suitable*. If only Ken, or even Glenda, could see her now. *Well, she's done all right for herself.*

'I've got an admirer,' she told Irwin as he counted up the takings.

'That surprise you?' Part flattering her, part amused.

'Yes. I suppose it does.'

Should she go to bed with him? All Saturday the question nagged at her. She flopped it around amid the washing, she squeezed it out through the wringer, she sucked it up in the vacuum cleaner then tipped it out and re-examined it. Still she was unable to come to a decision. She wanted to be recklessly and abandonedly sensual. She wanted to begin making amends for her distressing inexperience — thirty-three and three men, one a miserable drunken capitulation with a friend of Carol's, and another a pathetic effort at evening the score with Ken, an episode so excruciatingly embarrassing that Liz would have discounted it entirely except that three was a better score than two, however you looked at it. In her single years she had (until the encounter with Carol's friend) remained virginal not through inclination but due to the combined forces of ignorance of contraception and fear of pregnancy. That fear was sufficiently terrible to outweigh both her own inclinations and curiosity and the pleadings or threatenings of her partners. Her virtue had been saved. At thirty-three that seemed a matter for regret. Yet now she had the opportunity to redress the situation it loomed as an ordeal.

In the afternoon Ken rang to say he was bringing Michael over for the weekend.

'You can't. I'm going out tonight.'

'So am I. Really Liz, I thought you'd want to see him.'

'You can bring him tomorrow. You should have consulted me. I have my own life to consider.' Oh, triumph, small but rewarding. Except that Michael was in the middle.

She wore her black trousers, her red and black sweater and her diaphragm. Not, she consoled herself, a commitment but a precaution. She resolved to go back on the pill regardless of side-effects. Passion prepared for several hours in advance must be short on overwhelm and she longed for an overwhelming passion.

She met him in town as arranged. He did not drive, he said, cars made him nervous. She thought it showed a nice sensitivity. They went for drinks until the main movies started. His name was Jim Taylor. He was curator at the Arts Society Gallery, a post he'd taken up only three weeks before. For the past ten years he had been living in England, returning to New Zealand two months ago because of the death of his father. He'd had a woman in England but she was an editor in a publishing firm and preferred her job to the thought of trailing out to the remote underside of the world. It was that kind of relationship, he said with no apparent regret. He wore expensive denims nonchalantly. Liz was dazzled by her good fortune.

He took her to *Five Easy Pieces*. He'd seen it already. 'For me it clarified elements in my own life. And visually it's remarkable. It's worth abstracting yourself from the story-line at times and just looking. Many people are unable to do that. They're sloppy in their watching.'

She tried not to watch sloppily. She was nervous as a teenager, wanting his approval, but the movie finally caught her up and transported her. His taste was impeccable.

They took a bus to her place. He believed in patronising public transport. Home, they drank wine which Liz had thoughtfully bought the night before. She noticed how in certain ways Jim reminded her of Ken. Determined not to

59

chatter she found it more and more difficult to find things to say. It was him who threw words into the silences. He's nervous too, she thought in surprise.

He was talking about modern British artists. Her fault, she had asked. His words went round and round in descending circles, she sat on the rug beside him nodding encouragement and refilling their glasses. Having disposed with the Henry Moore influence he reached for her hand and held it. His hand was soft and dry, she restrained an unreasonable urge to draw hers away. He pulled her closer and kissed her. She felt uninvolved. His teeth indented her lip, his hands slid over a body dull with indifference. Surely he sensed that? Couldn't he feel the absence of current in her sullen, uncharged flesh?

No, it seemed. No and no.

She wanted to respond. Above all she didn't want to hurt his feelings. He was so admirable, he was so eligible. Her body didn't know a good thing when it felt it. She commanded her fingers to undo the buttons of his shirt and run dutifully over his chest which was covered with fine, surprising hair.

'Where's your bed,' he asked into her hair. And a martyr, she lead him to it.

He took so long. He was so unselfish and conscientious, concerned about her share of pleasure, busy as a beaver. Oh God, she thought, why should I land a scrupulous screwer instead of a wham-bammer! But she pretended pleasure to please him.

Afterwards he lay beside her smiling tenderly. *And now there were four.* 'Do you want me to leave?' he asked, making it a plea to stay.

'May as well stay till morning.' It seemed the least she could do.

She woke early. Asleep he looked worried, husbandly and she felt vaguely irritated that he should be there intruding on her fresh life. She slid cautiously out of bed and showered. The previous night seemed inconsequential. She tidied the house and took a book out on the kitchen steps to catch the pale morning sun. A while later, hearing the shower running, she made them a pot of tea.

He joined her on the doorstep. 'What a superb morning.'

'Yes.' She was impressed once again by his eligibility.

They talked about books. Liz noted that she had read more extensively than he had. It reduced his status to a more approachable level and she began to feel relaxed.

He declined her offer of breakfast. 'Ought to get back to my old mum. Anyway I don't want to intrude on your independence too long. I know how precious it can be. I shall see you, no doubt, Monday lunchtime.'

Her independence, thus acknowledged, settled about her; a personal achievement, a matter for pride. At once she wanted him to be gone, telling herself that once he was gone she would quietly look forward to seeing him Monday. They would have that kind of relationship; mature, respectful of the other's privacy. As he walked up the path she went into the bedroom, intending to make the bed. It was made already. She was unused to such helpfulness in a male. It made her quite weak with affection. *I rushed things, that was all, I was nervous, my body wasn't ready.*

Ken arrived at the door with an armful of stereo. He must, then, have seen Jim leaving. Hah, thought Liz in satisfaction. 'If you'll give us a hand,' said Ken, 'there's the speakers to come.' Ken had never made a bed in eleven years.

Michael carried in a pile of records.

'Some of those are mine,' Ken said, 'but you may as well have them in the meantime as I've now got nothing to play them on.'

She tried to make conversation with Michael. 'You didn't mind about last night, love?'

'I dunno, what about last night.'

'Never mind then. How have you been?'

'All right.'

'D'you miss me?'

He shrugged and scuffed his feet. 'Can I go outside?'

Ken finished connecting up the speakers. 'So? You've got a lover?'

'Have I?' She was watching Michael out the window, he had taken out his pocket knife and was stabbing it in the trunk of the elm tree.

'You don't have to tell me. Just that we more or less bumped into him. Good on you, I say. Who is he?'

61

'You wouldn't know him.'

'I know I don't know him. I mean what does he do for a crust?'

'What's that to you?'

'I'm curious, that's all. Was it good?' He came and stood behind her. She continued to look out the window. 'Well? Was it?' His hand grasped at her crotch with the confidence of ownership. She made no move to push him away. It was, after all, what she wanted.

'I've taken out my diaphragm.'

'I came prepared.' He manoeuvred her towards the bedroom. She watched him stretch the rubber onto himself with a kind of fascination.

'I didn't think anyone used those now.' His body was at once familiar and unfamiliar, the combination seemed irresistible. *Two men in twelve hours* a part of her scrawled in heavy letters on the prim blackboard of her mind.

But beyond the edge of relief she found regret. She got up and began to dress herself, her back to him.

'Have you had any thoughts about Wellington?' He asked.

'No. Why should I.'

'It's something we're going to have to work out together.'

'You can work it out,' she said. 'It hardly concerns me.'

'Perhaps it could.'

She felt a sudden weary distaste for him.

'No,' she said. 'I've got other plans.'

'In other words he's a better screw than me.'

'Oh God.' She turned to look at him lying on top of the bed naked, one knee drawn up. She noticed for the first time the network of fine lines etched across his pale face, the lengthening of his forehead. She felt pity and with it a sense of release. 'You can put it that way if you like,' she said, but gently.

She and Michael spent the afternoon at the beach. The beach was five miles away — they took a bus — and unremarkable. Liz had known childhood beaches of golden sand and small secluded bays, this grey and windswept sand seemed a poor substitute. They built sandcastles, ate ice-creams and rode the see-saw. It was a day in limbo. She had a sure feeling that part of her life was over and the remainder had yet to begin. She felt damp and empty; it was an effort to concentrate on Michael's chatter. The day was taking a long time.

Ken collected Michael punctually at 6.30 p.m. He sat in the car and tooted. Liz hugged Michael then watched him walk up the path ashamed of her sense of relief. She wanted to cry, her head felt like a queasy stomach, but no tears would come. The sherry bottle was empty.

She ran a bath and tried to think of Jim and his undoubted merits, she dressed him in his respective virtues as if he were a paper doll. He lacked dimension in her mind. She wondered if she was going mad, *really* mad. It wasn't a new fear. She kept adding hot water until the cistern began to run cold and she was forced to get out. She dressed quickly, warmly, in jeans and jersey, grabbed a jacket, cigarettes and matches and her wallet and ran out of the house.

Along the street the tears began, running down her face and soaking into the thick black cloth of her jacket. She turned the collar up to make her face less visible. What if someone should stop her and want to help? Was that what she wanted? Take me, look after me. And they would take her to their neat Sunday family home and trap her there, stifled, unable to explain that the panic had sidled in with her through their front door.

Reaching the main road she crossed diagonally, unaware of the traffic. A car braked sharply and the driver shouted at her. 'For Christsake Lady.' She didn't look at him. The street lights and car lights were lovely, expanded and distorted by the tears into sparkling jewels. The driver made her aware of the kindly lethal possibilities of motor vehicles. She thought of Nessa and turned and recrossed the street. Cars seemed to be all around her, bright and glistening, brakes screeched, but nothing touched her. She accepted that it was an omen, a calm acceptance without relief. After that she looked before she crossed.

She kept to the residential streets, skirting round the city. She thought she was walking blind and it seemed a coincidence when she registered Castle Street. But since she was in the area....

There was a motorbike parked outside and lights within.

She went to the back door and knocked. Max came to the door, but she did not know Max then and simply registered sharp blue eyes and sandy hair. She asked for Tug, standing back from the light of the doorway so he wouldn't see her swollen, blotched face.

'He's moved,' Max said. 'Dunno where to.' An abrupt scowling voice.

'Oh.' She felt utterly forsaken, yet a part of her was relieved. 'Thank you.'

She walked back along the side of the house, the curtains were all carefully drawn, and onto the street. A window slid up behind her and a voice shouted something indecipherable. She kept walking.

'LIZ!' A bellow. Tug's. She waited, heard a door slam and saw him coming towards her. When he could see her face in the streetlight he asked, 'Whassa matter?'

'I don't know,' she bleated. 'I just felt... miserable.' She felt the tears begin again. He stood there helplessly. She was afraid he would go off and leave her there, she made an effort. 'They said you'd moved.'

'He thought you was from Welfare, or a pro or something.'

'Pro?' Did they solicit door to door?

He grinned. 'Probation officer. It's cold here. You wanna come in?'

'Are there a lot of people there?'

'Quite a lot I s'pose.'

'Oh God.' She choked on a sob.

He swayed from foot to foot looking impatient. 'Whadda you wanna do then?' He sounded angry.

'I don't know.' She turned from him and began to walk away. He watched for a few minutes then caught her up.

'Got any money on you?'

She felt in her pocket for her wallet, thinking, of all the times to ask me! 'How much d'you need?'

'Taxi fare. There's a box over there. I'll take you home.'

He rang for a cab, tapping out the numbers subtracted from ten because they had no small change. They told him, about ten minutes. They waited inside the booth because it was warmer. Liz felt immeasurably better. Tug, squatting in the corner, told her about the house. Max had paid the rent in arrears and moved in, with Brent and Mitty and Nancy. Tony was in gaol for unpaid fines. Max had let Tug and Billy stay on, but they were sleeping on the floor with one blanket between them because the others had first claim on the beds and mattresses. And I come to him, Liz thought. From my cosy home and inner-sprung bed I come to him for help.

The taxi pulled up. Liz edged her way out of the 'phone booth and was about to open the back door of the cab when it abruptly moved off. They stood together on the curb watching it till it turned the corner.

'Cunt,' said Tug. 'The cunt.'

Liz stood in open-mouthed bewilderment. 'But why?.

'Why d'y'think? Cunt saw me.'

'Does he know you?'

'Course not.'

'But....' The light glimmered through. 'Do they often do that?'

'At night mostly.' He shrugged. 'Guess they're scared of being mugged.'

She looked at his skinny frame and the face, still a child's face, half hidden by the black curls that came down past his shoulders, bare feet, jeans and jersey. How did it feel to frighten taxi drivers out of their fare?

Tug patiently tapped out another free call. She took the receiver from him. 'The taxi we had ordered came then drove off leaving us standing on the curb. I'd like an explanation.'

The operator was professionally placating — the driver must have had an urgent call, they'd send another cab right away.

'If it had been an urgent call surely he could have told us so.'

'Leave it,' hissed Tug, 'or we won't get one at all.'

'Another cab's on its way,' said the operator and hung up.

'The bastards,' she seethed. Tug gave her a soothing smile and took her hand in his. *He understands the nameless misery. He knows how it feels. That's why my legs brought me here.*

The second taxi driver was a woman. They made the journey in silence. Liz felt them to be in the presence of an enemy.

Tug liked her house. He turned on all the lights and examined all the rooms, then put a record on the stereo. While Liz made coffee he executed random karate kicks and chops in the kitchen.

'Bruce Lee's a millionaire twice over.'

'Is he?' Politely.

'Don't y'know?'

'Of course I don't know. Don't really care, to be honest.'

'Bet he is though.'

She poured the coffee. He spooned sugar into his, not looking at Liz. 'That fulla stay here last night, did he?'

'What fulla?'

'I saw yous. Coming out of the movies with him. He your boyfriend?'

'Not exactly.'

'But you like him?'

'Yes. I like him.'

'Looked a bit of a dick-head to me.'

'He's a millionaire.'

'Is he? Him? Fuck!' He saw her straight face bending. 'Bloody liar.'

She made up the bed in the spare room.

'Sheets,' he said. 'I haven't slept in sheets since — I can't even remember.' He bounced the springs up and down.

'Thank you, Tug,' she said.

'What for?'

'You know, bringing me home and whatever.'

'Any time,' he said graciously.

He was still asleep when she left for work. She had stood at the door for some minutes watching him and remembering Ralph. Please, can I keep him, Mum? Of course you can't, her mother said, you don't know where he's been, he's bound to be diseased. You should have left him — and don't fondle him. If you really want a pup we'll get you a nice one with a pedigree.

But she had kept Ralph. She found him at the dump when she went with her father to dispose of a broken chest of drawers, and she kept him, despite her mother, in the old disused gardening shed. And he flourished. He grew large and handsome and devoted, and she loved him more dearly than she ever loved his pedigree substitute, Mickey. Loved him perhaps because he remained the gardening shed resident and was not allowed near the house and the injustice of it inflamed her. When Ralph was fully grown her father arranged for him to be given to a family who lived in the country some forty miles away, but he kept coming back to Liz. On his fourth runaway trip he was shot by a farmer who was keeping vigil for a marauding sheep-killer.

'You see,' her father had said. 'You let him get too fond of you. In the end you did him more harm than good. It would have been kinder to let him die in the first place.'

It was a slack day at the coffee bar, Irwin muttering about bankruptcy. Jim came in at twelve, his look implied a mutual understanding and made her uneasy. He asked if she felt like company that evening and she said an old friend was calling on her. Then she remembered how neatly he'd made the bed, and said, what about the next night?

She had splurged and bought steak for dinner. She went in the back door calling, 'Hi.'

No reply. No music. Nothing. She had been so sure he'd still be there. She looked into the spare room. The bed had been sort of made. She looked around for a note but of course there was none.

She put the steak in the fridge, she could share it with Jim tomorrow. The thought gave her no pleasure, steak would be no treat for Jim. She'd also bought a bottle of port. She'd opened it and poured her fourth glass when the 'phone rang.

'Liz?' he forgot his signature silence. 'We was raided.'

'What do you mean raided?'

'The dees, went through the house.'

'What'd they find?'

'Stuff.'

'What sort of stuff?'

'Transistors, clothes, stuff like that.'

'Was that what they were looking for?'

'How'd I know?

'Where are you?'

'In town.'

'Are they charging anyone?'

67

'They took Billy. Brent got away. They was the only ones there.'

'What'll you do? Is some of the stuff yours?'

'I dunno. If I go back they'll pick me up.'

'There's a spare bed here if you want it.'

'You sure?'

'Just for the meantime.'

He tapped at the 'phone, a little rhythm. 'Might see you later then.'

'Suit yourself,' she said.

SIX

TUG CHOSE TO remain in bed, where he had spent the whole day, and declined to eat. Over the steak Liz told Jim about the homeless boy she had met at Valleyview and now taken in. Sitting across from Jim, watching him scrape aside his mushrooms (of course, she ought to have asked) with a delicacy which proclaimed pedigree, she could believe it was that straightforward. Jim found her story unremarkable. He was accustomed to the dispensing of good deeds. His mother, he told Liz a little wearily, used to do Meals on Wheels.

He showed more enthusiasm over the discovery that she had been a psychiatric inmate. From his questions she realised that the possibility of madness lent, for him, an edge of mystique.

When they had eaten and were sitting in separate chairs in front of the fire, Tug breezed through the room and into the kitchen to slice and butter himself a piece of bread. She had earlier put his grimy clothes to soak and now he was wrapped jauntily in Liz's pink chenille dressing gown. On his return trip she introduced him to Jim who extended his hand with a conspicuously affable hello. Tug paused, glowered and moved on, slamming the bedroom door behind him.

'What did I do?'

'Nothing. I have a feeling that was aimed at me.'

'Are you sure you know what you're doing. I mean, is it safe for you...?'

'He's only a child,' she said.

69

'He looks capable of looking after himself to me.'

'Did you look after yourself at sixteen?'

'That's hardly the point, Liz. How long's he going to stay?'

'I don't know. I suppose until he finds somewhere.' She felt defensive. Good causes ought to manifest themselves as cherubic waifs pale with gratitude.

'You know,' said Jim, conversationally, changing the subject, 'I've never really known any Maoris. Not personally. There just never were any in my particular circle of friends and acquaintances.

'Then I wouldn't take Tug as representative. They come in all shapes and moods.' She had meant it to sound wry but it came out tart, a rebuke. Jim, she thought, looks at Tug and sees not Tug but a Maori. Tug looks at Jim and sees not Jim but a dick-head. Obviously it simplified things greatly for both of them. Were the complications simply her own invention?

She tried to retrieve the threads of earlier conversations, but an uneasiness remained. It was as if, Liz thought, they were being watched. Then she realised with dismay that this was possibly true. The house was old and the door to Tug's room had a keyhole. As if in defiance of the same possibility Jim moved his chair closer to Liz and took her hand onto his lap.

Tug appeared on cue. He swayed across the room, purposefully nonchalant, and positioned himself in front of the bookcase. Jim's voice tailed off limply in the middle of a memory of boarding-school humiliations. Tug studied the book titles.

'Are you looking for something in particular?' She asked him brightly, a nervous student teacher.

Tug turned to look at them. 'One with screwing in it.'

Liz felt herself, absurdly, blushing. 'Try Henry Miller,' she said, not looking at Jim. 'Second shelf to your left. The black cover.'

He found the book and thumbed through the pages sourly. 'Bet it's slack.' But he took it with him back to the bedroom.

Jim suddenly remembered his need for an early night.

'I'm sorry about....' Liz nodded towards Tug's door.

Jim shrugged. 'I just wonder if you know what you're letting yourself in for.'

She walked to the gate with him. He invited her to go with him to an exhibition opening on the following Saturday, and brushed her lips in a dry kiss.

She confronted Tug in his bedroom. 'This is my home and I won't have you being rude to my friends.'

'Whaddid I do?' Looking up at her in injured innocence.

'You know.'

'Aren't I allowed to read your books or something? Is that it? Stink book anyway.' He tossed it onto the floor. She left it where it was.

'You're a toad,' she said, but no longer angry. 'And I don't think you'll make it to a prince.'

'What's that mean?'

'I'm too tired,' she said, 'to explain.'

Tug spent almost all of that week in bed. When Liz left in the mornings he would be asleep and when she got home from work he would still be in bed, listlessly thumbing through a magazine or simply staring up at the ceiling. If he got up for dinner — and he had little appetite — they'd talk in a polite and almost formal fashion. His manner wasn't so much guarded as apathetic. After a few attempts at jollying him Liz let him be, telling herself that such apparently bleak inactivity must be fulfilling some need in him. And, even lying listless and silent in bed, he provided a certain reassurance, was a bulwark against the mindless panic. Someone to come home to.

On the Friday Ken drove her, in her lunch-break, to the lawyer's office where their separation was to be made official. She was allotted a third of the proceeds from the sale of their house if and when it was sold. A generous agreement, the solicitor said, the courts would probably have allowed her less.

'I gather this is an amicable separation? Good. And there is no problem about access? No? Right. If you wish to attempt a reconciliation and renew conjugal relationships but then resume living apart that will not be considered a breach of legal separation.'

So still nothing was final. The game went on. Did she want

or didn't she want? This pretence that people had a choice.

She let Ken do the talking, suspecting anyway that he and the solicitor had some kind of prior understanding from which she was excluded. She signed the papers thinking ruefully of the Treaty of Waitangi. How could you ever know the magnitude of what you were signing away?

'Perhaps we've got time for a celebratory drink,' Ken suggested, back in the car.

'I don't exactly feel like celebrating.'

'I still can't understand you.' He edged the car out of its parking space. 'I never did, all those years.'

She was tempted to say sourly, You never tried, but she knew it took two, and how hard had *she* tried? Besides, she felt an absolute need to have the whole marriage parcelled up nicely and prettily.

'I'm not sorry, Ken,' she said. 'I mean I don't regret all those years. I did love you.'

Ken was watching the car ahead. It had a sticker which said JESUS OUR ONLY HOPE. 'I've thought about that quite a lot. The truth is I didn't love you, Liz. I don't think I ever did.' He was still watching the car with the sticker.

Liz felt numbed with the pain of it. Eleven years of her life flushed down a toilet bowl. 'What a pity you didn't think to tell me sooner,' she said limply, looking at the people on the footpath who could not know that she had just been stabbed in the conjugal back.

'I think it's best to be honest about it,' he said.

'Oh yes,' she said, 'much the best.' She thought about people who died laughing.

'I mean what sort of shit is he? Maybe he's just bitter, d'you think? But he really seemed to mean it. It must be true then? All those years. I was just the cook and the cleaner and the bloody laundrymaid. Very convenient. Oh, it must have been more than that. No it probably wasn't. He didn't lose. He's got Michael. He's got his fancy women. But what was the point of saying it? Why couldn't he have just pretended at the end. Oh God.'

Tug jerked her wrist savagely towards him. 'Shut up,' he roared. 'For fucksake shut up. It's over, okay? There's no

72

point in stirring it round and round. You're screwed in the head I reckon.'

Liz tried with her left hand to prise his fingers from her wrist. 'At least,' she said venomously, 'I manage to get out of bed.'

Tug rolled his eyes sardonically, but released her arm. 'If you don't mind leaving the room,' he said, 'I'd like to get dressed.'

She lay on her own bed, afraid that he would leave her, listening to his footsteps. He came to the doorway sniffing at his armpits. 'Even smells clean,' he said of his jersey, pleased. He tossed her wallet onto the bed. 'I've taken some money.'

'Help yourself.' As sarcasm it was indifferent.

'Thanks, I have.'

She heard him slam the back door and pad down the path.

She lay on the bed and thought about mental cruelty and degrees of mental cruelty and whether there was something about her that invited it, and why. Then she heard him come back, knowing it was Tug for who else on these bleak winter nights travelled in bare feet?

He came straight to her bedroom and spread a feast beside her. Fish and chips steaming, a bottle of sherry, a bottle of whisky. He beamed as he opened the packets.

'Tug,' she protested, 'we couldn't afford whisky.'

'Only paid for the sherry. And the greasies. Here's your change. Go on, count it.'

'We'll take the whisky back. Later. I'll come with you.'

'Fuck off. It's a present. I got it for you.'

'But you didn't pay for it.'

'So what? Maybe I did and maybe I didn't.'

'I know you didn't.'

'If we take it back they'll book me.'

'I don't think so.'

'Jesus. Don't be thick. I got a record. Jus' say thank you and take it.'

She took it. He went for glasses and she prepared a speech.

'Tug, while you live here no more stealing, okay? It's just not on.'

He poured them each a sherry. 'Liz, while I live here no more crying and moaning your arse off, okay?'

'You need some shoes,' she said. 'We'll have to get you some shoes. Your feet must be freezing.' She reached to touch them. 'They are.'

'Last winter I had gumboots. I kept them on all the time so's they wouldn't get nicked and there wasn't nowhere to take a bath and when in the end I took them off I had weedy feet.'

She laughed. 'What do you mean, weedy?'

'There was weeds growing on them. Fungus stuff. True.'

They wrapped themselves in rugs against the cold and kept refilling the glasses until Ken no longer mattered. Raking out memories of his mother Tug said, matter-of-fact, 'Since she died you're the only person who's loved me.'

She was astonished. 'How do you know I love you?'

'But you do, don't you?'

'I suppose so.' Hedging it even then and amazed that anyone could expose himself so incautiously to rejection. With a certain shame she sifted his words for motive. Were they as innocent and trusting as it seemed? Was he trying to trap her into some kind of emotional obligation?

Later, he asked, 'Why do you stare at me so much.'

She was embarrassed. 'Do I?'

'You're always staring at me.'

She said, truthfully, 'Then it's because I think you're pretty. I mean I like looking at you. I suppose I envy you. Brown skin looks so much better than white skin. That's a fact, whatever people may say. It seems a bit unfair really.' She registered the unintended pun, but it didn't seem worth spelling out.

Tug studied the colour of the back of his hand judiciously. 'Yeah, you're right. That's why I only look at you when I really have to.'

The lady artist wore gold satin pants and high leather boots, her hair was straight, glossy black, her husband wealthy and old. She overshadowed her paintings which were abstracts in blues and purples and splotches of brown. If you joined them all together the paintings would have looked almost identical to the material of a dress Liz had bought from Kirkcaldies when she was nineteen. She had loved that dress, and at nine-

74

teen she would also have loved the exhibition opening and the party which followed when a selected few of them adjourned to the home of the lady artist.

At nineteen Liz had been a devoted admirer of the world and its people. She was continuously delighted by her amazing good fortune in knowing and meeting so many entertaining, talented and charming individuals. And here she was, deja-vuing in the same circles. But the familiarity lacked pleasure, she stood awkward in her black dress, remote and disengaged. She was not overlooked; her association with Jim lent her prestige and besides she was a new face and a fresh audience.

A plump little man with fleshy lips proffered a bowl of peanuts.

'I'm a criminal lawyer. You can take that however you like.'

'I believe you,' she said.

He laughed with his teeth protruding like a horse and gave a sweep of his hand. 'Did you ever see so much intellectual wankery?'

She smiled dutifully. He thrust his face towards hers. 'You wouldn't like a quick fumble in the spare bedroom I don't suppose?'

'No thanks.'

'Then you won't mind if I try elsewhere?'

She shook her head. He bowed and moved away.

Jim was in a corner being whispered at by the lady artist. A young woman warned Liz that there was a lot of bad acid being circulated these days, a young reporter boasted that he had never set foot on a rugby field, then a middle-aged man recited a poem about manuka bushes to the whole room. Leonard Cohen gloomed from the stereo speakers, joints passed from hand to hand.

A toothy woman in a caftan complained piercingly about the increasing number of louts in the city square, and Liz wondered if Tug was at home or out louting. The little lawyer was put in mind of a party he was once at where loutish males forced one of their women to lie on the table amid the beer flagons while they removed her knickers and shoved a saveloy up her. Then the men shared the saveloy. It was a most successful story. The toothy woman proclaimed it epitomised the average New Zealander. Someone else asked the lawyer if he liked saveloys and he smiled enigmatically. 'That's nothing compared to their gang initiation rites,' said another.

Liz moved away, less in disgust than anger. She felt, obscurely and drunkenly, defiled on Tug's behalf. She had a picture of herself standing, immobilised, with each foot on a separate iceberg and those icebergs incompatible and drifting apart. At some point, she warned herself, she would have to choose.

Jim was still wedged in the corner with the booted lady. He was tracing shapes on his hand, explaining something, with a frown of concentration. The artist's hand was nestled in Jim's crotch. She was smiling. Liz made her way quietly up the sumptuous passage and rang for a cab.

Tug was in bed. Checking on that, she stumbled against the doorpost.

'You're drunk.'

'A bit. Were you asleep? Shall I put the light on?'

'If you want. How was the party?'

'Awful. Full of stupid people.'

'Dick-head bring you home?'

'No. I got a taxi.'

'You left him there?'

'He seemed quite happy.'

'You left before it finished?'

She wanted to explain that she had chosen her iceberg and that the choosing had opened up another dimension of possibility which had seemed both shocking and inevitable. Coming home in the taxi she had made herself an unthinkable promise. Now she took a deep breath and dragged back the words that were cowardly fleeing from her mind.

'Tug, I'd like to sleep with you.'

He just looked at her, eyes widened.

'Well?' she snapped it out. The waiting was unendurable.

He squirmed beneath the blankets. 'I'm not sure what you mean.'

'Oh God,' she pleaded. 'I mean what you think I mean. Just say yes or no.' Her courage had abandoned her, she wanted to retract, deny, pass out.

He pulled the blankets up to his eyes and said something muffled from beneath them.

'I couldn't hear,' she said helplessly.

He lowered the blankets to chin level. 'No,' he said clearly.

The embarrassment was smothered in relief and a sudden sobriety. 'I'm sorry Tug. I'm really sorry. I should never have said it. You're quite right. We'll forget it. Okay? Everything just like it was.'

He nodded without conviction.

At breakfast Tug was polite and watchful. Liz was polite and regretful.

'Are you hungry?'

'No thank you.'

'There's some bacon?'

'No. Really, I'm not hungry.'

'But you'll have a cup of tea? I'm just making one.'

'A cup of tea. All right. If you're making one.'

'Michael's coming today. I thought he'd be here before now.'

'Might go out for a while. See some of the boys.'

'That's a good idea. You haven't been out for days. Shall I keep dinner for you?'

'Don't worry. I'm not sure what time I'll be back.'

I've frightened him away, she thought. I've betrayed his trust.

In the bathroom mirror she reminded her reflection that she was old. Her gums were receding, her skin was loosening. There were furrows and crow's-feet. She was old enough, as he'd once pointed out, to be his mother.

She wanted her times with Michael to be gentle with shared laughter and affectionate gestures, but there was an awkwardness between them. She wanted to explain, atone, be forgiven, but Michael watched her with veiled eyes remembering (she thought) her weeping past.

She walked with him to the park, aware that Ken had the car and access to more exciting diversions. He told her about the air-force bomber he had under construction at home; his hardest model yet. She listened but did not comprehend.

77

Michael was a small encyclopaedia of weaponry and warfare.

At home again they made gingerbread men and he talked about their plans to move north. 'Won't you miss me?' she pleaded. 'I s'pose so,' he said, looking down at the table. After tea he watched out the window for Ken's car coming to take him home.

At midnight she was woken from a dream about Toothless Neddy in a soldier's uniform crouching injured in a barn. She went to answer the 'phone. Did she wish, the operator asked, to accept a collect call from a Mr Morton in Dunedin? *Dunedin?*

'Liz?' He sounded anxious. 'Liz, I'm in... hangon....' She heard him open a door and ask, 'Hey, whassa name of this place?'

'Dunedin,' she said when he returned.

'Yeah, that's right. Always forget names.'

'What are you doing in Dunedin?'

'Nothing much. Standing in a 'phone box.'

'I meant... well how did you get there?'

'Drove down. Me and some of the boys. In this Holden. I drove from Timaru.'

'Whose car is it?'

'One of the boys.'

'He owns it?'

'He found it. Finders keepers doncha know?' He laughed. 'Mightn't be home for a few days so I's ringing to let you know.'

'Like how many days?' Wishing she didn't need to ask, wondering if in Dunedin it emerged as a plea or a threat.

'Not too many.' He was being reassuring, paternal. 'I'll be home by next weekend, okay? You won't give my bed to anyone?'

A whole week.

'I might,' she said off-handedly. 'It depends.'

An instant reaction. 'Go ahead then. I probably won't be coming back anyway.'

'As you like.' But she allowed him the satisfaction of being first to hang up.

'I was really tired so I just thought I'd slip away on the quiet.

I didn't want to mess up your evening. It just didn't occur to me that you'd be upset about it.'

Sitting in the Grand Hotel with its red leather upholstery and mahogany-stained tables Liz thought how easy it was to be sophisticated when you didn't really care.

On Monday she had decided there was little point in her continuing to see Jim. But this was Thursday and Tug had not come home and her resolve seemed perhaps a little hasty. Jim had been away attending an Indigenous Culture seminar in Palmerston North. He had told her about it, he said, though she had no recollection and would she have forgotten something as portentous as an Indigenous Culture seminar? Anyway here he was buying her drinks and almost nervously explaining that his association with Elly, painter of blue and purple abstracts, was a matter of ambition on her side and reluctance on his.

'You don't need to explain,' Liz told him. 'I don't own you. I don't want that kind of involvement.'

She could see that he was impressed, that her indifference attracted him. She felt ashamed of herself, yet after he had called at the coffee bar that morning to invite her for drinks she had made a deliberate decision to be encouraging. Jim was politeness, conversation, *normality*. When (if) Tug returned her role would be more clearly defined if Jim was around. No more embarrassing lapses.

She watched him walk across to the bar to refill their glasses. He walked with such confidence. Her mother would like him. From across the room the plump lawyer caught Liz's eye and waved. Liz waved back, smiling. It was so easy to be acceptable.

She'd been home an hour when the 'phone went. She ran to answer it. A wrong number. But it was natural to be worried, she thought. He could have been arrested. The car might have crashed. Both seemed more probabilities than possibilities.

If he was dead she wouldn't be notified — they'd track down some next-of-kin. For her he would just have disappeared.

She switched on the radio and waited for the hourly news

bulletin and the names of road fatality victims. There were none.

Friday night. A car slowed down on the street; all evening, cars had been passing and slowing, but this one had no muffler. Liz went on reading but the words were just words on their own and would not link into sentences. The car stopped. Definitely it had stopped. There were shouts and a slamming of doors, then the car drove off again. She began again at the beginning of the sentence; the street was full of houses expecting visitors.

The door was locked and he hammered on it with unnecessary force. Liz got out of bed and went to open it, remembering how much he could irritate her.

'You was in bed?' He smelt of beer.

'It's quite late.'

She went back to the bedroom, he followed her and stood leaning against the wall.

'You glad I'm back?'

'Well, I'm glad you're still alive anyway.'

'You was worried?'

'I suppose the car was stolen?'

'It was and it wasn't. Fat Boy paid the deposit. Only under another name.'

'What did you do down there?'

'Nothing much. Just mucked about. They wouldn't let us in at the prison.'

'But you had a good time?'

'Not really,' he said. 'I's homesick.'

She was going to laugh, but she saw he meant it. 'Well, you're home now,' she said.

He looked past her at the window with its curtains drawn and she knew in a curdling instant what he was about to say.

'You remember the other night, what you said.... Did you mean it?'

'I was drunk.' Her cowardliness shamed her. 'Yes, I meant it.'

He was crouching beside the bed holding her hand. The whole of her was a hand being held. His face was hidden against the bedspread; when he raised it his eyes seemed huge.

Blue eyes, she thought, were intrusive, they invaded you. Brown eyes looked inward; they went deep, you could float in them. Possibly drown.

At eleven Liz had been religious. She had planned to be a missionary in some dark tropical land tending the sparrow legged bulbous-bellied children who had eyes like Tug's eyes. She longed for selfless dedication and righteous anger. She wrote to Trevor Huddleston, care of his publishers, but he was no doubt too busy to reply.

Her mother sang in the Anglican church choir on Sundays, but Liz was privately scornful of her mother's style of religion — social introductions, descant harmony and a Sunday spiritual inoculation. The daughter waited to be overcome by some dark, tumultuous force; she longed for surrender and dedication and intensity. The feeling was strong in her that she had been Chosen, yet she hesitated, wanting confirmation; a sign; however small. She created opportunities for this to happen beyond the bounds of coincidence, but when no bushes burned, no telegraph poles split in two and the messages of the clouds remained obscure she finally lost interest.

She committed herself then to Ralph and his various successors — stray cats and broken birds. A few died but most of them recovered. The birds flew away or stayed around the home as semi-pets; the cats she took eventually to the S.P.C.A. where they were probably destroyed. Liz was aware of this likelihood but remained committed to tending her ailing strays.

After a time her spiritual aspirations began to seem nothing more than a childish phase. Watching her battered birds flap off awkwardly into the suburban skies she would tell herself that if there was some infinite truth this was it and it was beyond question or comprehension — just *there* like the hillside, like the sea.

And sometimes when she was alone, out riding Delilah, entranced by the shape of her horse's ears and the fall of her mane, she would get a sensation of pure happiness. Although the feeling itself was beyond description it was accompanied by a vague sensation of thirst. For herself she defined it as rapture. She had no doubt it had something to do with that

81

infinite truth.

And now, absurdly, with Tug's hands and mouth moving over her body she thought of religion. She remembered the sharpness of her longing for intensity and surrender and she recognised that incomparably exquisite thirst. *Of course,* she thought. *Of course.*

He was shameless. He presented his body as a chef might present his finest cuisine, confident that every morsel — every hair, every pucker and crevice — was delicious and desirable. And gradually, as he explored her own body without permission or hesitation she felt three decades of caution and apprehension crumble and fall away. For the first time in her life she felt unreservedly — well, *almost* unreservedly — lovable.

They lay tight in each other's arms.

'What are you thinking?' She whispered, feeling that dull thirstiness all through her.

'I's thinking what a lot of time we wasted.'

'That was your fault; you turned me down.'

'I's scared. I mean you're sort of...'

'Like your mother?'

'Not now you're not.'

She laughed. 'So what happens now?'

'We start again.'

'I meant.... I won't regret it,' she told him. 'Whatever happens I could never regret it.'

She woke at eight, exultant. She felt as she had felt after the birth of her children — permanently, cataclysmically altered. She had looked at the clock before she fell asleep and it said half-past five. Tug had fallen asleep about an hour before her, his arms still tight around her. When she slid a hand down over his buttocks he had thrust against her even in his sleep. Now, remembering that, she grinned to herself wanting him to wake so she could tell him.

He was buried beneath the bedclothes. She pulled them down carefully, wanting to look at his face. Unveiling it like a national treasure. His eyes flickered then opened wide and he grabbed at the bedclothes and pulled them back over his head.

'Tug?'

'I thought it was a dream,' muffled through the blankets.

'It wasn't, and you can't stay under there forever.'

He lowered the blankets slowly, fearfully, to make her laugh.

'What happens now?' he asked when they reached his chin.

'I guess we make the most of it while it lasts.'

'How long d'y' reckon we'll last?'

She thought about it. In her experience euphoria had never been more than momentary. 'Two weeks?' she ventured in wild optimism.

'I'd say nearer two months.'

She shook her head.

'Two months,' he repeated. 'D'you wanna bet? Two dollars, ay?'

'I don't want to bet.'

'Come on,' he urged, grinning already at his own joke. 'Make it a bit interesting.'

She cuffed at his head but he ducked. His face grew solemn. 'You wanna know something?'

'What?' Anxiety welled.

'It wasn't me who had the weedy feet. It was Bones.'

SEVEN

'YOU REALISE,' SHE said, searching for blackheads in the border forests of his hair, 'that we both happen to be at the peak of our sexuality.'

'How d'you know?'

'It's a known fact. Research has shown that men are at their horniest around sixteen and women when they're in their thirties.'

'So it'll wear off they reckon? What'll we do then?'

'I'll go back to knitting,' she said, 'and you'll just have to find another hobby.'

'Never. I like this one too much.'

'There's other things,' she said a little wistfully, trying to remember them. Insatiability had a lot going for it in terms of immediate reward, but she suspected it was an affliction and not the natural order of things. She could not decide whether she was supremely fortunate or helplessly depraved, but she acknowledged her addiction.

Nevertheless, apart from one lapse where she pleaded sickness, she dragged herself out of their voluptuous bed in the mornings and caught the bus to town. She buttered bread, cleared tables, poured coffee, smiled at strangers, chatted to Irwin and counted change into palms. And all the while her mind wriggled ecstatically over memories of the night past and anticipations of the night to come. Customers who had once been only smiles, frowns and small talk became bodies proclaiming their personal preferences and possibilities and Liz, checking her reflection in the washroom mirror was surprised, each time, to find that her compulsion was not etched there like graffitti.

Her fancies were most reckless in the mornings. By afternoon she would have tempered them, and sometimes by the time she wearily climbed off her homeward bus they would have diminished to minor and regrettable aberrations.

But in the living room or in the bedroom Tug would be waiting naked and erect ('What if it wasn't me but the meter reader?') or limp and languorously submissive. Once he was dressed in her long white nightgown and wearing her make-up. And though on close inspection the cosmetics lacked a certain expertise of application the general effect was quite lovely. It occurred to Liz, a bit resentfully, that even in younger days she had never looked as feminine and devourable.

Liz introduced games of another kind. They weren't as much fun but they were the kind she knew best and her playing of them was compulsive.

'Why me?' she would say. 'I mean, do you think of me as old? Doesn't it bother you?'

And Tug, ignoring the unwritten rules of play, would be flippant. 'Nah, doesn't bother me. I like a few wrinkles. I'm kinky.'

So, after a few attempts, she played it alone, except that he kept interrupting with interjections.

'It's like brown velvet,' she said. 'I'd wondered about that. Whether dark-skinned men were dark everywhere.'

'Did you think...?'

'I had no way of knowing. I thought maybe all men were that motley purple. I find dark skin so much more attractive. They say a lot of white women do. Like in America there's this mystique about sexy black men which attracts the white women. Maybe it's something like that with me and you.'

'Well aren't I sexy?'

'Of course.'

'Then what are you talking about?'

'Just that it's the wrong reason for wanting someone.'

'But I like Pakeha women.'

'Ah, but why?'

'I jus' do.'

'There must be a reason. I mean it could be revenge; a way of getting back at Pakehas for things they've done to Maoris.'

'Who told you that shit?'

'It happens.'

'How d'y'know?'

'I just know. I suppose I've read it.'

'Oh.' Eyes popping in phoney awe. 'Then of course it must be right.' Silently laughing at her.

'You're hopeless,' she sulked. 'I can't even have a proper conversation with you.' (Was *that* it — his lack of learning? Allure of the primitive; the Lady Chatterley syndrome?)

'You know,' she said one evening, digging into the stew he had cooked for them, heady with herbs. (Did she have a sub-conscious need to dominate — an unnatural desire to relegate her partner to the submissive wifely role?)

'You know,' she said, 'in some cultures young men are encouraged to get their early experiences of sex with older women.'

'So?'

'Just thought you'd be interested.'

'Well you'da been a waste of time. I had to teach you everything you know.'

'Not quite everything.'

'Near enough.'

She wondered; if they were sinning and, if she as the instigator and the adult was the guilty party, would her comparative inexperience be a point for or against absolution?

For guilt was always there lining the gingerbread of her passion. As his mother, she thought with doleful sentimentality, her love for him could have been pure and unconditional. (It being so much easier to love a child that is not rightfully yours — such love being free of the demands, self-accusations, duties and complex divisions of loyalty associated with true motherhood.) As his lover she was gross and tormented. She watched him for signs of emotional devastation due to their altered relationship, but on the whole he seemed happier.

Sometimes, glancing apprehensively into the future, she envisaged a time when they would revert to a platonic maternal/filial relationship. She would cast herself, convincingly, in the role of the dependable anchor in the drifting tidal confusion that seemed to have constituted Tug's past life and might be expected to constitute his future life. She would be his occasional refuge from an otherwise rootless and stormy life; he would be her vicarious excitement, her passing breeze of chaos and insecurity.

Beyond that she invented a tranquil day in the future when Tug, into his mid-twenties, would appear on her doorstep. (And she, having not heard from him for nearly two years, sometimes saying to her husband — that kindly, solid, good-provider whose features remained indistinct — 'I hope Tug's looking after himself. I do worry about him.') Then there Tug would be at the door with a pretty young woman beside him and an infant — a boy — in his arms (wide-mouthed, black haired, the image of Tug). And Tug would say, 'Liz, you've got a grandson,' and he would introduce Liz to his wife, proud of them both. And Tug and Liz would exchange glances; a bond of understanding, of shared memories and affection, of a rare and fragile secret shared.

She described to Tug this happy vision. He thought about it for a while.

'You wouldn't be jealous of her?'

'No. As long as you were happy I'd be delighted for you.' She believed herself. It was such a satisfactory happy ending.

Tug was teaching himself to read. He could handle the little words, it was those with more than two syllables which confounded him. He had discovered some of Liz's treasured childhood books and had worked his way up to *The House at Pooh Corner*. At first, when Liz found him struggling through *Snow White* she had laughed because it seemed so incongruous.

'Don't laugh at me,' he'd rebuked her. 'I'm trying to improve myself.'

Later he explained that he was working up to *Sexus*. 'I tried but it was too hard. Does it really have screwing in it?'

'You're obsessed. Have you always been so interested in

sex?'

'Of course. Haven't you?'

'Not really. There were always so many other things.'

'I'm interested in other things too.'

'Like what?'

'Pills, drinking, dope, music.'

'Oh God!'

'I might change,' he said consolingly, 'when I'm grown up.'

But he was bigger than her, and stronger. When he put his arms around her it felt like protection. 'I think you need me' he would say then, with more hope than conviction. There were wild moments when she could even believe they had some kind of future together — perhaps for as long as a year. Then she would try to channel his 'improvement' along her own lines of interest. One night she searched through an anthology of poems and read to him; a sample of Baxter, a little of Auden. After which she looked up hopefully. He was wearing his tolerant, paternal smile.

'You finished?'

'What d'you think of them?'

'Boring rubbish.'

She sulked. Not over his lack of appreciation but over his way of conveying it. To her it was second nature to cushion her words with tact. As a child it had seemed necessary, as a wife obligatory. She had thought it a civilised and universal verbal currency. Tug not only ignored this convention but seemed to delight in insult and provocation. Each time she would retreat from him, withdraw injured into her own resentment.

'What's the matter?' he'd ask eventually.

'What do you *think's* the matter?'

'I dunno.'

'What you said's the matter.'

'Whad'I say?'

She would have to remind him.

'I din mean anything.' Caressing her thin skin. 'You take everything so seriously. It was just a joke.'

'But it wasn't funny.'

'Wasn't that kinda joke. It's just.... If you's a Maori you'd come right back at me. You'd know how to take it.'

'But I'm not a Maori. I just get hurt.'

'No wonder you ended in the funny farm. You're so wet, you are.'

'Tug!'

'I'm sorry, love. I'm sorry. I din' mean it.'

Together they would examine their pasts for signs of predisposition (perhaps predestination) which might explain their unlikely union.

'About two years ago or more, so I'da been thirteen or fourteen. She was a student teacher so she musta been about nineteen. Gave me a taste for older women.'

'When I was at school I used to draw faces in my books. In the margins, you know. Maori faces I suppose — wide noses and big lips. I didn't know any Maoris, not one, but those kind of features sort of fascinated me. It was always the same face I drew, more or less. It could have been your face.'

'I wouldn'ta been born then even. Perhaps you invented me?'

'Yeah, perhaps. Did you fancy me? Before, I mean?'

'Dunno really. I didn't think about it. Least not straight out.'

'All those days when you lay in bed — what did you think about?'

'I slept mostly. Yeah, and sometimes I wanked. When you's at home I listened to what you was doing; your footsteps.'

'Did you think about sleeping with me?'

'Fuck no. Well, not that. But I thought about you and that dicky Jim. Thought about that a lot.'

She watched his hands; slim brown hands with nails like delicate pink shells. HATE tattooed, amateurish, between the knuckle and first joint of a middle finger. She touched it; 'Why?'

'Why not?'

'Sit down,' ordered Irwin. 'Have yourself a break. You want to make out I'm a slave-driver?'

He had poured them both coffee. Liz sat down with him, knowing he was going to talk about his family. Irwin talked about his family more and more often. His children (he lamented) weren't as children should be; this was his wife's fault, she had strange New Zealand ways. Irwin and his wife didn't have much to talk about any more.

'Eva's changed,' said Irwin, as if taking up where he'd finished the day before. 'She's lost all her courage.'

'Her courage?'

'That what I call it from the way I see it.'

'It's hard,' said Liz, 'being at home with small children all day.'

'Poof. She has all the machines. I give her everything.'

'It's still hard. Even with machines.'

'But you still have your courage.'

The expression pleased her. 'I'm not at home with small children all day.'

They'd had the same conversation in several different versions. Liz felt sympathy for Eva whom she had never met. On Eva's behalf she would try to explain to Irwin the feelings she had never been able to explain to Ken. It was possible, of course, that Eva didn't share those feelings but it was the only kind of contribution that Liz felt able to offer.

'Why is it I can talk to you but not my wife,' bewailed Irwin, and Liz wondered whether Ken had felt like that. Had her hardening resentment finally prohibited any real communication between them? She also wondered, a little uneasily, if Irwin imagined their conversations were leading to something more intimate, that he might think he was falling in love with her simply out of gratitude for having someone to air his problems to. He kept remarking upon how different she was to Eva, and Liz kept insisting (though how could she know?) that they were the same and the difference was in their circumstances.

Should Irwin seek more than a sympathetic audience Liz would align herself firmly on the side of Eva and fidelity (though it was entirely her own assumption that the two went together). She wondered if any of Ken's extramural interests had displayed that kind of loyalty to her. But in honesty she admitted to herself her moral decision was not made in the face of temptation. She could not imagine Irwin's naked arse proffered up as a delicacy, or Irwin in blue eye shadow and

90

satin nightgown.

Eva, Irwin now complained, was extravagant. She insisted on buying coloured toilet paper and he'd checked at the supermarket and found that it cost more.

Liz laughed at him. 'A couple of cents a fortnight. Divorce her, why don't you! Blowing all your hard-earned cash on luxuries like that!'

'That was just an example,' he said defensively. 'I could tell you lots of others but you're in the wrong kind of mind.'

They were sitting at the table nearest the counter. It was the lull time before lunchtime. Liz was still grinning over Irwin's claim when Jim walked in. It was only a little over a week since she'd last seen him but he seemed like some distant acquaintance from her past. In that week her world had rolled over.

Irwin cleared away their cups while Liz made Jim his pot of tea. Jim had been in Auckland buying paintings. Auckland, he said conversationally, was frantic.

'They're all crazy up there,' put in Irwin from the kitchen. 'All thinking they own the world and running round trying to catch their tails.'

'Well I didn't catch any tail,' said Jim loudly to Irwin, but looking at Liz. She avoided his eyes. As she set his tea on the table he asked, not casually, 'What have you been doing with yourself?'

'I've met someone,' she said, feeling bad about it, 'sort of special.'

He was of course gallant. 'Well, I'm glad for you. Anyone I know?'

Cowardly she lied no, ashamed of the denial.

Irwin had been listening in. He quizzed her later.

'So you've got a new lover. Or was that just a way of getting rid of the old one?'

'Irwin! That was a private conversation.'

He smirked. 'I'd like to get a look at him. See what I'm up against.'

She laughed to show he must be joking.

Lying in bed nose to nose, breathing his breath like a deep sea diver she considered the rapture.

'The only other times I felt this way were when I was quite young. When I was out riding my horse.'

'Well of course,' he said.

'What do you mean, of course?'

'Horses. For girls it's a kind of wanking. Everyone knows that.'

'Bullshit. Anyway I was talking about something more than that. Something to do with my soul.' She thought about saddles. 'Tug? Maybe it is only sex, maybe that's all there is in the end. D'you think so?'

'No, of course not.'

'What do you think then?'

'I don't think about anything. I jus' wait to see what happens.'

She would wake in the middle of the night to switch off the transistor radio. He insisted on having it on until he fell asleep, claiming that silence kept him awake and made him lonely.

'If you did something during the day....'

'I did. I tidied the house.'

He made her sleep on the outside of the bed in case something horrible crept in on them during the night.

Michael came for the whole weekend. Liz wanted to be delighted but thought of it as an intrusion. 'He'll be the fly in our ecstasy,' she said to Tug. He looked at her blankly. 'Never mind,' she said, 'never mind.'

The weekend weather was cold and windy with sporadic rain. On the Saturday afternoon Liz took Michael to a Disney movie which seemed to her almost unendurably long and foolish. Nevertheless she wept near the end when the dog died because fictional sorrows almost always made her cry. And when they walked out into the grey afternoon light Michael looked at her reddened eyes and winced.

'You're so embarrassing, Mum,' he said. She felt mildly pleased, he made so few personal comments.

Tug spent much of the weekend in bed. She had insisted that he move back to the spare room and Michael should sleep on the living-room sofa. Tug had objected.

'Just tell him 'bout us.'

'I can't.'

'Why not?'

'Because....' She floundered. 'Because I don't want Ken to know.'

'Why not?'

'It might go against me in a divorce,' she prevaricated. 'He might stop me seeing Michael.'

Tug could be acute. 'You're ashamed of me.'

'That's not true. Maybe I'm ashamed of myself.'

'It comes to the same thing.'

Having returned to the single bed Tug stayed in it until well into the afternoons. Liz would have preferred him to stay there the whole time. To Michael, Tug was impersonal, neither friendly nor unfriendly. He kept his attention on Liz, contorting his tongue into open invitations, gesturing, posing — a charade designed to punish Liz by arousing Michael's curiosity. But Michael was oblivious to Tug's performance and Liz, though resentful, could feel her body responding to Tug's lewd mime acts. Yet at night when Michael was asleep and Tug came to her bed she was tense and constrained.

On the Sunday afternoon, in unspoken consent, they adjourned to the bathroom which alone had a door that locked. They fucked, barren and urgent, on the cold hard lino. *This is the under-side to our coupling,* Liz thought, *another perspective.* She wasn't dismayed. There was something sharp and hard and fundamental about their pleasure.

But she also presumed it to be a truce. 'Try and be a bit nice to Michael,' she coaxed as she replaced her clothes. He had his back to her, washing himself at the handbasin and he took his time about replying.

'You ask a lot from me, y'know. Y'ask too fuckin' much.'

She felt he had deceived her. She had believed she had already been the repository for his anger — that it was spread now warm, damp and impotent between her legs. This reserve of fury seemed an insult and his accusation outrageous.

'I ask a lot from *you*! Jesus, Tug, I ask nothing from you. But *you* expect me to go to work, to buy the food, pay the rent, mother you. I mean what do you do? You do nothing.'

He was looking at her, his eyes narrowed, black and cold and his mouth twisted into the sneer — but this time she no

93

longer thought it theatrical and amusing. It was a mask of hatred.

'Yeah,' he said, his voice very soft. 'Din't you know that. It's a bludge. I'm just a bludger.'

She felt fear trickling cold inside her. She had never before in her life felt physically threatened and the fear was mixed with astonishment. She had not thought to feel afraid of him. She made an attempt to placate, keeping her voice neutral, conversational.

'I didn't say that, Tug.'

'It's true anyway. You're a mug, always knew it. Whaddya think I'd be with an old woman like you for?'

Fury swamped her fear, though she kept her distance. 'Get out,' she ordered. 'Get your things and go.'

'Make me.' He leaned against the door, his top lip was drawn into a snarl, like a dog's. Liz thought with what seemed to be great clarity, he's evil — this is the real Tug. His refusal to leave confirmed this; it was so *unreasonable*. It reduced everything to nonsense. For even though he was bigger and younger and meaner and could, if he wanted, beat her up she had still held the trump card for she was the householder and he the guest. Now she had played that card and he had torn it up. Yet her dismay at the situation was tempered by a certain reluctant admiration for his disregard of the rules.

As he appeared to be staying she asked him tersely, after a time of silent hostility, to let her out the door.

'Why?'

'I have to cook dinner.'

He held the door open and closed it again after her.

Later, while she stood at the bench shredding cabbage, he walked past her through the kitchen with a tentative pause. She concentrated on the cabbage.

'I never asked you for money,' he said. It was little more than a mumble, then he walked on. She made no reply. She struggled to retain that clear vision of him as a monster, unclouded by compassion or need, but her anger was abating and already the vision seemed less sure. She added more sausages to the pan; at least he should leave on a full stomach.

And it was true that he had never asked her for money. When she had given him a couple of dollars here and there he had always seemed embarrassed and reluctant to accept it. *Of course,* said a sharp voice in her head — the voice she was later to identify as the Upbringing. *Of course. He's cunning. That's part of the act.* But the vision was now confused, Tug's character had become a moot point. She could not throw him out, but she would *ease* him out.

She heard Michael's high voice from the living room. 'Are you going away?' Then the sound of the front door opening. She went into the living room. Tug was standing in the doorway as if waiting for her. Under his arm he had the old jersey and jacket she had given him and the spare pair of jeans she had bought him, second-hand, from the Red Cross shop. Those were his 'things', the sum total of them. She felt an ache of pity. She had so much. She stopped a few feet away from him, aware that Michael was watching, trying to convey casual concern.

'Where will you go?'

He sneered — a classical sneer, prolonged for full effect — then turned away.

'See y' round,' he said and started down the path.

Liz registered the melodrama of his exit and part of her wanted to laugh, but she went after him, it seemed imperative that she did.

'Tug, I'm sorry. Let's talk about it. Please? Couldn't we?'

But he went out the gate and turned up the road without even looking at her. She went back inside, shivering in the chill wind.

After dinner, for which Liz had no appetite, she played snakes and ladders with Michael until Ken came to collect him. Liz and Ken now treated each other like business acquaintances — or, more accurately, business competitors. She found it hard to believe there had ever been anything more.

On this night Ken was cheerful, pleased with himself. He had a buyer for the house and had settled on a moving date. As (he pointed out) Liz had got out of their separation lightly, without having to pay maintenance, she would be happy, surely, to fly Michael down to be with her in the holidays.

That was assuming she wished to continue seeing him.

Liz agreed with his arrangements though she sardonically registered his use of the word 'lightly'. She didn't dwell on the thought of Michael as an occasional holiday visitor. She was distracted, listening for the 'phone or footsteps. She was indifferent to Ken's talk of settlements and mortgage repayments. She wanted to be alone. She didn't want to be alone. Whichever, she was relieved when they left.

The 'phone rang at twenty-past-one in the morning. She wasn't asleep. The operator asked if she wished to accept a collect call from a 'phone booth — a Mr Morton calling.

'It's me,' he said.

'I know.' Silence. 'Where are you?'

''Phone box. Manchester Street.'

'I never knew you could make collect calls from 'phone boxes.'

'I tried to tap it an' I got an all-night service station.'

That seemed to demand no particular reply. The silence expanded, not even the tapping of fingers or that familiar shaky breathing sound. She began to fear he had gone away.

'Tug?'

'Mmm.'

'I wondered if you were still there. I'm sorry Tug.'

Now she could hear him breathing — that shaky rasping sound. 'Can I come home then?' A small abject voice.

'Of course.'

He made a small noise like a sigh. 'See you, then.'

'Yes.' She waited for him to hang up first and felt anxious when he did. She began to think his voice had had an edge to it. She went back to bed, installed her diaphragm and waited. The diaphragm seemed like a lost cause; the stable door past which the horse had, in all probability, bolted. Pregnancy loomed like the ultimate disaster, yet she supposed it may be inevitable and beyond her control. It seemed greatly to her credit that on all but a couple of occasions she had displayed sufficient forethought or mustered enough last-minute willpower to ensure that the yellow rubber obscenity was inside her before Tug was. She thought of returning to pills and perpetual nausea for she had no faith in the diaphragm's powers of prevention. She conceded it may improve the odds, but she couldn't believe that in the battle for her womb that dingey, flabby apparatus could win out against Tug's rampant and unflagging virility.

She waited. Her mind was needled by apprehensions but her body was smug with anticipation. The mind carped; Tug had devised this night of humiliation for his own sadistic pleasure; he had her by the shortest hairs, grovelling; right now he would be laughing with the boys — old money bags, the waitress.

There are other things, murmured the body.

What things?

You know.

That!

Other things too. His warmth. His realness. How he can make me laugh.

Nebulous value judgements. Look at the facts.

Fact: to walk from the city would take at most an hour. But he may have been inadvertently delayed. He could have been knocked down by a car. He could have been hurt in a fight with the local Hell's Angels. Hadn't Tug said they hated the boys?

Finally she fell asleep and dreamt that Tug was on the pavement beside a motorbike, with blood trickling from his mouth and a bikie who was Irwin was kicking Tug in the stomach and Michael was there waving a gun and laughing. Liz was watching but she was also playing the piano. She was watching Tug stretched on the footpath and she was thinking, funny, I've never learned the piano and yet I play it so beautifully.

At seven-thirty the alarm woke her, still alone. She told herself that it was for the best. She allowed herself relief and a little sentimental nostalgia. It was over. The heights had been lyrical. She was richer for it, and wiser. No cause for regret.

The mood sustained her through breakfast and half-way into the city centre then began to crumble at the edges.

Two of the boys appeared about mid-morning. She knew at once they were the boys because there was a familiarity about their dress and demeanour. She noticed them immediately because the people in the street had been of particular interest all morning and it was astonishing how many of them had dark skin or long black hair making her think for a moment that....

They stood for a while outside the plate glass window watching Liz and talking between themselves. Joking, no doubt. She recognised one as the young man who had told her Tug wasn't home when he was. The other had an exotic appearance; he was tall and dark-skinned and he wore a black hat festooned with gold chains, a scarlet scarf around his waist and heavy copper bracelets on each arm.

After a time they came into the shop. Irwin who was refilling the Cona machine froze and watched them, eyes bunched like fists. The fair one came up to the counter.

'I'm Max,' he said. 'You've met me. We gotta talk to you.'

'Would you like coffee?' she asked, aware of Irwin behind her.

He gestured, palms up and empty.

'I'll pay,' she mouthed and said aloud, 'I'll bring them over.' She took coins from her pocket — a tip from an American hung with cameras — and jangled them into the till.

'This is Lua.' Max pointed across the table as Liz set down the cups. Lua smiled shyly, a glimpse of white teeth.

'Is it about Tug?'

'He's in the cells,' said Max. 'They picked him up last night.'

'Why? What for?'

'A job. You know. In Dunedin.'

'What job?'

'Burglary,' said Max with a tinge of impatience. 'He's coming up this morning.'

'Coming up?' A bewildering vision of Tug surfacing like an injured goldfish.

'In court. He was gonna ring you but he said for us to come and tell you in case they wouldn't let him. He should say he didn't do it, you see. But he won't know. We didn't get a chance to work anything out. But if you come you could bullshit a bit and they might let you see him. Unless he's up early and we miss him.'

'I don't understand.'

'Jus' come with us and you'll see.'

'I can't. I'm working.'

They exchanged glances. Lua shrugged.

'Fair enough,' Max said. 'You want us to come back and tell you what he gets?'

'Reckon he'll be sent away this time,' said Lua. He spoke softly and quickly, as if words were a reckless exposure.

'Where to?'

'Borstal,' said Max.

Liz went up to Irwin who was spying through the cake stand.

'I've got a crisis,' she said apologetically. 'The boy who stays with me was arrested last night. He'll be in court this morning and he needs someone there.'

'Can't his mates go?'

'Please, Irwin?'

'You better be back by twelve. I can't manage lunchtime on my own.'

'Thank you.' She beamed at him, grabbing her coat and handbag.

Walking down towards the courthouse — running at times because they strode so fast — she tried to catch up on her education.

'I thought everyone was allowed a 'phone call?'

'Nah. Depends on the cop. What kind of mood he's in.'

'Should we get a lawyer?'

'There's lawyers there. Duty lawyer. Mostly worse than useless anyway.'

'Did Tug do it, this burglary?'

Max gave her a sharp look. 'We were with him — me and Lua — all the time. Driving round, then at the pub. So he couldn'ta done it could he?'

Liz looked at Lua, wanting an answer.

'Better ask Tug,' he said.

'You gotta tell him we'll be his witnesses about being with him,' said Max. 'Or maybe tell the duty lawyer.' He thought for a minute. 'Tug's seventeen, right?'

'Sixteen, he told me.'

'Sixteen? That's sweet then. Be Children's Court. We might be able to talk to him before he goes up. Mightn't need you after all.'

The Children's Court was Dickensian. Narrow, winding passages, stone floor, thick wooden doors with brass rings for handles.

'Oh,' said Liz in delight. 'What an incredible place. I didn't know it was here.' Her words echoed in accompaniment to their footsteps, hanging around to embarrass her in their banality.

Around the third bend in this ancient burrow they came on a cluster of youngsters and a few adults waiting on benches. Among them was a policeman, a policewoman and a harassed-looking man with a sheaf of papers. A boy, leaning against the wall, smiled at Liz. It took her a moment to place him — Billy, of the Castle Street flat. She smiled back.

'Tug gone in yet?' Max was asking a girl, amateur blonde and dumpy, who sat sullen-mouthed, smoking. She shook her head.

'He's not going up,' said Billy. 'I seen the list. There's only me an Steph and Fat Boy but he h'nt turned up, and a couple'a others.'

'Whatta you up for?' Max asked the girl.

'Nicked a coat.' She ground her heel along the stone floor, looking sideways at Liz.

'You'll be all right.' Max was paternal, reassuring. 'That's just petty theft.'

Steph's friend, slouched on the bench beside Steph, gave a sharp cackle of laughter. 'Fuck that. Was real fur, man. That ain't petty.' She threw an arm around Steph who gave a small grin of restrained pride.

Max went to the man with the sheaf of papers. 'You got a Morton down there?'

The man scanned the top sheet. 'Thomas Morton. Been crossed off. He'll be in Magistrate's. You know where that is of course.' He gave a wearily sardonic grin.

Max ignored it. 'You sure?'

'Been crossed off,' the man repeated.

'He's only sixteen,' said Liz, 'so shouldn't he be here?'

'Depends.'

'Depends on what?' Her voice had become aggressive. The man was accustomed to aggressive voices, he gave her his

100

bored, implacable stare.

'Depends on a lot of things, miss. You'll have to ask at the court office or somewhere if you want to know more. It's nothing to do with me.'

As they crossed the road to the building opposite Max explained, 'It's no good asking them. They don't have to have reasons. Them cunts do what they like.'

Court was in progress. Liz followed Max and Lua, trying to walk silently, aware of the stares from the public benches, relieved when they too were seated. She had never before been inside a courtroom and compared to the movie versions this one seemed somehow shabby.

In the box was a sharp-faced man, thirtyish, slicked-back hair and tapered trousers. He looked bewildered, as if he had just emerged from the early sixties into a harsher era. From the front benches a uniformed constable was reading something, Liz couldn't hear for the murmurings and shufflings around her. *Silence in the court,* she remembered inappropriately, *the monkey wants to talk. Speak up monkey.*

'I'll see what I can find out,' Max whispered at Liz, and edged himself off the bench and across the room to an official who stood beside a closed door.

'He's still in the holding room,' Max reported back to Liz in a loud whisper.

'Where's that?'

'Through there.' He pointed. 'He hasn't been up yet. You'll have to come outside.'

It was a relief to be out. Max led her round the back of the building to another door.

'Now, what you do is go in there. There'll be a cop around, or someone. Ask if you can see Tug. Lay it on real thick. If you see Tug tell him plead not guilty, get remanded. They won't let you see him, ask to see the duty lawyer or leave a message. Say he's got two witnesses that he didn't do it.'

'Can't you come with me?'

'Better I don't. You're kind of one of them, if y'see...' He hesitated then said, embarrassed, 'Tug really likes you. I mean, it's good you came. Like you're kind of his family.'

'And what about you?' she asked. 'Why did you come?'

101

'The boys stick together. Like we're his other family.' He said it firmly, as if it were a slogan, and for a minute he looked like a crafty-faced boy scout. Liz felt an inclination to salute.

Through the door she found a solitary constable in an empty room.

'Excuse me,' she said deferentially, 'but I wondered if I might be able to see Thomas Morton for a couple of minutes? It's most important.'

'Sorry.' He was young, blue-eyed, his face expressionless.

'Just for a minute?' She was older than him, but he had friends in high places.

'Why do you want to see him?' He spoke down at her. Height was another advantage.

'Because,' she improvised, 'I'm his guardian. And I wasn't told of his arrest. I mean, he would have 'phoned me if he'd been allowed.... (Would he?) I believe he has a right to one 'phone call.'

'It's not a right,' the constable interrupted. 'It's a privilege that must be earned.' That victory pleased him and his official face softened a little.

'He's sixteen!' said Liz. 'Surely he has a right to have an adult concerned about him. I mean shouldn't he be in Children's Court, anyway? Why is he here?'

'It's not my decision, but I *can* tell why. Someone has decided that Morton's criminal record puts him in the adult criminal class. I presume you do know the extent of his previous convictions?'

'Of course,' she lied, wondering if he too was bluffing. 'But he's still *legally* a child and therefore I should at least have been informed.' The irony of her protest mocked her, she imagined her hypocrisy smeared on her face like jam.

Perhaps he felt pity. 'Well,' he weakened. 'Just one minute. No more. If you wait here.'

The waiting reminded her that she had had only three hours' sleep. She fumbled through her bag for her cigarettes and lit one, nicotine to prod at her exhaustion. Tug came in alone, and looking at him she felt a flush of righteous maternal indignation. He looked so lost and waif-like. So *young*. When he saw her his face lit up with pleasure, or

102

relief. Checking to see that the policeman hadn't yet entered he kissed her on the mouth. She relayed Max's instructions hurriedly.

He said, still holding her hand, 'If I get a remand I'll have to have bail. Will you do my bail?'

'Of course,' she said, not really knowing what it entailed but so glad to have him there, smiling, beside her.

The constable came in and stood tall against the wall.

'I wish you'd rung me,' Liz said, for his benefit.

'I asked,' said Tug gesturing his head copwards, 'but them cunts wouldn't let me.'

The constable's eyes moved in Liz's direction but his head stayed erect and motionless.

'I had a good breakfast,' Tug offered. 'One thing they always give y' good breakfasts.'

'Righto Morton, back you go now.'

'Thank you,' Liz said to the blue eyes. They brushed over her, saying nothing back.

By ten minutes to midday Tug still hadn't been called. 'I'll have to go,' Liz whispered to Max who was engrossed in a horror comic he'd borrowed from a girl in the seat behind them. 'I'll try and get back later.'

She ran back to the coffee shop, dodging pushchairs and dawdlers. 'He didn't come up,' she explained, panting, to Irwin. 'They thought he would but he didn't.'

'So you want to go back!' An accusation, not a question.

'I don't know. Perhaps I can do it after work. I have to go bail, whatever that entails.'

'They sure know a sucker when they see one.'

'If you say so,' she said, too tired to care.

As the afternoon-tea crowd was thinning Tug came in, on his own.

'Can I have coffee? And sandwiches? I'm starving.'

'What happened? What about the bail?'

'S'okay. Judge gave me bail on my own. Two hundred dollars.'

She was horrified. 'Where will you get that?'

'Don't have to. Only if I skip and don't turn up.' He piled a plate high with sandwiches. Liz fetched her purse, as she passed Irwin he shifted his eyebrows and gave her a look which combined in approximately equal portions pity and contempt.

'Max says we gotta sign the forms for something. Legal you know.'

'Legal aid?'

'Yeah. That. Have to go soon or they'll be closed.'

'You need me to come with you?'

'Can't do it myself.'

'We'll go tomorrow, in my lunchtime. One day can't matter. What else happens?'

'I gotta report is all. Each day, at Central.'

'Why?'

'So's they know I haven't shot through.'

When he'd cleaned up the sandwiches and coffee, Tug left. No word of thanks, she glowered and gritted into a sink full of cups; nothing. But when, after work, she reached the bus stop Tug was waiting. 'Let's walk,' he urged.

'I'm tired, Tug.'

'Please?'

'But why?'

'I jus' want to. Hate buses. We'll walk through the park.'

He strode ahead of her until they were through the gates and into the park, then he waited for her.

'Why do you walk way ahead of me?'

'People stare at us. Haven't you noticed? If we're together.'

'They do seem to. But so what? Let them stare.'

'I can't stand being stared at.'

'You would've been stared at in court.'

'It's horrible, you don't know.' He took her hand and they walked between the monkey-puzzle trees. 'D'you love me?' he asked.

'I don't know. Yes, I suppose I do. In a way.'

'You never tell me,' he complained.

A woman appeared ahead of them, turning off the side path that ran through the rose garden and walking towards them. Tug began to slide his hand from Liz's but she grasped it and held it tight. The woman looked at Liz, at Tug, at Liz, at their clasped hands. She passed them. They both turned to look behind and she was looking back at them. They looked at each other and laughed.

'See that tree,' said Tug. 'Bruce Lee could chop it down with the side of his hand.'

'He's dead,' Liz said.

'Bullshit! Who told you that?'

'I heard it on the news, yesterday.' (I was listening for traffic fatalities. Was it only yesterday?)

'I bet he was killed outa jealousy, gunned down.'

'He died from taking an aspirin, something like that they said. I was only half listening.'

'My arse! He's still alive, I know. Bet they're just putting it about that he's dead. I bet it's a conspiracy.'

'Conspiracy, eh? That's a big word.'

He pulled a face at her. 'You'd be surprised at some of the words I know.'

He ran ahead of her, lunging, raging and chopping down assailants bare-handed, then he threw himself on the grass and waited for her.

'He's a millionaire,' he said when Liz drew level with him. 'And he can beat anyone.'

'Well, he's dead,' she said. 'Bruce Lee is dead.'

EIGHT

'I LOVE YOU,' she said. Not lightly, yet not with total conviction. How could you ever know for sure? Could intensity be taken as evidence, or should one expect a degree of consistency?

'I love you,' she said, 'God help me.' And the saying of it was like rolling back skin and leaving herself more naked than naked, obscenely exposed.

Tug smiled and fluttered his eyelashes. He was lying belly down; his face turned towards her, distorted by the pressure of the pillow, looked bulbous and rubbery, a clown's face.

'Tell me why,' he urged.

'Because you make me feel so....' she struggled to find some fitting word.

'Old?'

She grinned. 'Mmm. Old. Young. Pretty. Ugly. Real. Unreal.'

It was true. They had a fluidity. Their roles converged, merged, interchanged. She was mother, woman, man, mentor. He was child, nymph, man, woman. The possible combinations seemed boundless and far, far removed from the constrictions of the housewifely role she had so meekly (willingly? reluctantly?) fulfilled for so many years.

Yet this new freedom frightened her. With Tug there were no norms, no guidelines. They were pioneers, or so it seemed, and Liz was short on intrepidity. She longed for the comfort of signposts, the familiarity of beaten tracks, she was weary (already) of the smell of danger and the hostility of the natives.

When she had gone with Tug to apply for legal aid and had struggled through the forms (*Do you own shares in a business or company?* Ha ha. *Declare your assets.* Two pairs of jeans?) the clerk had scrutinised Tug's laboriously printed replies and asked with only a shadow of disdain, 'If you haven't been working, Thomas, how have you been living?'

'I live with her.' Nodding towards Liz.

'You mean she supports you?'

'Well... yeah.'

The clerk looked at Liz, from head to toe and back to head, then back at Tug. His face rearranged itself into an expression that seemed perilously close to hatred.

'How very... providential for you,' he hissed through closed teeth.

The incident had shocked Liz profoundly. Her immediate reaction had been embarrassment and humiliation. Later, dwelling on it, she had found a kind of irony. If the roles had been reversed — if she was a man and Tug a nubile teenage miss — that same clerk would probably have leered, even winked, at lucky Liz in conspiratorial envy.

In fact Tug would have made a lovely concubine; tidying the house, playing about in the kitchen, working at ways to make her laugh, dreaming up new sexual delectations. But Liz could no longer believe in fulfillment-as-a-homemaker and did not wish to inflict its dull futility upon Tug. And anyway waitresses just weren't in the mistress-keeping income bracket.

'My love, you're going to have to find a job. You know that?' (I love you and therefore can no longer support you.)

'I've been trying, Liz. You know I have.'

Which was, to the best of her knowledge, true. Since the night of his arrest he had stumbled reluctantly out of bed at the same time as Liz and fetched in the morning paper so that they could go through the situations vacant columns together. And at night he would glumly describe to her the hopelessness of his efforts.

'You know what I'm like on the 'phone, love. I never know what to say. I get muddled and these women are on the other end squeaking What? What? Sometimes I just hang up.'

In ten days he had managed to obtain four interviews. The first was at a shoe factory several miles out of town and when Tug had got to the central bus depot he had found the area wasn't served by buses. He went home. The next two, a woolstore and a foundry, had kept him waiting an hour and an hour and a half respectively for the personnel officers who then took one look at him and said sorry but the vacancy was filled (and maybe it was). The fourth was a timber mill. The boss looked at Tug and said, 'No dice, boy. We had one of you people before. Only turned up the first two days.'

'That's really shitty,' Liz commiserated when he told her.

'That's really shitty,' he mocked her savagely. 'Well you oughta know, he was one of yous people. And you're all the fucking same underneath.'

'Then you're being as stupid and bigoted as he was.'

'So? I gotta right to be.'

She had given up. Perhaps it was true. If those with the power named the game and drew up the rules how else to play but with the same tactics? She washed the dishes in silent resentment — rationalising his jibe did not ease the sense of injury. Tug glanced at the tea towel but made no move in its direction.

'Perhaps,' she said eventually, 'if you cut your hair...?' She was, after all, her mother's daughter.

'Stuff that. Why should I? It's not my hair that'd be working for them.'

'I know that.' Placating. 'You shouldn't *have* to cut your hair. It's not their business. You're right in principle.'

'There,' he brandished the word, triumphant. 'It's principle.'

'I agree. But the thing is it's *me* who's paying for *your* principles.'

He glared. 'You're always moaning. If it's just money you're worrying about I'll get us some.'

'No Tug. Not that. You promised. Has to be honest money.'

'There's no such thing.'

'Mine is,' she snapped. 'I work for it.'

'Then you're a mug, aren't you.'

(Oh Irwin, oh mother, how right you are. He is a monster and an opportunist, he is idle and amoral and indubitably lower-class.) She sniffed disparagingly and tossed her head — her mother again — but she let his retort go unfielded. It had only recently occurred to her that when they had arguments Tug was at a considerable disadvantage. She could trot out worn old homilies and regurgitated theories with some semblance of authority. He found it difficult to organise and present even the words he was familiar with while under stress of battle. She could twist and tighten sentences around him while he struggled to sharpen up one small salient word. Was it any wonder that, almost always, he took refuge in the familiar bad-lot stereotype?

Besides, she rationalised, holding her tongue though difficult was a form of victory, for Tug enjoyed an argument if only for the sake of the making-up which followed.

He *had* tried to find a job, and she would have thought that sufficient except that now she had acknowledged out loud that she loved him. That declaration placed on him certain obligations.

'You come with me, then,' he demanded. 'Monday. They might give me something if you come. And at least you'll know I try.'

'I can't take more time off work, Tug. I can't.'

Irwin had Tug summed up after one good look. He had then passed his insight on to Liz. Lazy, he said. Never amount to much, you can tell. Can't change those kind of people, they are the way they are. I'm not prejudiced but they're not like us. Cunning, mind you. Know a soft touch. You want to learn the most hard way that's your business. Just don't say I didn't warn you.

So Liz took a sickie, salving her conscience with the thought that Irwin owed Tug, at the least, a day's opportunity. Severe period pains, she claimed, feeling there was also a kind of justice there. A blow struck for Eva.

They searched the paper first thing in the morning and Tug made the calls while Liz stood beside him, prompting and feeding him lines. The result was three interviews. They checked on a street map; all the places were miles apart.

The warehouse was the closest. Tug had been told to ask for a Mr Person and they giggled together over the name. He was, at least, a prompt Person, but Liz, watching his face as he emerged from his office to greet them, knew they had come for nothing. He didn't invite them into his office.

'Right, boy, what experience have you?' The question was barked out like a rebuke. Liz was astounded — never had a stranger spoken to *her* like that.

'I was at a biscuit factory for a while.' Tug mumbled it, looking down at his hands.

'And what else?'

'Few days on a building site.'

'And?'

'That's all.'

'Why did you leave?'

Tug looked at him in apparent confusion. The man raised his voice.

'Why did you leave the factory?'

'I... I jus' got sick of it.'

Mr Person smirked. 'Afraid we need a bit more experience than that, boy.' He turned to Liz with a bleakly polite smile. 'Good day, and thank you for coming.'

'A nasty Person,' said Liz when they were back on the street. Tug didn't even smile.

'Do they always talk to you like that?'

'Like what?'

'Like... well, like they're talking to a dog.'

'He was all right, that's 'cos you were there. Should hear some of them. Always, boy. Yeah boy, no boy, lick my arse boy.'

Two buses and two and a half hours later the personnel officer from the plastics factory arrived back from wherever he had been. Tug, at Liz's prompting, introduced himself. He looked Tug up and down.

'Afraid the job's gone.'

'Maybe it really had,' Liz consoled Tug over sandwiches in a cramped suburban milk bar.

'It's always gone. A waste of bus fares. Let's go home.'

'There's only one more. It's worth a try.'

But when they eventually found the building Tug jibbed.

'I'm not going. What's the point? It'll be gone anyway.'

She had the same feeling of futility. 'The 'phone box,' she said. 'You can ring and see if they still want someone. That way we won't need to go in if....'

Tug rang. Yes, they still had vacancies. Yes, it was unskilled work. He replaced the receiver, grinning. 'Okay, let's go.'

It didn't take long. It was a small firm and the boss himself greeted them. 'I came about the job,' said Tug.

'Sorry. It's been taken.'

They called at the police station so Tug could report in, and they blew part of her 'phone bill money on a flagon of cheap and syrupy port wine.

'We'll get drunk,' she promised. It seemed a shabby substitute; she wanted to shower him with riches and prestige and electric guitars and tickets to kung fu movies. She owed him. The day had left her heavy with shame.

'I'd no idea,' she told Tug later, her guilt awash in port.

'It's not your fault,' he said with more pity than conviction.

'You could go on the dole I guess. If they won't give you work they must have to give you the dole. If nothing turns up this week we'll get you on the dole.'

'You'd have to come with me.'

'In my lunch-hour,' she said in her innocence.

The next day at around lunchtime Tug came into the coffee bar with Lua and a stocky youngster in school uniform. Lua paid for the coffees and they sat at a corner table. They stayed there talking and laughing among themselves while the lunchtime customers came, ate, and went. Irwin did not conceal his displeasure.

'I don't want that kind of element in here.'

'Savoury mince for two.' And back to the customers.

Then. 'Who you have as friends is your own matter but I don't want ruffians in here.'

'One chicken salad, no potato.'

And. 'I want them out of here.'

'They're customers, Irwin, like anybody else.'

'They'll frighten decent people away.'

'We're getting low on milk.'

Finally he trapped her against the fridge. 'Have you not understood? Tell them to go. They are not welcome here.'

'I thought you were a fair man.'

'I'm a businessman. I have to make a living.'

She told them. 'I'm sorry but the boss says I have to ask you guys to leave.'

'Why? We're not doing nothing.'

'I know, but....' She rolled her eyes towards the kitchen.

'Tell him to get stuffed.'

'Tug! I'd lose my job.'

'So? You could get another one. They'd love *you*.'

'Please?' she pleaded.

'You'd sooner boot us out?'

'I need the job.'

'C'mon.' Lua stood up. 'A job's a job, man. Not her fault.'

Tug hesitated then got to his feet. He pushed Liz out of his way. 'So now we know how it is,' he said to her, his contempt like spit on her face.

She did not speak to Irwin for the rest of the day, a small satisfaction. She wanted to hate him but a part of her had to acknowledge that he was, in his own way, a good man and a fair boss.

Tug was not at home when she got there. It was a relief for she feared he would be waiting, stoking his anger.

He didn't come home that night, nor did he come near Irwin's the next day. She presumed it was a matter of pride. Tug's pride, prickly and vulnerable, was to Liz a continuing source of amazement — steeped as she was in the lugubrious art of humility. *A proud people.* She remembered the phrase (also lugubrious) from tedious text-books on the country's colonisation. A genetic virtue? But *pride comes before a fall* sneered the voice of her mother.

In her lunch-break she went to the library and selected an armful of books. It felt like a sentimental reunion. How long since she'd enjoyed a good read?

He didn't come home that night either. She was being a little heavy on the sherry in the evenings, but on the whole she felt pretty good. Released. She began to hope he had left forever.

On the third evening he strolled into the kitchen as she was finishing her dinner, book propped against the toaster, heater warming her toes.

'Well, hello,' she said. In the region of her stomach she was suddenly less nonchalant.

'Hi.' He was strung up, tense. He pulled up a chair at the table and began drumming his fingers, rocking in the chair.

'So? Where've you been?' It didn't come out as lightly as she had intended.

'Nowhere much.'

She waited but he offered nothing more. She looked down at her book and began to read again, but without comprehension. He waited until she turned the page.

'I needed to get away from you a while. Being with you messes up my mind.'

She looked at him in surprise; it hadn't occurred to her that the problem might be mutual. 'Why does it mess up your mind?'

'Dunno. Well... you expect things of me. Get a job. Act like a married man. Stay home nights.'

'I never asked you to stay home nights.'

'But you expect me to.'

'I s'pose,' she admitted.

'I wanna do other things.'

'Yes,' she said, feeling guilty of gross self-absorption. 'Of course you do.'

He looked relieved. 'I been with the boys. I's missing them a bit. I'm staying at Marty's.'

She noticed his use of the present tense and some small emerging bloom in her intestines closed up and withdrew. 'Who's Marty?' A casual query.

'Don't think you know him. He's waiting for me. Jus' came to see how you are.'

'I'm fine.' Glowing with conviction. 'Have you been reporting?'

'Yep. Haven't missed.'

'You'll take care, won't you, Tug?' Maternal concern was in order. 'No doing jobs or anything?'

'Promise,' he said solemnly. 'Won't get into any trouble.' He touched her cheek. 'Like you worrying about me.'

She thought, when he touched her, he doesn't really intend to leave — this is just a try-on. But he withdrew his hand, mouthed a kiss at her and went. He may as well, she thought bitterly, have been a whirlwind — barging unbidden into her fragile contentment and reducing it in minutes to shattered and pitiful ruin. She couldn't read, nor finish her dinner; to defrost the fridge would be unendurable. Why had he come at all? Why hadn't he stayed?

She would have to go out.

As the bus pulled in at the city square she saw from her window Tug strutting jaunty rooster along the footpath, a head of fair curls tucked beneath his arm. Beneath the curls, neat little features and unpainted lips. Beneath that a suede coat with lambswool trimming, tight jeans and long brown leather boots. Turning the corner to offer her a new perspective — a tight denim arse with a black crease flashing like a duty pointsman's arm. *I wanna do other things,* she remembered.

Yeah, boy. Sure you do.

She watched till they were out of sight and the bus had emptied. Her mind was fixed on the clothes. That was no waitress, that was my heiress. An exaggeration of course, but the unmistakeable impression had been good school, select suburb, Daddy's darling. Whatever, thought Liz with grim satisfaction, would Daddy say if he could see her now?

In the disinfectant-smelling darkness of the cinema she assured herself that events were taking the proper, reasonable — inevitable, in fact — course. She relocated and propped up the vision of herself as a bonny foster-grandmother but it teetered precariously and seemed in danger of falling flat on its face. The problem seemed to lie with the identity of the Tug replica infant's mother. Liz tried to censor out a shadow of fair curly hair and neat little features — and was forced to acknowledge that the woman she had envisaged had been plain, impoverished and barely educated. *Tug's type! Tug's class!* That arrogance a thorn in the open wound.

The film was *Who's Afraid of Virginia Woolf.* It reminded Liz of herself and Ken, thought they had never scaled the

114

heights of acid repartee. She watched it coldly, uninvolved. How phoney such people are, she thought. Artificial, cosseted, over-indulged. How they deserve their self-induced misery.

Knowing that a few months earlier — a few weeks even — she would have been awed and devastated by the movie's reality. Could Tug have made that much difference? So altered her perception? Would the world she had considered normal (not particularly congenial but unquestionably normal) never seem that way again?

He returned the following night, late. A heavy knock on the door. She went in her nightgown to open it.

'I need to talk to you,' he said.

She went back to bed and he followed her. He sat on the edge of the bed, tentatively; a visitor. His hands were shaking, he saw her watching them.

'They got worse again. Booze I guess. Soon as I go away from you I get the shakes. Maybe it's not booze.' He shoved his hands between his thighs and clamped them there. Liz waited, propped on pillows.

Tug looked at his straight-jacketed hands. 'I been going round with someone,' he said. 'Another woman.'

She had an inclination to smile at the 'woman', but who was she to quibble over a few years given or taken?

'I knew,' she said. 'I saw you with her last night.'

'Where? Where were you?'

'I went to the movies.'

'Who with?'

'On my own.'

'Shoulda gone to the Clint Eastwood one. There's this shoot-out. Bamm, bamm. POW.' Aiming for the light bulb, eyes asquint from the long hot prairie sun. Replacing the gun in its holster. 'So, what'd you think of her?'

'Pretty.'

'Yeah. Good legs, ay? Loves herself a bit though.' He looked her finally in the eye. 'You don' mind then?'

Mind? She wrapped herself in the cold comfort of mature reason. 'It was bound to happen. There wasn't ever a future in it for us. Still you might have told me last night instead of

115

all that shit about your mind being messed up.'

'It wasn't shit. It's not *just* her. It was us.'

'Then you're doing the right thing. And I *did* expect you to behave like an old husband.' She wanted to prolong the moment, finding a satisfaction in the mellow pain of it now; moved by an image of nobility and self-sacrifice. 'If you really like her Tuggie, I'll be happy for you.'

He withdrew his hands from between his knees and reached one out to her, she took it in hers tightly. 'I won't abandon you,' she promised.

He shrugged, 'I thought you would.' He squeezed her hand in return. She saw them, framed; a tableau of devotion. Her eyes moistened with the sentimentality of it all. Then Tug said, matter-of-factly. 'But I don' really like her that much. She's a bit of a silly bitch, really.'

Liz withdrew her hand sharply.

'I jus' like the look of her.' He made it sound comical and Liz, despite herself, began to laugh not just at his words but at the mood now shattered and silly.

'What a bastard you are,' she told him affectionately.

'I can't help it.' He pulled a mournful face. 'Can I come to bed?'

Why not? She moved over to make room for him. Watching him undress, his jack-in-the-box cock springing up from his jeans, unwieldly and absurd like a coathanger. One night she had arrayed it with beads and bracelets, wishing for a grander accolade — a coronet at least — for her velvet display rack.

While she thrashed against him, even in those moments when she was exquisitely convinced of her absolute, universal, eternal and infinite insatiability, and in the moments after when she admitted that her insatiability could be, if not finally cured, at least temporarily (and gloriously) assuaged — even through that a small part of her mind was warning her that he was only there for the exercise; afterwards he would dress and go back to the girl with good legs.

But he showed no inclination to leave. He snuggled against her, wrapping her in his arms, his flesh glued to hers in their warm and mutual damp.

'I forgot the diaphragm,' she worried.

'Good,' he said. 'I want you to have my baby.'

She felt wide awake. 'I thought you were just going to screw me then go back to your new lady.'

'Don't be silly.' She could feel his breath against her forehead.

'Well that's what I thought.'

'You're disgusting. I think you want me to be evil.'

'Then you're going to stay?'

'If I'm allowed.'

'Of course you're allowed.' She tightened her arms around him.

'Just for tonight,' he said.

Her arms went limp, she turned her face away from him. Closing her eyes she saw a coat with lambswool trim above slim denim thighs. She disengaged her body from Tug's and turned onto her back.

'What's her name?'

'Julia.'

'How did you meet her?'

'She hangs around with the boys sometimes. A few of the others have been with her.' A pause, then. 'She reckons I'm the best though.'

Liz ignored that. She knew he would be grinning.

'Does she work?'

'She's a model, sometimes. And she goes to University.'

'Bullshit. Don't believe you.' Looking at him now.

'She does,' he protested. 'True. She's eighteen.'

'She can't be too silly then.'

'She is a bit. Thinks she's cool. She says far out and dig that, man.'

'Does she think you're far out?'

He grinned.

'If she goes to University what's she doing hanging round with you lot?'

Tug let his lower lip hang and ran the tip of his tongue slowly across it. 'Y'oughta know.' He reached over and edged his hand between her legs.

And she was helplessly receptive. He knew, he must know, that the jealousy which had forced the questions was part pain and part aphrodisiac.

The house was sold. Ken had begun packing up his possessions. He rang Liz about the bedroom suite which they had bought second-hand — imitation antique, mahogany finish.

'You may as well have it. I know you really loved that suite. I can probably borrow a trailer.'

Had she loved a bedroom suite? How absurd. 'I don't want the thing. You may as well sell it.' She felt impatient about even discussing it.

'Well, if you're sure? Any stuff you do want?'

'I thought we'd agreed that you kept it all. There's one thing — what about Mitzi? You taking her?'

'Oh.' An uneasy pause. 'Actually I'd told a friend she could have her. But if it's important?'

'It is a bit. I thought you knew I wanted her.'

'All right,' he said. 'I'll see you get her.'

How easy to be amicable when only a cat was at stake.

Ken had told her that her share of the house sale would arrive in due course from the solicitor. Ten thousand dollars. The figure danced in her head offering wild possibilities and hidden dangers. She wouldn't believe in it until she saw it.

Ken delivered Mitzi on the Friday night when he brought Michael for the last weekend before they would leave for Wellington. After a brief inspection the cat settled in without objection.

'Will you miss her?' Liz asked Michael.

'Who? Mitzi? Don't expect so.'

'That's good then,' she said. The cat purred beneath her hand, unperturbed by dispensability.

Liz hadn't seen Tug for three days. Not since that morning when she had left for work. He had rung twice and they had exchanged cautiously friendly and entirely meaningless conversation punctuated by pauses, tappings and heavy breathing. She had given up on trying to draw conclusions; she felt suspended and almost calm, waiting for the next storm.

She had bought Michael a large box of plastic soldiers complete with a fort for guarding, an arsenal of weaponry and two tanks. It was a bribe to inspire fond remembrance but also, for Liz, an acknowledgement of defeat. She had fought for years against his having such playthings, fought for a principle or just an instinct, and when Ken had overruled her she had resorted to sabotage by way of casual broom swipes or treading accidently on whole platoons.

The choice of gift was painful, too, because it marked another kind of failure. She had wanted to buy him something grander, but toy shop salesmen could not be placated with promises of wealth-around-the-corner, and she had no savings. There was the expense of feeding Tug and then the expense of her increased consumption of sherry and cigarettes when not feeding Tug. All of it indefensible when her son should be her first priority. Had Michael some certain foreknowledge of his mother's propensity for extravagant dissipation when he opted for Ken?

'If you had a car we could go somewhere.'

Saturday morning and already Michael was bored. Should she give him his farewell present so soon?

'Where do you want to go?'

'Anywhere. Coulda gone to the beach.'

The day was clear and crisp. She calculated bus fares but felt a reluctance to leave the house. What if the phone rang unanswered?

'When I've done the washing we'll go somewhere,' she compromised. The washing would take the best part of an hour, and if he hadn't rung by then....

'Sometimes,' she said gaily, into the receiver, 'I think you've got ESP.'

'What?' He sounded tired, his voice flat and faint.

'I was just thinking about you.'

'D'you miss me?'

'Yes.' Why should she pretend?

'I miss you.'

'Do you?'

'I'll be home tonight. If that's okay?'

'Course,' she said, but casually. For a couple of hours, a couple of nights, a couple of years? 'I'll be out for a while. With Michael.'

'What are you doing now?'

'I'm doing the washing. What are you doing?'

'I'm standing in a phone box. The boys are outside. There's Tony, Billy, Max and Solly and Solly's girlfriend. Billy nicked a pair of shoes yesterday but he got lady's shoes by mistake. Solly's wearing them anyway and he looks real dicky in them. I got some new jeans.'

'Where from?' Her suspicion showing.

'Tony. They don't fit him.'

Tug hadn't been so communicative in a long time. As he had made the call Liz could afford to be off-hand. 'Tug, I gotta go. I've got the washing machine on.'

'See you later then.' A damp chirrup of a kiss before he hung up.

They stayed at the beach longer than she'd intended. By the playground she met Ailleen.

'Remember me?' asked Ailleen.

'Mother helper,' said Liz, remembering Ailleen less clearly than the jars of paintbrushes, the easels, the lumps of dough — pink and green — that stuck on the soles of your shoes, the wide judgemental eyes of the children. Ailleen's husband was a General Practitioner; that she remembered. It had been the important thing, what your husband did. And she remembered now that she had liked this pale, thin lady better than most of the mothers she did duty with. The kindergarten mothers had frightened her with their confidence, their easy talk of problem readers, home appliances, clothes, committees and prices. They were so shiny and unworn without scratches or chips. She had made no overtures of friendship, she didn't want those women in her home drawing comparisons and breathing her diminished air.

'Are you still living...?' They began together, and laughed.

'We've moved,' said Ailleen. 'I left Tom two years ago.'

'I thought you seemed different. I suppose that sounds silly, but you seem more real. Or maybe it's me. I'm separated too.' It suddenly seemed a creditable achievement.

'Oh, I'm much more real.' Ailleen was smiling. 'I've decided single people are. How long've you been on your own?'

Liz told her about Ken, about herself, even about

Valleyview. She omitted Tug.

Ailleen had custody of her three children. 'It's tough for a while. There's a lot to work through — as you'll know. The thing that got *me* through was becoming a feminist.' She made it sound like conversion. 'You should come along. We meet every week.'

'I don't much like joining things,' Liz demurred. 'I never have.'

'You don't have to join. You can just listen if you like.'

Ailleen drove Liz and Michael back to the city so they only had one bus to catch. They exchanged phone numbers and Liz promised to think about the feminist meetings. It had been a good day, even Michael had enjoyed himself.

Tug arrived as she was preparing dinner. Max was at his side, Lua hovering apprehensively in the background. She welcomed them all, still feeling bouyant. She recalculated her food supplies, repressing qualms. Dinner won't be long. Max and Lua protested lack of hunger. Liz insisted; and watching them eat she knew they had been ravenous. Her eyes kept meeting Tug's over disguised smiles. He had missed her. He was back.

She left them, at Max's insistence, to do the dishes and followed Michael into the living room where she began to lay kindling for a fire. Tug came up behind her and turned her face to be kissed. Michael was watching. Well, let him watch. Was Ken so cautious?

Tug wore a worried face. She prodded at the corners of his lips with two fingers. 'What's the matter?'

'Them.' Nodding towards the kitchen.

'What about them?'

'They got no place to stay. They been kicked outa the Mission.'

'Oh, Tug!'

'Well I said maybe, jus' for a coupla nights?'

She sighed.

'I can't come home to a warm house and leave them on the streets. Those are my mates.'

'I know, love, but....'

'They're gonna lie for me in court.'

'You didn't tell me it was lies.'

121

'Look, do you want that they send me away?'

'No,' she said. 'No. Okay, they can stay then. A couple of nights. But I wish you'd picked some other time. It's my last weekend with Michael.' She looked around for Michael but he'd left the room. 'Besides there's nowhere for them to sleep.'

'There's the spare bed. Or the sofa if Michael's got the bed.'

'One sofa?'

'Better than the footpath.'

'Do they know about you and me?'

He shook his head. 'Guess they'll find out soon enough.'

'Just two nights.'

He smacked a kiss on her forehead. 'Thank you, darling.'

After Michael had gone to bed the four of them played cards and the boys told her street tales.

Billy you know Billy well once we was having this party and Billy was really out of it I mean zonked right out of his mind and he's flaked in the corner then he musta needed a leak so he gets up just like he's you know a sleep walker and staggers cross the room and he pees right into this gumboot and we's all cutting up laughing. And then he goes back and curls up asleep and just a bit after that these bloody demons come and they grab Bones an' they gonna take him to the lock up and they say get some shoes on and he dun' know about Billy an' he puts on the gumboots and he's squelchin off between the dees Jeez it was funny ay.

Old Bones Tug told you about Bones? Well he useta have these boots and' he never took them off 'cos they mighta got nicked see and' he wore them for months alla time till one day some of the boys held him down an' they drag off his boots and you might not believe but he had weedy feet. No for real he had this green fungus sorta stuff *growing*. Real filthy bugger Bones and since that he's been famous for weedy feet.

'What's Tug's claim to fame?' Liz wanted to know.

Max looked at Tug, grinning. 'That's easy. I'll tell y' how I'm gonna remember Tug when I'm old. He's gonna be walking down the street with some chick an he'll have one hand round her neck clutching her tit and' the other in her pocket holding her purse.'

'Fuckin' arse,' roared Tug. 'That's bullshit.'

They laughed at him. Liz laughed too, but uncomfortably. She fetched them bedding. 'There's only the sofa, I'm afraid.'

'Tug can have the sofa,' said Lua. 'It's his home, ay.'

Liz looked at Tug.

'S'okay,' he told them. 'I got somewhere to....' He looked at Liz.

Max thumped a fist between his eyes. 'Ah. Shoulda guessed. Morton, you're a dog.' Grinning at him. Lua beginning to smile too. Tug and Liz stood smiling back at them, embarrassment giving way to relief. Liz felt a warm glow of gratitude, both for their easy acceptance of the situation and for the fact that they didn't somehow belittle her affection for Tug, or Tug's affection for her. She might have known that in a world of weedy feet most things were acceptable, but she was surprised by the benign sentimentality she saw in their smiles. As if they believed in love, wherever it happened.

Watching Tug undress, still holding her tongue about his clothes — flashy red corduroy jacket, green sweater (not new), jeans with red stitching.

'You admiring me or my gear?'

'Both.' Having to ask. 'Tug, you didn't lift them, did you?'

'I never. I swapped the jersey with Solly, and Tony give me the jeans.'

'What about the jacket?'

He climbed over her to his side of the bed against the wall. 'Julie bought it for me.' He lay looking at the ceiling, waiting for her response. She made none.

'You don't look after me good as that, do you?'

'No. I don't do I.' Without apology. 'What'd you do with your other gear?'

'Dunno. Guess someone's wearing it.'

'You should've hung on to it. Clothes are so expensive. You've got even less than you went away with. You're hopeless.'

'I know. I need looking after.' Cuddling against her.

The subject, having been raised, occupied too much of her mind and would have to be dealt with.

'And what about Julie?'

'Fuck Julie.'

'No thanks.' Her voice softened. 'What happened?'

'She's a moll. I found her with Tony.'

'I thought you knew she was like that?'

'Thought it was different with me. Don't care anyway, only liked her for her legs. And she was an easy touch.'

'One hand on her tit and the other in her purse?'

'Yeah. Guess it's true a bit. You wouldn'ta known me when I's with her. I's doing this big act all the time. Mister-Cool stuff. Tough. Come here, woman! Like that. I'm only real with you.' He ran his blind finger round the rim of her nipple. 'It's good to be home.'

They lay around listless with boredom, drawing matches over who next should make the arduous journey to the stereo to change the record. Liz felt oppressed by their presence. The three of them seemed to have taken over her house and her Sunday, leaving Michael and herself sliding around the edges. The conviviality of the previous night was gone. Even Tug was no company for he was now one of the boys, their Tug, not hers. And she could tell he was aware of that distinction and not happy with it but found it impossible to be both at the same time.

She gave Michael the soldier set. His delight was hers. Some, he explained to her, he had already but a general could not have too many troops. He took them to the living room and arranged them across the floor. It provided a diversion.

'You ever get presents like that?'

'Thassa joke!'

'Not even for birthdays. Hey, Michael, is it your birthday? Whew. What you get for a birthday then?'

'*I* got the animals out of the cornies.'

'More'n I got.'

'Din' even know when my birthday was till I read it on my Welfare report!'

It's not his fault, she wanted to shout at them. You can't blame a child for having more than you had. He's lost a sister and he's losing his mother, isn't that enough? You don't have a monopoly on misfortune.

Michael's back was turned to them. She wondered if he could feel the resentment, was shielding his face from it.

She had planned a festive dinner for two, or possibly three. In the kitchen she tried to expand it to five, seeking a miracle. No eggs, no milk and only a lick of butter. Sixty cents in her purse.

Tug had succumbed and was playing at soldiers with Michael, happily engrossed. She asked him to go down to the dairy and see if he could book up some food in her name.

'Me? You know he'd never let me.'

She saw that was most likely true and went herself, taking Michael, wanting that time with him alone.

'Why are those people living in your house?' Michael asked, nose wrinkled in disapproval.

'They've got nowhere else to live.'

'That's silly. Everyone's got homes.'

'Not everyone, love.'

'But why do they live at your house?'

'Because. Just because.'

The dinner was a disaster. She had not dared to extend the dairy man's credit to another chicken and the one she had wasn't large. Michael, partial to chicken, complained about his share. Liz gave him some from her plate but still he complained. Lua gave some from his plate, saying he wasn't too keen on chicken, but Michael wasn't entirely placated. Liz saw the exchange of 'spoiled-brat' glances and wanted to say: it *is* his farewell dinner, and you too lack some social graces. But she said neither.

Kneeling beside his small suitcase in the privacy of the bedroom she put her arms around Michael. 'I might not see you for a long time.'

'It's all right, Mum,' he said awkwardly and gave her a small tentative cuddle. She was determined not to cry.

She wanted Michael ready when Ken arrived for she didn't want Ken coming beyond the front door. But she didn't hear the car and Ken didn't bother to knock. She was still folding Michael's pyjamas when Ken walked into the little bedroom.

'My God, Liz,' he said, and she had a fleeting impression that he was pleased, that her companions vindicated his good sense in having got free of her. She clicked shut the suitcase, offering Ken no explanation.

'I won't come out to the car.' She handed Ken the suitcase and bent towards Michael uncertainly. He gave her a small solemn peck on the cheek.

'Well,' Ken said, 'good luck.' He hesitated, but she knew of nothing to say.

They left, and Liz, lying on her bed in the dark, thought about reconciliation. Things may have been different for the three of them in Wellington. Maybe if she were stronger... if she could learn to accept things...? She lay very still and the thinking stopped; her mind was dry and empty, small pieces could flake off and drop and they would echo.

After a time Tug came and sat beside her. He reached for her hand and held it and they stayed there in silence.

In her lunch-break she went with Tug to the Labour Department. They waited for the whole hour among the careers brochures (*Have you thought about dentistry?*) and fellow job-seekers — a sad-faced man, a plump girl accompanied by her mother and a dark-skinned boy in a navy-blue suit — then they left. The girl had been called into a side office by the time Tug and Liz gave up, the man and the boy were still waiting.

Liz invented a dentist appointment for the following morning. Her tongue informed her it should have been true, as there was a vast cavity shared by two of her back teeth; but solid teeth were an indulgence that must wait for more secure times.

Again they went to the Labour Department. After a wait Tug was given a form to be filled in. After another wait he was called aside and told to return after ten days if he still hadn't found employment.

Lua and Max wanted her to go with them to the Labour Department.

'I can't keep taking time off work. Anyway you two don't need me to go.'

'We've been,' said Max. 'We've been and been. You fill in the form and it's not right so next time it's do another form. Come back next week. So you do and they've lost the form. Or some other thing. Always something.'

'Be just the same if I went with you.'

'Maybe it wouldn't.'

'I can't Max. I just can't.'

'S'okay,' soothed Lua. 'You don't wanna lose your job. You worry 'bout Tug first.'

She looked at his handsome face for signs of sarcasm but found none. 'I'm sorry. I really am. I wish I could help.'

Max put an arm around her shoulders. 'You're helping. Course you are. We gotta roof over our heads thanks to you.'

She couldn't ask them to leave.

They were, the four of them, a kind of family. The days passed at increasing speed as if, Liz thought, they were all hurtling down a hill. She tried not to think about what might lie at the bottom. Nothing was predictable any more.

There were the good days when she loved them all, when their need of her and her need of them was a comfort and a virtue. On those kind of days she felt tender respect for their easy humour, their vulnerability, their *style*.

And there were the other days when they were the dead weight around her neck, when she was the fool and they the opportunists. Desperate days when she felt herself being dragged under.

There were now two of Tug — the disarmingly candid child and lover who emerged only when he was alone with Liz and the tough and brooding delinquent of the streets. The more truculent Tug became the more she relied on the other two for companionship and the more reassuring and agreeable Max became. Liz could see what was happening but not a solution. Even in bed their friendship was becoming hedged by his suspicions and divided loyalties and her increasing exasperation.

He had begun to drink heavily, sometimes with Max and Lua, sometimes with others of his friends. Usually one of the boys would get him home. Sometimes they would ring her then pour Tug into a taxi whose driver she would pay when they arrived. There were the occasional nights when he didn't come home. Sometimes when she had helped him in from the taxi he would collapse just inside the door and she would have to leave him there until a degree of sobriety or the cold would bring him to bed.

How could he afford to get plastered? The boys, he said, had money. And indeed sometimes Max or Lua would give her several dollars towards food, though never quite enough to cover costs. She didn't ask them where it came from. The money seemed more essential than moral indignation and besides she was wary of the involvement that would come from knowing too much.

Enough to worry about Tug and the large possibilities (burglary, mugging, assault) let alone the small probabilities (obscene language, obstruction, under-age drinking, disorderly behaviour). She nagged him about remembering to report in — his case had been remanded for another two weeks.

Money. That was what her worries all boiled down to in the end. Money and the lack of it. How to pay this bill or that bill. How to make the food last out till the end of the week. (A small comfort was her discovery that Lua had a talent, born no doubt from past necessity, for making a meal out of damn all — a few scraps, a bit of stock, a fair bit of water). They had no concept of the cost of eating and they thought that electricity like the sun shone freely for all.

But hope was always there, beckoning, pulling Liz's leg. Lua got a job in a clothing factory pressing clothes. He lasted at it three days.

'Better be dead than go back there.'

'What's so bad about it?'

'It's.... You won't understand. I feel like I'm in there forever. Like being inside, like that. Pressing clothes!'

'I don't like waitressing much, either.' Making a point.

'I'd like to be a waiter.'

'So you'd be looked at?' She'd observed the vanity behind his shyness. He grinned.

'It's a job, the factory,' she persisted. 'We need the money.'

'I'll get another job. I'm not gonna be stuck like this. May as well be inside.'

'It's not the job,' she guessed. 'You think you're missing something 'cos the others aren't working. I may as well chuck it in too, what the hell's the point?'

He flinched at her anger. His eyes had a distant veiled look. He turned and walked away from her into the small bedroom he now shared with Max, closing the door quietly behind him.

The next evening he handed her a silk blouse in greens and blues. An expensive peacock shirt.

'For you.'

She fingered its slippery softness. 'I don't think I should take it.' Shoplifted, for sure, like his own colourful gear.

'I got it for you.'

'At great risk?'

A small grin. 'I can't take it back. You may as well have it.'

'Lua, I understand what you meant last night. You get stuck in a job you hate, you might get trapped there forever. I can see that, but we've got to eat. I wish you could have a decent chance, but you have a family.'

He shook his head. 'They don't know me. I've shamed them.' He shrugged. 'You give young Tug a good long chance. He needs it. You can't do it for us all.'

'It's a lovely shirt,' she said. 'Thank you.'

'Don't tell Tug I give it you. Might mash me up.' Smiling down from his superior height.

She hid the shirt away in the bottom of her wardrobe. It even seemed to smell stolen.

Life was eventful. Always a new surprise in store. There was the day Tug was picked up for unpaid fines and spent three nights in gaol until Liz, with a little help from Max and Lua, got together seventy dollars. And the day Lua was picked up in the street and put in an identity line-up of possible rapists. ('The guy didn't look nothing like me.') The night Tug was arrested for drunkenness and Liz paid five dollars for his release; and the night he came home bleeding from a bottle wound and they spent four hours at casualty. And the visit from Max's brother who had got religion and promised Max grimly of sure-fire hell and sure hellfire.

Max, so easily articulate (or was it glib?) yet remaining an unknown quantity. Max, mature in his twentieth year. 'Am I just a joke to Tug?' she asked Max after a night spent alone.

He shrugged. 'One thing, he's loyal. I mean he gets a hard time about you from them others, but he never says nothing.

129

Just tells them to fuck up.'

Yet it was Max, Liz felt, who fostered the matehood and made her increasingly an alien. Max who initiated the conspiratorial glances and exclusive undercurrents. What was it she mustn't know about? Girls? Plans to pull a job? Drugs?

One day when she arrived home from work she found Tug curled on the floor beside the sofa. He was awake, trembling, mumbling nonsense. She knelt beside him and he crawled into her arms whimpering. His body was damp with sweat. 'What did you take?' she asked him, but could make no sense of his mumblings.

Should she call a doctor? But what to tell him? How to explain this to a doctor whose world revolved around respectable matters like pregnancy and earaches? And would he take Tug away from her, hand him to the police or to Valleyview? And what good would that do? What good had it done?

Lua and Max came home much later. Tug was by then sitting upright, breathing heavily and clinging to Liz's arm in a vice-like grip. Liz thought, on seeing the other two, that they were high on something, so glistening their eyes, so benign their smiles, but she could not be sure.

They pleaded ignorant. 'He's okay when we left 'bout four, eh Lua?'

Lua nodding assent, his eyes absent.

'What'd he take? You must know?'

'We dunno. Really Liz.'

She didn't believe them. They helped her to put Tug to bed. 'He'll be okay,' said Max, 'Don' worry. He'll come down out of it.'

She sat with Tug till he fell asleep, seeing the generation gap gaping and wondering what kind of vaudeville was happening inside his skull. It wasn't until the next day when she came home to find Tug, convalescent, in her dressing gown that she had a chance to question him.

Acid, he said. The three of them had taken it, but Tug had taken more. 'Mostly it don't affect me much. Only this stuff musta had something else in it. I feel awful.'

'How did you feel then?'

'Not something you can.... Dunno really.'

130

It frightened her, this infinite unknown. Hers had been a drinking generation, coming to marijuana later — and then only, she suspected, because Ken considered it fashionable. She was a drinker, preferring the blurring of her reality to the distortion and exploration of it.

'Tug, what's happening to you? To us? If that's what you want there's no point in you being here.'

'It's not what I want. It's them being here.'

'You brought them here.'

'Make them go, love.'

'You. They're your mates.'

'I can't, you know that.'

'I'll try,' she said.

'After the court case.'

'After the court case.'

Her money from the house came in the post. She touched the cheque in disbelief, and foresaw the pitfalls. If the others knew they would expect a display of largesse and certainly a substantial rise in their standard of living. Word would get around and the boys and their satellite girls would descend like locusts. They must not know. The money was her security, compensation for the glass-cage years of marriage, for the two children she had borne and lost, for being at thirty-three a waitress despite early promise. Yet how could she coolly stash it away when the needs of her friends — and they were her friends, weren't they? — were so pressing? Could she perpetuate privilege?

She would try. She banked the cheque in her lunchtime. The eight days needed for clearance would give her time to consider its fate. But she had never been good with secrets, she confided in Tug that same night.

'Ten thousand! Why din'you show me?'

'It was a cheque.'

'I jus' would've like to've seen the words. D'they have thousand dollar notes?'

'Dunno. I suppose so.'

'What colour are they d'you reckon? Don't tell them others whatever you do.'

'I wasn't going to. I don't want to start spending it. It can

131

be a deposit on a house.'

'Why don'you get a car?'

'I'd thought of that, but....'

'I could get a job then. I could get around properly to look.'

'You don't have a licence.'

'But I can drive. You know how hopeless it is getting to them job places on a bus.'

'I'll think about it.'

'We could get away on our own in weekends.'

Tug's case came up. Liz, having already arranged for an afternoon off later the same week, went to work on the day. She worried about whether he would turn up at court. The possibility of his being sent away to some reformatory had made the night before — or what remained of it by the time he had rolled home — tender with anticipated loss. She was fatalistic about the outcome, thinking that if he *was* put away her life would be more manageable.

They arrived at the coffee bar as she was about to have lunch. Rowdy in their triumph. The magistrate had dismissed the case, not because of the bare-faced witness of Max and Lua but because the prosecution witness who was supposed to have seen Tug running from the building felt unable to make a positive identification.

'All you Horis look alike,' said Lua.

'So do all yous Coconuts.'

'See that dee though. He was right pissed off. He's gonna be after you, my son,' Max warned.

'Yah, what can he do?' scoffed Tug.

Liz as St George flailing her sword at the Department of Labour, learning that the meek do not inherit the kingdom of the dole queues.

Tug approaches the desk and gives his name. The woman behind the desk hands him a form to fill in. Tug takes it to Liz.

'Tell her you filled one in last time.'

He does and the woman goes off and returns with his file card. 'I'm afraid we have no jobs that would suit you.' She

132

smiles her dismissal.

Liz goes to stand beside Tug. 'He wants to apply for unemployment benefit.'

'I see.' She purses her lips as if this is an impertinence then tells them they must wait so that Thomas can be interviewed. They wait for over an hour. Other people come in, some leave, some are ushered into adjoining offices. A man puts his head around an office door and calls Tug's name.

'Come with me.' Tug whispers fiercely to Liz.

They go into the man's office. He looks at Liz with suspicion. 'You're with him?'

'Yes.'

'May I ask for what reason?'

She hesitates. 'Moral support.'

'I assure you there's no need for moral support here.' He gives a thin smile. 'If you'd both sit down then.'

The questions — education? jobs? qualifications? And Tug's hesitant replies — to the third form, no training, no skills — being noted down in case some small inadequacy should be overlooked among the larger ones.

The man hands him another form. 'You take this to the Department of Social Welfare and they'll see to you.' He speaks slowly and clearly now that he has Tug's limitations on record.

It's two blocks to the Social Welfare office. The building is older but the atmosphere is the same. The people standing in tentative queues at the counter look worried and deferential. Tug finally reaches the front of his queue and proffers the form he was given. He's told to wait and half an hour later his name is called. Liz goes with him to the counter.

'Are you a relative?'

Liz smiles slightly. On appearances it would seem unlikely. 'A friend,' she says.

'I see.' The man studies the form on the desk before him. He is grey and middle-aged and entirely unremarkable. 'I see here that you haven't worked for some months.' He stares at Tug, waiting. Tug looks back blankly until the man adds, with slight impatience, 'Well? Why is this?'

Tug looks at Liz.

'Valleyview,' she prompts.

'I was sent to Valleyview.'

'I see. And when did you leave there?'

'Bout two or three months ago.'

'Three,' Liz says.

'But why haven't you worked since then?'

'Couldn't find a job.'

'In other words you haven't been looking.' Lowering his head towards Tug like a bull or a schoolteacher.

'He has,' Liz objects. 'I've gone with him myself.'

The man smiles. 'There are still plenty of jobs going for people who want them.'

'He has tried,' Liz repeats firmly.

'I could get a job tomorrow if I wanted one.'

'Maybe,' she argues. 'But you're not unskilled or Maori.'

He snorts and looks back at Tug. 'How have you been supporting yourself if you have no income?'

Tug turns to Liz.

'What's the matter? Can't you answer for yourself?'

'Okay,' Tug's voice is raised. 'I been stealing. That what you want?'

The man takes a deep breath. He does it noisily and for a second it looks as though his eyes are being sucked inside his head.

'He's been living with me,' Liz intervenes quickly.

'You're supporting him?'

'I've been buying the food, yes.'

'I see.' His face brightens to something like happiness. 'Then he doesn't need a benefit. He has you to support him.'

'He's entitled to a benefit if he cannot find work.' Liz is emphatic about this.

'Madam, no-one is *entitled* to a benefit. They are given at our discretion. And if a person does not apply to us within six weeks of becoming unemployed we presume that he does not require a benefit in order to live.'

A lash from the dragon's tail. Liz can feel tears of hopeless anger welling and struggles to keep them back. She doesn't want to allow this man the satisfaction of her tears. 'How were we to know that?' she asks limply. 'Isn't there someone above you we could talk to?'

He shakes his head. 'It's in the regulations,' he says.

'You'll know next time.'

'You tried,' Tug said as they went down the stairs. 'You really gave it back to him.'

But on the bus he was withdrawn and wouldn't speak to her and as they walked from the bus stop he turned on her. 'Fucking Pakehas. See what you're like. Y'all the same, a pack of cunts.'

She crossed to the other side of the road to be away from him, not wanting to argue. When he turned up their path she walked on for a few blocks, trying to walk off the sense of having failed and the helpless frustrated anger, reminding herself that for her the afternoon had been an insight but for Tug it was a way of life. She turned to walk home to him.

In the living room an armchair lay upturned and one-armed with two broken legs. A window was smashed, a cushion ripped open. She went into the bedroom and found Tug lying on the bed.

'I'm sorry,' he said. 'I'm sorry Liz.'

She shrugged off her coat and lay down on the bed beside him.

They bought a rather battered Vauxhall for $300 from a dealer on a Friday night, and drove it home waving magnanimously at pedestrians and bus passengers. They examined the moving miracle of machinery with awe and apprehension. And on the Saturday, after dropping Lua and Max in the city, Liz and Tug went driving in the country.

They looked at lambs and at houses and tooted at cows and strangers. They bought ice-creams. He drove with her hand on his crotch and she drove with both hands on the wheel (because she was a nervous driver) and his fingers probing between her legs. Then they chose a clump of bushes and crawled to find a private spot within sight of the car in case it should be kidnapped or converted, and found a place only moderately damp and partially prickly and quite good enough for their urgent purpose.

She suggested that they might stop in at a pub, but he declined, which pleased her.

'I hate the way you've been drinking.'

'At least I don't go impertinent when I drink.'

It confounded her for a minute. 'You mean impotent, I think.' She giggled.

'Impotent then.'

'Impertinent means cheeky.'

'I'm never that either.'

She let him do the driving, it gave him such pleasure. She had never liked cars, they had killed her father and her daughter, but she was rapidly warming to this one. She couldn't remember when she had last felt so happy.

'Now we can get away,' she said, 'it won't matter too much about Max and Lua.'

'You said you'd tell them.'

'I hate to. You know that.'

'I don' want them there.'

'Then you tell them to leave.'

'How can I? They got nowhere to go?'

'Exactly.'

'But I'm weak,' he said. 'They make me do things.'

'What things?'

'Not things exactly. Can't explain.'

'I think they're just an excuse for you. You can't spend all your life saying, Look after me 'cos I'm weak.'

In reply he trod hard on the accelerator and kept it down. They skidded around corners and for a time he drove deliberately on the wrong side of the road. Liz shouted at him then pleaded then was silent. As they approached the outskirts of the city he zoomed through red lights. Liz prepared to die, eyes closed, her head pressed against the seat and covered by her arms. She stayed like that until they screeched to a stop and Tug jumped out slamming the door behind him.

She opened her eyes and peered shakily at the crumbling and torn upholstery of the back seat. Could it be that the car was not to be, after all, their passport to happiness?

In the week that followed the boys drove her each morning to work and sometimes remembered to pick her up after work. They said the car was of great assistance in job hunting, and it may have been true but sometimes she didn't see it again till after the pubs closed.

On the Friday they showed her the bad news. The right

front side of the Vauxhall was smashed in. Not their fault, they impressed upon her. It was that cunt Bones who had pinched the keys from Tug and gone for a joy ride. Liz oughta make Bones pay for the repairs. When Bones got a job, that was.

'I could lay a charge then,' she said. 'If he really did steal the car.' But she knew she wouldn't. She was the only one with a licence and she hadn't been there. And anyway Bones was one of the boys. There was a matter of loyalty.

She put the car into the garage for panelbeating. Common sense told her she should sell it but she remembered how the country drive had for a time seemed to offer a glimpse of possibilities.

'I suppose you were waving the keys about,' she lectured Tug. 'Skiting.'

'Max was. Then he threw them to me. He always insists on driving. But I suppose really we was all skiting a bit.'

'You stay with that lot and you'll never get anywhere. Maybe you better choose.'

'How can I? I know they're taking me away from you and I can't stop it. Darling, you gotta save me.' She saw he meant it.

How could she save anyone? She was way out of her depth already and the current was getting swifter all the time.

NINE

'I'LL TELL THEM tomorrow,' she said. 'Definitely. I was going to tell them tonight but then Max came home with that big bunch of flowers so how could I? But tomorrow.'

'Nah, maybe we should let them stay.'

'Bloody hell, Tug, it's you who's been nagging me....'

'Well maybe I got used to them. They go I'll be bored, won' I.'

'Then you can go with them.'

'It's because you took so long. When I needed them to go you just farted around and did nothing.'

'You could'a told them to go.'

'You know I couldn't. They're older than me. Anyway it's your house. You should'a chucked 'em out right after the court thing.'

'I was going to but....'

'But what?'

'Well it's so hard, and anyway I kept thinking, if you really want to know, that why should you deserve a home more than them. They behave better than you, they're not as much trouble.'

'Shows I need help more.'

'Oh my God.'

'Anyway, you love me.'

'I'm going off you rapidly.'

'Don't say that. Jus think about my beautiful body.'

She began to giggle but dodged the hand that grabbed for

her. Out of his reach she remembered her morning inspiration.

'Tuggie, I had an idea. Now listen. Maybe if we let them stay and you went to a doctor and told him how you are lately.... Well, doctors are there to help people and maybe he'd put you on tranquillisers or something. Surely he would. And if you took them properly — *only* the prescribed dose — it might help a bit. At least until we sort things out.'

Tug lay on the bed looking at the ceiling out of one eye with the other screwed up. When he did that he looked every bit as crazy as the hopeless cases at Valleyview. He knows that, she thought, he pulls that face to frighten me. He also deliberately takes a long time to answer because he knows it provokes me. She picked up a book and pretended to read.

'Whadda you reckon they'd give me?' Tug asked the ceiling. 'Mandies, you reckon? Or them mogadons? Maybe speed, eh?'

'Tranquillisers,' said Liz primly. 'I don't know what. Not speedy, they'd calm you down. Look,' she laid down her book, 'you'd have to take them properly or there's no point.'

'No point anyway. No doctor'd give 'em to *me*.'

'They give them to housewives.'

'I don' look like a bloody housewife, do I. An' I'm no good with words. You know that.'

'But I thought there were some doctors dished them out like ice-creams?'

'You think you know everything. There was just one did that here and he's pissed off somewhere. I never went to him anyways, just some of the boys did. Mostly they was from chemist shop jobs, that kind of thing. You ask Max about them.'

'Well, that's that then.' Liz was resigned to the way that, for Tug, even the smallest actions and transactions were fraught with insurmountable problems.

He had picked up her transistor radio and was undoing the screws with the tip of her scissors. 'You could get 'em for me,' he offered. 'You know all the words. You could explain what it was for. What about the dozey old doctor you had at thingee? He'd do it.'

When she asked for Dr Wray the receptionist replied, in a

cautious voice, that he was no longer on the staff. Was it a personal or medical matter? Medical, said Liz.

'Then I'll put you through to Dr Manson.'

She could not recall a Dr Manson, but he was on the line before she had time to reconsider. His voice was young and encouraging.

'I have this friend, and he's been behaving a bit... well, *irrationally*. We have two chaps staying with us because they have absolutely nowhere else to go, but it's... well, the situation is very *stressful* and my friend's not coping with it well at all. And I thought... we thought that maybe if he could be put on something to cool things down. But he's not very good at explaining so....'

'I don't really feel,' interrupted the doctor, 'that it's our territory. He should see his own doctor.'

'He doesn't have one. And he was a patient at Valleyview, about six months ago.'

'I see. And what did you say your friend's name was?'

'Morton. Thomas Morton.'

'Thomas. Wasn't he the young lad in F Wing?'

'Yes.'

'And what's your relationship to Thomas?'

'I'm a friend.'

'An intimate friend?' His voice was so kindly.

'Yes,' she said. 'And that's probably part of the problem. You see I'm much older and.... Oh, it's all very muddled, but I was in Valleyview too for a while, and I thought that maybe Dr Wray would be still there and could help.'

'I think,' said the doctor, 'it might be a good idea if you came to see me. Thursday afternoon? About three?'

'And I'll bring Thomas?'

'I don't think that's necessary. It's really you who has the problem, is it not?'

'Three o'clock Thursday. Thank you.'

He'll save me, she thought. He'll see it all clearly and know what to do.

He was the doctor who had talked to her the night she took the taxi to Valleyview. Strange how after that night she had not seen him around. His office, he said, had been usurped,

140

but he would find another private space.

As she followed him along the polished corridor she saw, down an intersecting passage, Dr Wray shuffling towards her in a plaid dressing gown and scuff slippers. It can't be, she told herself. But she knew, with a kind of panicky horror, that it was.

Dr Manson stood leaning against the windowsill while Liz sat on a chrome and vinyl chair. It seemed to give him an advantage. She saw he was not young, as she had thought when they had first met. In daylight he looked at least thirty, but his manner was younger. He wore a wide floral tie which didn't suit him. Liz wondered if he wore it to please a wife or girlfriend.

The telling was more difficult than she'd expected. She aimed her words at the tie; at its navy blue cornflowers and twisted green vine. She felt she was giving only the bones of a story and the truth was in the flesh which she couldn't properly portray. She wondered as she talked if he didn't perhaps find her case a little more interesting than run-of-the-mill psychiatric problems. Might he even be titillated by it? But she did not dare to raise her eyes above the tie until he began to ask questions.

'These car rides,' said the doctor, 'how did you feel about them at the time?'

How would anyone feel? But she answered, obediently, 'terrified', disliking her own pallid predictability but unable to give the kind of reply she could imagine Tug offering. 'Horny. I mean it turns me on, donnit?'

Dr Manson studied his fingernails which were pink and clean. 'Have you considered,' he said slowly, 'that the problems that surround your... idiosyncratic household may only exist because you are there and you identify them as problems?'

'I'm not sure what you mean. If I wasn't there the problems might be different ones, but they'd probably be worse mostly. I mean for one thing there'd be no income, so they wouldn't have food, and the rent wouldn't get paid, and they'd all be back on the streets and then they'd be picked up.'

'Picked up?'

'Arrested. You can be, you know, just for having no place to live.'

'But my point is,' he stabbed his finger towards her, 'it's only *you* who sees these things as problems. You with your middle-class values. I'll guarantee Thomas never thought of himself as having problems until some well-intentioned social worker told him he had them. He should never have been admitted to this place, for one thing. But that's what happens when people start shovelling their white middle-class values onto other races.'

Liz felt cowed by this astonishing logic. 'I would have thought,' she said, but diffidently, 'that not having food or shelter was a problem no matter what race you belonged to.'

The doctor shrugged. 'Well of course, to some degree. But problems is such a broad word. We need to define our terms. What I'm saying is that I'm sure Thomas and his friends don't regard their difficulties in such a dire light as we undoubtedly would in their circumstances.'

He means that, she thought, watching him in amazement. He really believes that. 'I only wanted,' she said, defining her terms, wanting only to get away, 'some tranquillisers or something to at least stop him running down an innocent passer-by.'

Dr Manson shook his head, smiling slightly. Liz felt humiliated by his smile, an angry humiliation made worse by the welling of tears. 'What do *you* think I should do then?' She meant it to be edged with sarcasm but the constriction in her throat made it sound like a plea.

Dr Manson placed his fingertips together and studied the orb he had created. The gesture seemed familiar. An affectation, Liz told herself, borrowed from the movies. At last he said, 'You know I can't tell you what to do. You must decide that for yourself.'

'But you must have some opinion,' her anger made her a little bold. 'I'd like your opinion. Otherwise it seems we've been wasting my time and yours.'

'All right,' he said hastily, almost nervously. 'Let's put it this way. If it wasn't Thomas it would be some other young man. Or possibly a succession of young men. Where there is that need... that tendency...?' He shrugged.

If he had hit her Liz would not have been more shocked. Even in her continuous and apprehensive examination of the relationship between her and Tug this was a possibility that hadn't seriously occurred to her. In Dr Manson's professional opinion she was a Dirty Old Woman by unnatural inclination.

'I don't think,' she protested, but without confidence, 'that I have a... tendency. He's not *just* a boy. He's a person. We were friends first.'

He shook his head sadly. 'You would like to believe that, of course. Well, surely you don't think this is a viable relationship? You can't imagine there's a future in it?'

No, thought Liz, I don't; there's too much of you in me. Yet she wanted to believe it, to have that kind of faith in the way things ought to be. She stood up, ready to leave, clutching her old leather bag.

'Why not?' she said. 'Why shouldn't it be possible? I believe in fairy stories and happy endings.'

Dr Manson laughed in a gentle ripple of condescension.

She could hear Carlos Santana from the bus stop. Someone was home. As she got closer the notes rose to meet her. She used to feel this to be gull music, pure and soaring, but it was acquiring undertones. Already she knew that in years to come the sounds of Santana and Hendrix and Stevie Wonder, no longer little, would hold for her between the notes an image of this house and those who sailed in her in the year of 1973. This gallant if dilapidated craft adrift without compass in the inner city suburbs, manned by a wholly incompetent crew of small-time criminals and heading, almost inevitably for the rocks of retribution. And Liz, the only one aware of their predicament, was immobilised; lashed to the mast by bonds of love. Or was it lust as Dr Manson had so confidently diagnosed? Or simply the shabby little fear of being alone, unwanted?

Today Santana was not soaring but wailing. Writhing. His music slithered from the house in threads of anguish. Liz prepared herself for disaster. It had become a habit; she always prepared herself for disaster as she walked up their front path. And she walked the last hundred yards in quick,

143

nervous steps, partly because she looked forward to being with Tug but also because she felt that a disaster known was a disaster halved.

Max and Lua were in the living room stretched out in front of the heater. The heater went constantly. You get very cold, lying around all day. Around them was spread an assortment of cups — some doubling as ash-trays — a couple of plates edged with dried tomato sauce, two forks and an empty spaghetti can. Liz picked her way through the crockery and turned down the volume on the stereo.

'Hi,' she said. 'Where's Tug?'

'He went out.' There was pity in Max's voice.

'You don't know where?' Ashamed for asking.

They shook their heads. Of course. Not out *somewhere,* just out. Who goes anywhere else these days? And if they did know they wouldn't tell her. That's loyalty. That's being mates. They were the boys and she was the interloper.

She turned the volume up again. *Don't turn your back on me baby. Stop messing around with your tricks.* Lua did a virtuoso drum roll on the dirty plates. The room was cold in spite of the heater. Liz shivered inside her coat.

'Might'a gone to pick up the car,' Lua shouted, helpfully — or hopefully — above the music.

Liz shook her head. 'Not ready yet,' she mouthed at him.

In the kitchen, still in her coat, she made herself a mug of coffee. She held the mug in two hands to warm her fingers and carried it to the bedroom. An inventory check of her valuables — five rings and two pendants (decorative only), the fur jacket, the Chinese ivory pelican and under the mattress, her camera and transistor. All there. It shamed her, this ritual checking, but Tug insisted it was prudent. 'They'd rob their mothers. We're all the same.'

The room was cold, a penetrating and hopeless cold. In winter the sun never reached its windows, but this was theoretically spring. Liz kicked off her boots and slipped her legs beneath the blankets, still wearing her coat. She thought of Dr Manson in a centrally heated office drinking coffee with a staff nurse, wryly describing the chiropractor's ex-wife who was living out her fantasies with a juvenile offender. A nod and a wink.

Where was Tug? Whose pub, whose house, whose car, whose bed? *Where have you been Lord Randall my son? Where have you been my handsome young one?* Incest was everywhere.

She retrieved her radio from beneath the mattress and switched it on. 'There's no need to live in drab surroundings,' a woman told her. 'People are doing such brilliant things with colour these days.' Liz switched her off. Joe Cocker drifted through the wall. *What do you feel when you turn off the light?*

A knock on the door, and Max looked in. 'You wanna cup of coffee?'

'Thanks, but I just made one.'

'You okay?'

She nodded, but the gentle concern of his tone weakened her, the nod dissolved into a shrug.

'He should treat you better than this.' Max came into the room. 'D'you mind if I have a fag? I've run out. Ta.' He settled on the corner of the bed. 'He should, y'know.'

'Yeah,' Liz said, 'he should. You're right.'

Max lit two cigarettes and handed her one. 'I know it's not my business, Liz, but I jus' can't understand... well, you with Tug?'

'It's the mystery of the century.' She said it lightly. Watch him, Tug had warned. That Max's a sly cunt. He'll be into your pants first chance he gets, into your purse the next.'

'You wasn't at work this afternoon? I called in. Said you'd gone to the doctor. You crook?'

'No. As a matter of fact I went out to Valleyview and saw a doctor there. About Tug. You know that it makes it harder for me and Tug, having you two here....'

'Yeah. Yeah. I 'preciate that, Liz. And I mean if you want us to piss off right now you jus' say. We was just sort of hoping to stay till my tax money comes through, then we could get a flat 'cos they all want bonds and things. Otherwise, well, we just gonna get picked up.'

'What,' she asked cautiously, 'if I borrowed some money and lent it to you for a bond?'

'We couldn't ask you to do that. Nah. My money'll be through in a few days.'

145

'You said that ages ago.'

'But I rung 'em. Today. They said it's gone through the system, be here soon.'

He made her feel ashamed. 'It's Tug,' she said, 'who gets upset about you two being here.'

'Sure he does. But you know why, don' you? He's scared we'll move in on his missus. He knows when he's onto a good thing and he don't want to lose you. Fair enough. Neither would I. Only I'd treat you better — wouldn't go buggering off who knows where.'

'I went to Valleyview,' she said, wanting to divert the direction of the conversation, 'to try and get some tranquillisers for Tug, just to keep things together in the meantime. But he wouldn't give me any. He said it was my problem.'

'Why din' you say *you* needed them?'

'I never thought of that.'

Max thought about this. 'Look, maybe I could get you some, if you told me what it was you wanted exactly.'

'I don't know what he needs. Anyway, no. I don't want to be the cause of.... No thanks, Max.'

He patted her shoulder. 'Me an' Lua was going out for a while. Wanna come?'

'Where to?'

'Anywhere. Bit of action. You wanna go somewhere in particular?'

'No. No thanks. I'd just want to drag you round the pubs looking for Tug.'

'That's cool. I can understand that. We'll do a pub crawl then.'

On her money? 'No. I'll stay here. Thanks anyway.'

'Don't like leaving you on your own like this.'

'I'm fine,' she said. 'Really. Think I might paint my drab surroundings. What do you reckon about leaf green?'

'Sure,' said Max uneasily. 'That'd be great.'

On their way out they looked in to say goodbye. Liz noticed that Lua was wearing her long black cardigan but she hadn't the heart to mention it.

Lua was twenty-three and had only been out three months after serving a four-year sentence for manslaughter. Tug said the other man had started the fight. Lua had kicked in his

146

skull with a pair of traffic cop boots he'd stolen from his uncle. But Liz had only seen him gentle.

'We see him, we'll send him home,' Lua said now.

She smiled. 'Take care.'

When the front door slammed she was tempted for a minute to call them back. Don't leave me alone. But it was not them she wanted.

The record-player could be heard from the living room stuttering for relief. The switch-off mechanism hadn't worked since one bored day Tug had dismantled it to see how it operated. Liz got up and went to switch it off, then automatically began to clear the dirty dishes strewn on the floor. I'll write a letter to Michael, she decided as she dried the dishes. A good, long letter.

Dear Michael, It was so good to get your letter. I'm glad you're liking your new home. And perhaps you'll get to like the school better once you get used to it. It's always hard at first, not knowing anyone. It must be a posh school if you have to wear a cap. Your bike sounds fantastic. Do you ride....

She was interrupted by a knock on the door. A heavy, aggressive knock. Dr Manson's anti-depravity squad coming to take her away?

They had let themselves in before Liz reached the door. The sight of their uniforms set in motion a kaleidoscope of ghastly possibilities.

'A Peter Maxwell Hughes lives here?'

Deny. Hadn't the boys impressed that upon her? Never admit, never assist, there will always be a trap. But there were two of them and her loyalties were ambivalent.

'A Max Hughes stays here, but he's not home.'

They pushed past her into the living room. 'Where is he?' 'We'll just have a look round, if you don't mind.' It wasn't a question.

She felt a surge of anger. 'Yes,' she said. 'I do mind.'

'You live here?' asked the older one.

'Yes.'

'Where does Hughes sleep?'

'I want you to leave.' It sounded, even to her, more like petulance than authority.

147

'What's your name?'

'Have you a search warrant?'

'Hughes sleeps with you, eh. Getting into you, is he?'

'No,' she shouted. Then regretted that they had provoked her into even a denial. 'I'm asking you to leave.'

The older one laughed. They moved about the room lifting cushions, peering out the windows, reading the book titles, glancing through the letter she had begun to Michael.

'The stereo. Where'd that come from?'

'It's mine. Why?'

They trailed into the spare room where Max and Lua slept. Liz followed them. 'I want to know why you're here,' she said.

'Keep your hair on,' said the younger one. 'We're leaving soon.' He kicked at a pile of bedding on the floor.

She followed them to the front door. As they let themselves out the older one said to her, 'What are you doing with these bums anyway? Bit out of your class aren't they?'

'Just get out,' she said.

He laughed as he closed the door.

She had been lying on her bed in the dark, thinking about leaving, of shedding it all like an old skin and just going somewhere she could have a normal, simple, everyday life (but where would she go? What would she do?). She had been lying there for perhaps an hour when she heard Tug's footsteps clumping up the path in the shoes she'd bought him. He began calling her name even before he opened the door. She didn't answer. She listened to him going through the house, switching on lights, calling for her like a child, with a child's fear and need.

The bedroom light blazed.

'Why din' you answer me? I thought you were out. You heard me. Liz? Darling are you mad at me? Please don' be? I was coming home early but I met that guy Steve. You know Steve. Well you musta seen him round. Anyway he was driving this big car, belonged to his uncle and we went to these people's place an' he stayed an' stayed, an' I wanted to come home, but I couldn't till they was ready. Truly.' His arms around her. 'Please? You're not mad at me? Hey,

148

what'd the doctor say? You get them pills?'

'No,' she said. 'He wouldn't give them to me.'

'Why not?'

'He reckons the thing that's wrong with you is me.'

'What you mean?'

'He thinks I'm depraved.'

'What's that?'

'Oh...kinky...filthy.'

Tug's face spread into a grin. He pushed his tongue between his lips and narrowed his eyes in sensual parody.

'Depraved,' he whispered. 'Depraved. I'll remember that one.' He tugged to free her jersey from the waistband of her jeans and inserted his hand. 'Aren't you glad,' he said as his fingers closed around a nipple, 'that I'm so eager to educate myself?'

TEN

MAX AND LUA left. Without pleas, threats or financial assistance they found themselves a flat. Max's tax refund hadn't turned up but he had found a job in a wool store and on his first pay day the two of them shifted out. Liz felt it to be a small triumph for optimism. She was ashamed to recall how threadbare her own faith in the pair had been at times.

On the day that they moved, which was also the day she collected the car from the repair shop, she withdrew an extra forty dollars from her house fund. And when she and Tug transported Max and Lua to their new home — a barren yellow fibrolite house that smelt throughout of mildew and cat's piss — she pressed the money upon them, ashamed even then of her parsimony. They refused it.

'Hell, Liz, you done enough for us already. You give us a chance, not many'd'a done that.'

She thought of her nightly inventory of 'valuables' and her shame increased.

When they got home Tug leapt about the house. 'It's all ours again. Just us, on our own.'

She watched him, smiling, wishing she could believe he'd continue to feel that way.

It wasn't until they were in bed that he said, plaintively, 'But what am I gonna do all day? Could'n you stay home? You could stop working. We could live on the money you got in the bank.'

150

It was a cool, fine, colourless afternoon and she was returning to work with an armful of groceries when she saw Martyn.

He walked right past her and it had been so long that she couldn't be sure, but when she turned round he too was looking back with the tentative beginnings of a smile.

They hugged each other.

'I *thought* it was you.'

'Me too. What are you doing down here?' She felt suddenly nervous of her pleasure at seeing him, doubting that it could be mutual.

'I'm just down for a few days.'

'From Wellington? You're still there?'

'No, I left there years ago.' He was staring at her with a bemused sort of smile and she wondered if she had changed so much. 'Are you still with Whatsisname?'

'Ken?' She shook her head. 'Where are you staying?'

'With my sister-in-law. My brother died, I'm down for the funeral actually.'

'I'm sorry.'

'Don't be.' He grimaced and began to look uncomfortable as if their meeting was already regrettable.

Liz remembered the time. 'Martyn, I have to get back to work. Look, I don't suppose you'd like to come round tonight? Have dinner? I could pick you up?'

'I'd love to.' He seemed to mean it. 'But I'd better eat there first, they'll expect me.'

She gave him the address, half-thinking as she did so that he wouldn't come. His life was probably too full for nostalgia. It was only Liz who kept the past stored away to be polished and pawed.

Liz and Martyn had worked, for three years, for the same agency. Martyn had been the junior artist, a bony, pale young man intense with ambition. With Kath, Carol and Geoff they had visited and passed judgement on Wellington's available night-life, had spent hours discussing The Arts and applauding each other's creative talents and admiring each other's wit.

But reason told Liz now that her memory was selective and

151

unreliable. If her single days had been so bright with hope and confidence why had she allowed herself to marry? Could it really have been just because Ken asked her and marriage seemed somehow inevitable? Or because she had slept with him and that seemed to involve some kind of commitment? Or because he had countered her reservations with such convincing logic?

As she polished up the salt and pepper shakers, stacked dishes, swept away crumbs, Liz almost began to hope that Martyn would not come round that night. In the pleasure of meeting him she had overlooked Tug. But how monstrous, she thought, if I can't even invite an old friend into my own home?

'He's okay,' she promised. 'Really he is.'

Tug sneered. 'Another Jim?'

'No. And he was never my boyfriend. Nothing like that. Actually I think he's probably camp.'

'You *think*?'

'Well, he didn't seem to have girlfriends. We never talked about it, but it was harder in those times, people were more against it. I guess it wasn't something you would talk about.'

'You can'ta known him very well.'

'Well I did. But we talked about other things. There *are* other things, you know.'

He glowered. 'A bloody pouff. Whadda you want to go asking one of them round for.'

'He's a friend.'

'I can't stand them.'

'He's not a them, he's a him. Anyway do you know any?'

'Course! They're always hanging round them toilets. Some've even offered me money.'

'Did you take it?'

'Yeah. Then I ran like fuck.'

'I think you're a shit,' she said and meant it.

His eyes slid away from her uneasily. 'I needed the money, ay. Woulda taken off anyone who was silly enough to hold it out. Off you even.'

'Look, if you don't want to meet him why don't you go out?'

'No thanks, don't feel like it.'

'There's only a few desperate ones hang around toilets,' she said, 'so what have you got against the rest of them?'

'You *know*.'

'Damned if I do. You tell me.'

'They're perverts.'

She thought of Tug fluttering his eyelashes, the pleasure he took from passivity, his moments of unashamed femininity.

'You're amazing,' she said. 'Just bloody amazing.'

'He won't come for a while,' said Tug. 'We could go to bed.'

Perhaps it was that that mellowed him. At any rate when Martyn arrived he and Tug seemed to like each other on sight. Liz who had grown accustomed to the discomfort of undercurrents felt loose and light-headed without them. They talked about music, about funerals and God and grieving and forgetting, then Martyn and Liz about their Wellington days. Tug went off to make supper.

Martyn hadn't lost contact with their friends as abruptly, as finally, as Liz. Carol, he said, had died two years ago of an alcohol-related disease. He had gone down to her funeral. One of only eight mourners. Geoff was editor of a country paper and an aging father of young children. Kath, the dazzling Kath, was last heard of in France married to a rich count.

Liz sifted through his information looking for something, a pattern or a conclusion. People coming together in friend-ships, leaving smudges of their being on each other then drifting away. Time gone and existing only in shared but different memories. It made her feel empty; plundered.

'Martyn?' she asked clutching at the present. 'Tell me about you?'

'Me? I live with fisherman Pete. A pom with a voice like Tennessee Ernie Ford.' He laughed. 'You'd like him. We've been together three years. More. I'm happy Liz. We live at a place called Wai Bay. I'm still painting but mostly illustrating, that kind of thing, for the money.'

Tug brought in tea and biscuits. 'Who's Tennessee Whatsits?'

Martyn sang in a husky but unrecognisable imitation. *'Saint Peter don't you call me 'cos I can't go. I owe my soul to the company store.'*

Tug looked blank and they laughed.

'Where's Wai Bay?'

'Out of Auckland. Little bay. Beautiful, you can't imagine. You two'd love it. Lot of good people. Quite a few freaks — I mean the smokers and the oddball eccentric types. Accepting kind of people. Pete and I can walk down the street holding hands and the neighbours still smile and say hello.'

Tug gave Liz a quick so-you-were-right look, but without disapproval.

Liz felt emboldened. 'We wouldn't dare. As it is Tug walks seven paces behind me like the Duke of Edinburgh and still people glare.' There was a relief in saying it. Martyn's smile was empathetic and free of surprise.

Tug reached over and took her hand now their togetherness was official. 'Which one's the Duke of Edinburgh?'

Liz glanced at Martyn anxiously. Again he showed no flicker of surprise. 'The Queen's husband. I mean the *royal* Queen's husband.' Grinning at that.

'That one!' Tug was now entirely at ease. 'He only gets to screw her when she decides, doesn't he? She sends a guard to bring him in.'

'That's when they fire the cannons off,' said Martyn, straight-faced. 'Once a year.'

Tug almost believed him then his face spread in a grin.

'You should come and visit us,' said Martyn. Asking them both, not just Liz.

'We should move there.' She surprised herself. 'There's nothing to keep us here.' She meant *me* but Tug's hand still lay warmly in her own.

'It'd be good for you. I know it would. It's kind of... benign.'

As she drove Martyn back to his sister-in-law's (he had come by taxi), glad that Tug hadn't insisted on coming with them, the idea took firmer root. She waited to find out more. Martyn was talking about his dead brother.

'We never really got along. And *her*! She called me a faggot once, to my face. *I don't want faggots in my house.*

Almost funny I suppose. But it humiliated me to come down for the funeral. Still, I did. Pride doesn't seem to measure very large alongside death.'

'If it was me,' she said, 'I'd have come.'

'Oh, I know *you* would've.'

'Why do you say that?'

'I'm not sure. It's just the way I remember you. On top of everything — no grudges.'

'I've changed, then.'

He caught something in her tone. 'I think you two are miserable in this place. You will come and look at Wai Bay? If you ask me this city's a two-faced upright, uptight, arsehole of a place.'

'I hate it here.' Her vehemence surprised her. 'But I want to leave on my own. There's no future in me and Tug. We're gonna have to split up some time and this would seem like a good way to do it.'

'Why will you have to split up some time?'

'He's only sixteen.'

'And?'

She was startled. 'Well that's enough. And there's all the other differences.'

'You'd be all right up home I'd say. Different's normal there.'

'It's not just outside things. It's us. I'd be better on my own. What about work though? Is there any?'

'Not much unless you're prepared to travel a long way. But work's no worry, you'd find something.'

'What if I flew up next week and had a look?'

'Great. Send us a telegram and I'll meet you at Auckland.'

'I'm glad I ran into you.'

She didn't want him to go, knowing that once he was gone her resolve would shrink and his assurances would begin to seem suspect. Once he was gone the prospect of deserting Tug would seem impossible.

Irwin was angry that she should ask for three days off.

'But I've been here nearly six months. Surely I'm entitled to a bit of leave?'

'Leave? Yes. Maybe you should do that!'

155

'Okay then. I will. I'll finish right now.

It was just before the lunchtime rush. He backed down as she had thought he would. 'Liz, you're being irrational and it makes me irrational. Workers need holidays, of course they do. Only the bosses get no holidays. I'll manage. Eva can help. So, you go off to Auckland. You'll have a good time there. The streets are full of Maoris up there. You can have all the Maori boys you want.' He had turned away from her, busy slicing sandwiches, a mountain of them sliced precisely into two triangular mountains.

She stood searching for a retort, wanting it to be a slap, hard and quick. Looking at the elbows of his pale beefy arms beneath the rolled up sleeves of a powder blue shirt. Ginger hairs and freckles. And beginning to feel sorry for him. It was always the way — her rage going damp and dissolving into a puddle of sympathy, at least with men. For men always seemed so transparent in anger, like a glass clock with little wheels of insecurity, fear and injured pride revolving, one turning the other.

Irwin looked over his shoulder almost cautiously as if expecting blood and gaping wounds. She smiled at him. The sight of his jowly face made her feel again the desire to slap.

'That's exactly why I'm going,' she said. 'I can't get enough of it.' She recognised something of Tug in her voice.

Irwin was staring at her, disbelieving, believing. His eyes gleamed and his face was animated yet furtive. She watched him with fascination, seeing the excitement in him. All the erotic fancies about dark skin and light skin, the imagined wet ecstasies offered by wide and fleshy lips, the delights of firm young flesh — they were there in Irwin's face. Liz turned away and began to stack plates into the warmer. Looking at Irwin she had had a sudden and unnerving flash that she was seeing herself.

Am I just the same, she thought, except that his fantasy has become my reality?

Tug turned seventeen. She made him a chocolate cake with seventeen candles and bought him a Led Zeppelin album. Seventeen was a relief, so much less innocent-yet-corruptible-sounding than sixteen. He now had a sparse collection of wiry black hairs growing on his upper lip. Strangely she had never thought about his hairlessness until the first stragglers appeared like a rebuke. Now she watched his face anxiously for new growth as if the hairs were daffodils heralding the end of a long hard winter.

He was still growing. Another mute condemnation of her frail moral fibre. He must have grown almost three inches since they were at Valleyview, although some of that may have been improved posture. He now stood straight, his slouch being saved for special occasions. And his body had filled out.

Liz, disregarding time and nature, gave herself personal credit for these changes. Although he still wasn't notably energetic he was no longer given to the listlessness which had once puzzled and exasperated her. She gave herself credit there too (with more justification) for his improved diet.

Tug's birthday was clouded by her planned departure for Wai Bay on the following day.

'You'll stay up there. I know.' She could see the fear in his eyes.

'Don't be silly. I have to come back anyway. All my stuff's here. Mitzi. Everything.'

He drove her to the airport. He would have the car while she was away. She knew that was foolhardy, much better to have driven herself and taken the keys with her, but the car was her peace offering for leaving him alone. He hated to be alone, she knew that. He seemed so desolate at the airport that she found herself reassuring him over and over that it would only be for a few days.

She even had the thought that his unhappiness may be a kind of premonition. The plane would crash. Or was it that he knew by some sure intuition that her plans didn't include him? She could believe that. Sometimes lately it had seemed that Tug could, not read her mind exactly, but tune in on her feelings more accurately than she could.

'Don't forget Mitzi,' she said against his neck — risking the finer sensibilities of all the other intending passengers. 'And please, love, don't get into trouble.' Thinking, even as she said it that she was asking the almost impossible. For trouble wasn't, for Tug's lot, something they had to seek out

157

— trouble surrounded them and pressed in on them like the smog that gathered over the city and suburbs on winter evenings with stealthy menace.

Wai Bay had a startling and extravagant beauty. Liz, who some two and a half hours before had been standing in sleety rain on a southern tarmac, felt weak with disbelief as they stood alongside Martyn's aging Citroen and looked down from the hill. Grey-yellow sand stretched beneath them broken here and there by clusters of rocks, the sea sparkled and glinted, the bush came down to the sand in tight little curls of manuka, fat pungas and boastful palms. She saw that Martyn was beaming with pride as if it was all his own creation on a giant canvas.

'It's at its best in early summer,' he said modestly.

He had parked at the top of the hill to give her this first look. The road wound down to the bay quite steeply and the bush around it was dotted with houses, rough beach baches mostly, littered like lolly-papers on a lawn. To Liz at that moment even the houses looked perfect. She thought with a heady certainty, I've come home. It was one of those clear-headed moments of *knowing* so that even if later events belie the accuracy of it, the moment itself remains somehow pure and true in its conviction.

The decision having made itself, Liz was left with four days of just being. Which meant, for a start, sleep. In the tiny spare room of Martyn and Pete's cottage she slept almost the whole of her first full day. 'Sea air,' she apologised, finally awake and feeling a lightness as though the exhaustion had been a burden shrugged off. She'd awoken to a smell of wood smoke, sea food, salt air and the encroaching bush. The little patched-up cottage was yellow-lit and shadowed by lantern light. Pete cooking at the stove, Martyn at the table rolling a joint. She felt safe and enclosed and grateful.

Three more days. She knew it was three days, but time contorted and it was much more and much less. On the first of those days the three of them went out on Pete's boat. She lay on the deck burning happily, dangling a fishing line. The still day was suspended entirely by a lungful of spicy smoke. She was finding the stuff had hidden attractions. Above them a petrel soared and plummeted on magnificent wings. Liz had a sudden childish urge to run into the cabin and hide herself from that great Killjoy in the sky. As far back as she could remember she had believed that pleasure, undisguised, invoked celestial wrath.

On the two remaining days she sampled an assortment of dubious homemade wines and inhaled on passing joints. She explored the beach with a sense of wonder and privilege and was reminded of Tug. His body. She talked with the procession of visitors who called at the cottage, spent an hour or two, and wandered off. The talk revolved around Wai Bay — its residents, its store, its soil, its weather, its houses. Houses for rent were hard to come by, snapped up by the oldest grapes on the grapevine.

'No hurry for that,' said Pete. 'You could stay here long as you want. You know that.'

Pete was in his forties. Thoughtful, watching eyes above a grizzled beard. Gruff-voiced with a broad provincial accent; Yorkshire, but she had to ask having no ear for such things. A big man with legs like kauri trunks.

Liz wanted to capture moments so she could unwrap them afterwards like barley sugars to sustain her till she returned to Wai Bay, but in the alcohol blur and cannabis warp the moments melted together sweet and inseparable. It was difficult even to extract herself, her departure seemed a daunting project which demanded a superhuman effort of organisation.

They urged her, 'Don't go Tuesday. Stay a bit longer. What's another couple of days?'

'I can't,' she regretted, wanting to stay curled in that patched-up fairy tale of a cottage for ever and ever. 'I have to get back.'

I have to get back because Tug is there waiting, and in the middle of all this I have missed him. And not the screwing, surprisingly, but him.

They barely made it to the plane, no one having a watch and the transistor batteries having run flat. By the time Martyn returned from a trip to the store to check the time they should have long since started for the airport.

The plane was a shock. The moments before had been too rushed for sensations, but in the plane, tethered, drained — but feeling that little glow of importance she still got from being an *air traveller* she looked around and knew she was back in the real world. And she realised that she had done nothing, while in Wonderland, about finding work. True she had raised the subject a few times but it had met with shrugs and 'Something always turns up,' or grins and 'Work? Wassat then? Some nasty foreign habit?'

And Wonderland, she thought looking through the window at the matchbox cars on matchbox roads, the crushable miniature houses and people the size of wood-slaters, was a lousy description. There it had been all bright, sunny, daylight. It was now she was gliding down the rabbit-hole, falling back into the chill and problem-filled dark.

But he would be there at the bottom to meet her. Hair blowing wide in the inevitable airport wind, making his shoulders look narrow and frail. His mouth beaming in wide welcome. White teeth — a golliwog, waiting for her to pick him up and take him to bed.

He wasn't there.

In a taxi — thank God for the house fund — she drew conclusions. He had simply forgotten. (But how could he forget? He loved her. How dare he forget? He was driving her car.) Something more substantial then? Circumstances beyond his control. An accident? (Yes, something like that. Better an overdose than an oversight. *I take that back. It was a joke. I didn't mean it.*)

The car was there, uncrumpled, in the street. A light was on in the kitchen. (*I did mean it. How dare he forget!*)

The front door wasn't locked. The living room was tidy, so was the bedroom, the bed neatly made. She went into the kitchen wondering why he hadn't heard her parading about the house; sharpening up a sarcasm.

At the kitchen bench a girl was pouring steaming water into Liz's teapot. She put the lid on carefully then turned to Liz. Her face was vaguely familiar — or was that because it was that kind of everywhere face; pretty in a soft youthful way but unremarkable? An assembly-line doll's face, fluffy light brown hair to just below the shoulders, blue-green eyes, a

160

pink tinge to the cheeks — nature's doing or else a reflection from her jersey.

'Do I know you?' asked Liz. It was a start.

'I'm Paula.' She brushed her hair from her face, a nervous feminine movement. 'I's just making you a cup of tea. Do you feel like one?'

'Absolutely.' Liz sank onto a kitchen chair and fumbled for cigarettes. She had a curious feeling that she had suffered some kind of time lapse and returned to the right house but the wrong year. Should she have gone easier on the Wai Bay green, being a bit inexperienced in that field?

Paula was pouring milk into their cups. 'You do take milk?'

'Yes please.'

'D'you remember meeting me?' Placing a cup before Liz, pushing forward the sugar bowl. 'In town once, d'you remember? I's with Tony.'

Liz couldn't remember. 'I thought I'd seen you before,' she said, as if she could. She had got to know at least a dozen of the boys and some of the girls but they moved in packs inconsistently and were often so alike in style that she barely noticed them as faces, names. Now she watched Paula pulling herself in at the table across from her and lighting up a Rothmans. There was an awkwardness of unfamiliarity about her actions. *Where's Tug*? But Liz felt she must not ask, at least until she established where she stood in this new household.

'The sugar's there if you need it.'

'No thanks.'

Paula wore a pink mohair sweater above jeans. It was the kind of sweater that had been the rage for a while when Liz was seventeen, she was surprised to see the fashion revived so soon. Could a shared experience of mohair be taken to constitute a bond between them? Paula put down her cup and looked at Liz squarely.

'I thought you should have the tea first,' she said. 'I came to tell you Tug's been arrested. Tug told me to come and tell you.'

Liz propped her head in her hands and looked down at the tea, sitting there in the cup as if everything was easy and calm. She looked up at Paula. 'What for?'

'So's you'd....' She realised she'd got the question wrong and paused. Her cheeks grew pink. 'Oh he didn't *do* it.'

It was possible that Tug would have asked Tony's girlfriend to convey a message, but why should Tony's girl be flushed with indignation on Tug's behalf?

'Do what?'

'Didn't do *anything*. They reckon he assaulted this dee, only Tug swears he didn't. He said to tell you it was the same cop that was out to get him.'

'When did all this happen?'

'S'morning. I *know* he didn't do anything.'

'Can you tell me from the beginning?'

'It was this morning, see. 'Bout seven o'clock 'cos I's just gonna get ready for work. And these two cops just barge straight in. I mean they didn't even knock, how's-your-father, nothing. Marched into the bedroom.'

'You were here? In the bedroom?' Liz hoped she sounded capable, a Miss Marples, but the question had been fired a little too urgently.

Paula wriggled uneasily, sensing something in the question. She decided on boldness. 'Yes.' She squared her shoulders. 'I was in bed with Tug.' She smiled too vividly. Her parted lips said, We're women of the world, and her eyes pleaded Don't growl at me. But it wasn't a big-deal thing; it was between generations, not between rivals. She doesn't know, Liz realised. She smiled back in reassurance.

'Sorry. Go on.'

'Well we was in bed and they barged in and ordered Tug, Get up. And when he asked they said they wanted to question him 'bout some burglary, so he said he didn't know anything 'bout any burglary and why didn't they piss off — I mean I only say it like that 'cos that's the word he said. I don't usually use them words. And I know I should say *those,* and mostly I do.' Liz was nodding for her to go on. 'So they took him down to the station. Well first they told him to get dressed and how he was only making more trouble for himself if he didn't go along with them and all that. So he got up and put on some clothes and then they started on me, asking my name and that, and Tug said it was none of their business.

162

Then one of them got really nasty at Tug and said to go through the other room with him and answer some questions. And the other one — he was younger — stayed and asked me my name and said what was I doing hanging round with the likes of Tug. And he was looking at me... you know, and he said he'd like to go out with me some time. I said no thanks very much. I was still in bed 'cos I had no clothes on. And he grabbed at the blankets and put his hand down under the bedclothes and touched me. Laughing. Like who does he think he is? I told him to shove off and then the other one called him and he went. So I put a blanket round me and went to see what was happening and they were taking Tug out to the wagon and he called out for me to tell you tonight and that he hadn't done anything, just that dee was out to get him.'

'I'll ring,' said Liz, 'and see what they tell me.'

'Would you like something to eat? There's eggs in the fridge. I could make something.'

'No. Thanks but I'm really not hungry.'

'Me neither. It's being so worried. Bet we won't sleep either.'

Paula would, Liz reflected, waiting for the call to be put through to the watch-house, make an amiable daughter-in-law. She imagined the girl nursing Tug's son on an exposed and pendulous boob and felt a pain in the region of her own chest.

The voice at the watch-house was friendly and apparently eager to oblige. Yes Thomas Morton was in custody. He would be appearing in the Magistrate's Court in the morning. The charge was — he went away to look up this detail — assault on a police officer and resisting arrest.

Liz felt the anger seeping through her so her fingers tingled. She wanted to throw, hit, break.

'I understand,' she said, the Lady Bracknell voice coming to her in this moment of need, 'that the officers concerned walked into my house and took Thomas from his bed. I wish to know whether they had a warrant to enter the house?'

'Just a minute lady, the detective who made the arrest is right here. You better speak to him.' The voice was almost sympathetic. Liz was sorry for having had to inflict her superior breeding onto him.

'Yes? Detective Warren here.' Very brusque. She repeated her query, it seemed a bit insubstantial.

'A warrant isn't required under those specific circumstances.' He sounded bored by the need to explain the obvious.

'I understood it was,' she persisted but knew she was losing ground.

'Then you understood wrongly. Perhaps next time you'll check your facts.'

'Oh, I will.' She hated him. 'I'll certainly check them. I have another query.' She was afraid he would hang up.

'Which is?'

'I understand you came to enquire about a burglary, yet he's not being charged with burglary so how can he be charged with resisting arrest if you had no reason to arrest him?'

'He was arrested for assault.' Bored again.

'Yet *you* came into the house and dragged him out of bed?' She knew she was getting nowhere but she wanted to keep him on the line, something definite to aim her anger at.

'Madam, I've got work to do and people like you waste my time. Good day.' The receiver crashed in her ear. Liz wondered if that was a small point to her.

'That's the way to talk to them.' Paula was pink with excitement — or was it admiration?

'Didn't achieve anything.' She slumped into a chair.

'Shoulda told him about that cop touching my breasts.' She said the word with a wriggle of embarrassment.

'You should go down to the station tomorrow and make an official complaint about that.'

Paula looked impressed. 'What would they do if I did?'

'Probably give him an award for initiative.'

Paula giggled. 'That's about it.' She stood up. 'I may as well make another pot of tea.' It seemed that they'd known each other for years. Liz watched her rinsing the cups, filling the electric jug.

'Have you known Tug long?'

'Ages. Since before he went to hospital. But I didn't know him well, just really to say hello to. We didn't really, well, you know, until this last weekend.' Her voice became shyly confessional. 'I think he's really neat. I s'pose I'm in love with him.'

Liz prodded this admission around in her mind gingerly in case it exploded. Paula saw something like dismay in Liz's expression and added kindly, 'Tug really admires you. The way he talks about you. He says you've done so much for him, just like you were his mother.'

Liz lit a cigarette. How bizarre, she thought, but mildly. She felt somehow abstracted from the whole situation, a spectator at a play. A comedy. For part of her had a great urge to laugh. Paula talked on and Liz saw that the girl felt sorry for her.

'He told me — I hope you don't mind that I know — that you and him used to, you know. I don't mind. I guess you musta got lonely not having your husband around. I mean I can understand that.' She looked at Liz for response and took her bemused smile as encouragement. 'Problem for us is I'd like us to get a place of our own but Tug doesn't want to leave here. So I wondered if maybe, after the court case and all, we could both of us live here with you? That is if you wouldn't mind? But of course it'd have to be clear that... well you understand I wouldn't want him going off to your bed in the night or anything. I mean not that he would but....'

She was waiting anxiously for a reply. Liz the spectator had been dragged centre stage fumbling for her lines. The three of them together playing happy families and musical beds? Or Liz graduated to den mother, no pleasure and all responsibility? But since Liz intended to flee as soon as possible to the warm womb of Wai Bay shouldn't she welcome Paula, under any conditions, as a means of weaning Tug from her all-too-appreciative bosom? Or had he weaned himself in her absence? An anguishing thought.

'Tug hasn't quite told you the truth,' she said. 'You see he and I were sleeping together until I left on Friday. I came back presuming we still were.'

'Oh,' said Paula. A small breathy noise. Paula punctured. She gave Liz a pleading look. 'What are we gonna do then? I really want him.' The look reminded Liz of Nessa standing longingly beside the chocolate bars in the supermarket.

Pleease.

'I think,' she said, 'he should be with you. It'd be better for him in the long run. There'd be some kind of future in it.'

'I'd marry him,' promised Paula. 'I'd love us to get married.' In white, Tug tame and embarrassed in a suit. Liz could see it.

'He's a bit young to get married yet. And he'd give you a few problems — you know that?'

Paula smiled. 'I know he's a bit irresponsible, but I could look after him, I've always been very responsible. I'm the oldest in our family and I'm a year older than Tug even. Besides men are always kind of irresponsible aren't they? And the thing about Tug is he's such a loving person, don't you think?'

'Yes, he is.' Knives slicing into her heart, having to remind herself hard that this was the best possible ending.

'Of course we won't be able to stay here, not now I know about.... It wouldn't be fair to you or me.' She gave Liz a look of concern. 'I hope you'll be all right. I mean I know you'll miss him.'

'I'll be fine,' Liz said firmly, but feeling things were being resolved a little too fast. 'But you know we can't really sit here and decide about his future. I mean Tug hasn't been asked what he wants. He's the one that has to decide.'

'Yes, I s'pose so.' But Paula gave her a look of disappointment as if Liz owed her a irreversible and dignified abdication. She poured the tea and stirred sugar into her own cup then forgave Liz with a sunny smile. 'I can't help it,' she confided. 'I'm hoping he chooses me.'

Liz smiled back feeling ancient and decrepit in the face of girlish confidences and enthusiasm. 'If he's wise he will.' She offered Paula a cigarette.

They sat until it was past three in the morning, drinking tea and talking Tug. Liz wanted to ask the girl such thorny or horny questions as, How do you find him in bed? What did he do to you? What did you do to him? Does it stay firm for you, too, for ages inviting re-use? But Paula's face had the soft mistiness of romance and a primness about her little mouth. She would be repelled by such loose and dirty talk. Paula preferred to suffer for Tug. 'Poor Tug, I'll bet he's

166

cold. They probably only give them one blanket. And just a mattress on the floor.' And, 'I bet Tug's not sleeping either, poor love.' And, 'I hope they didn't bash him about.'

Liz, old and flinty, reflected but did not say that a cold hard night in the cells might give Tug the opportunity to consider the times when he had been hateful and had abused her hospitality.

As time dribbled by, Paula's confidence increased. Liz seeing Paula's wide bright eyes studying her with a kind of curiosity, felt if she leaned closer she would see her own reflection in those eyes. See the small corrugations that ran towards the lips, the permanent furrows between the eyebrows, the network of lines beneath the eyes, the loose colourless flesh, the thickened waist. All those horrors so malevolently dwelt upon by glossy magazines. Paula was smooth, firm, fresh, pink-and-beige, juicy. She had every reason for confidence.

'See you in the morning,' said Paula, demoted to the spare bed, at twelve minutes past three.

'Good night,' said Liz. Already the Wai Bay sky would be lightening and in a couple of hours Pete would be leaving the house to bring in his set lines.

In the morning Liz rang the sewing factory where Paula worked and said she was Paula's flatmate and Paula had a temperature and wouldn't be in. Then Paula rang Irwin and told him she was Tug's girlfriend and that Liz had rung to say she had missed her flight and would have to catch a later one. Then Liz drove them both to the courthouse and they took seats side by side on the public benches.

More than a hour and three traffic offences and a shoplifting later, Tug was called and escorted in. As he walked to the dock his eyes searched the public benches, when he saw them his eyes widened above a grin.

The duty solicitor entered no plea and asked for a remand. The magistrate requested a probation report and set bail at $200 surety. Brief and businesslike. Tug was escorted back through the door he'd come in by. Liz and Paula crept out the public entrance, Liz stopping to ask the policeman who appeared to guard it where she should go to sign as surety, and feeling a certain pride in being no longer a complete greenhorn about such matters. She was directed to the door Max had previously shown her to. Paula opted to wait in the car.

Liz was given a form to sign. It committed her to forfeit $200 if Tug didn't appear in court on the due date — a fortnight hence. They had to go and fetch Tug from the paddy wagon which was about to take him to the police station. She waited, reading the posters on the wall. VD is a social disease, and how to identify a cannabis plant. Tug was escorted through an inner door. On seeing Liz he beamed and came to her holding out his arms. She cuddled him fiercely, it seemed they had been separated, cruelly, for years. He kissed her indiscreetly, regardless of the man with the bail forms and the middle-aged officer.

'I missed you,' he whispered.

She waited until they were outside. 'What about Paula?'

'Tell her to go.'

'I can't, Tuggie. She says she's in love with you.'

He put his hands over his face and peeped at her between his spread fingers.

'It's not a joke, Tug,' she said crossly.

He took his hands away. 'But you gotta admit it's kinda funny though.'

She grinned despite herself. Back there inside when Tug had come through the door and looked at her she had felt something between them that had seemed both inevitable and indestructible. It was a feeling that she didn't wish, given her present intentions, to probe but it had left a warmth within her.

'Why did you move her in,' she asked, 'if you don't want her?'

'I's lonely. And you're planning to leave me anyway.'

She said, non-committally, 'If that's what you think shouldn't you hang on to Paula?'

He gave her a look of suspicion.

They took a roundabout route to the court office to avoid passing the car and Paula. This time the application for legal aid was taken by a young woman who was courteous and not interested in reading between the lines.

Coming out of the office Liz demanded, 'What do you plan to do about her? Paula?'

He shrugged helplessly. 'I dunno.'

'You'll have to tell her something.'

'I can't. She's all right, you know. She's a nice chick.'

'Then you *do* want her?'

'Don' be stupid.'

'Then you'll have to talk to her. Go on. I'll wait here.'

He returned in a few minutes. 'Come on, I said we'd drive her home. It was awful, love. I just din' know what to say.'

Paula sat in the back of the car. Tears ran softly down her smooth cheeks. Liz drove, following Tug's directions. (How often had he been along this route?) She wanted to say something to the girl but the words she assembled in her mind seemed fatuous and depressingly adult. Paula lived in one of a cluster of ugly brick flats.

'I'm sorry,' Liz said as the girl left the car, but Paula's eyes, with their accusation of betrayal, were fixed on Tug.

'I hope you'll both be happy,' she said to him softly, looking young and determinedly brave.

'See what you've done,' Liz rebuked Tug as they drove off.

'It was your fault,' he insisted. 'You shouldn'ta left me.'

'I never noticed that before.'

'What?' Lazily.

'The skin on your balls. It moves. It writhes around, like there are lots of little amoebas or something all moving round underneath. It's really weird. You don't know what you're missing.'

He pulled at her arm. 'Come up here and talk to me.'

'What about?' She moved to lie alongside him. She waited for him to answer, not impatient for once at his slowness.

'Us,' he said at last. 'Is it just sex, d'you reckon?'

'I don't know,' she said. 'Sometimes I think yes, sometimes no. Whadda you think?'

'Same. You really going up north then?

'Yes.'

'What if they put me away this time? Will you wait for me till I get out?'

'Well,' she said, moving the words out cautiously, 'maybe

after you got out you could come up there and join me.'

'But you wouldn't stay on here and come an' visit me?'

'Tug, how can I be expected to make decisions about something that most probably will never happen?'

But in her mind she was already arriving at Wai Bay alone. Free as a gull.

ELEVEN

'I THINK YOU'RE probably just imagining it was victim-isation,' the solicitor said. 'And even if it's true it's not relevant to your defence.'

'Surely it is.' The sumptuousness of the lawyer's office made Liz feel aggressive. From the smug comforts of such luxury how dare he presume to understand Tug's circumstances?

The lawyer was young and overweight, straining at the seams of his elegant three-piece suit. He sat holding a pencil, then dropping it the inch or two onto his blotter with an abstracted air.

'You can't criticise the police in court,' he explained. 'Magistrates won't tolerate it.'

'But if the complaints are true....'

'No ifs. We can't afford to upset the magistrate.' He turned to Tug. 'I want you to describe exactly what happened in your... interaction with the police.'

Tug looked at Liz.

'What happened? What you did?' she prompted.

'Like I told you,' he said to the lawyer. 'I din' do nothing really. The dee twisted my arm round behind my back, you know, an' it was hurting so I kneed him in the balls. Well, anyone woulda.'

'Then what happened?'

'He let go and kinda came at me an' I said if he touched me I'd do him. Then he called the other cop in and they took me out to the car. I jus' went with them. Wasn't gonna take on two.'

'But what else did you do besides kneeing him in the testicles?'

'Din' do nothing.'

'Was the girl in the room at that time?'

'Nope.'

'She was being molested by the other officer,' offered Liz. The solicitor gave her a wearily cautioning look.

'Don't you believe me?' she demanded.

'It's beside the point. I've already explained that.' He turned back to Tug. 'The police report tells a rather different story. It claims you attacked both officers and there was a lot more than a knee in the balls.'

'Then they're lying.'

The lawyer sighed. 'Maybe, but we can't claim that as defence. We can of course say you deny it, but magistrates almost always choose to believe the police, especially when, as in your case, the defendant has a lot of previous convictions. If you plead not guilty it'll be your word against theirs. I really think your best course would be to plead guilty and try and present a case for lenient sentence. The probation officer's report may help us there. It's a pity you're not working because that'll go against you, but your rate of convictions has rather slowed down in the last few months.'

'But if he's not guilty why should he say he is?'

'I've explained that to the best of my ability.'

'All you've explained is that a person's considered guilty no matter what.'

'You might put it that way.' He gave a faint smile.

'Then it's all a farce.'

He shrugged. 'If Thomas would prefer me to find someone else to handle his case? Would you Thomas?'

'No,' said Tug, glaring at Liz.

Outside, in the corridor, he said in fury, 'You stupid bitch. Why did you go on like that for?'

'Because,' she said, hurt by his anger, 'it's all so unfair. Well, I know last time you cheated your way out of it and I thought that was wrong, but it was probably the only way. I mean it's all stacked on their side.'

He snorted and strode on ahead of her, but at the building's entrance he was waiting, 'Don't you *see*? He's all I got, an' you were tryin' to screw it up for me.'

'He's worse than nothing.'

'He might be right. He must know.'

And she thought, walking beside him, that perhaps Tug was right. When your enemies were legion, an indifferent ally was probably better than none at all.

'But maybe you want me to be put away,' he said. 'Make things easier for you.'

Liz was no longer working at the coffee bar. Irwin had, in the end, been gracious about her departure, even to the extent of giving her, as a farewell gift, an engraved copper bracelet. When she'd thanked him he'd said sardonically, 'It's to ward off the rheumatism. It tends to hit you, rheumatism, as you approach forty.'

Unemployed, she spent her time organising the move to Wai Bay — arranging for railways cartage of her aging stereo, giving notice to her absentee landlord, sorting through her clothes. It seemed a bit like a game of pretend, for between Liz and Wai Bay lay the painful dilemma of Tug.

Tug himself, as if preparing himself for desertion, had begun once again to hang out with the boys. He came home each night, though sometimes very late, and there was a hardness about him, a deep anger, that even when they made love did not disperse. Liz reminded him daily to report at the police station and took him to keep an appointment with the probation officer, leaving him at the steps of the probation office; but beyond that she left him to his own devices.

She told herself that the growing gap between them would ease a final separation, but she couldn't prevent herself seeing, beneath his anger, a deep and accusing pain. She longed for a just and honourable solution but the alternatives seemed to offer only degrees of deception, betrayal or martyrdom.

When Harry Daniels had rung to ask if he might come 'for a chat' Liz had agreed only reluctantly. The prospect of a visit from Tug's probation officer wearied her; conversations with officialdom concerning Tug had been, in the past, unpleasantly predictable.

But Daniels turned out to be a surprise. They sat at the table over cups of tea.

'He depends on you.' Harry Daniels, a large, ungainly individual with shoulder-length curls and a small disorderly moustache, gave Liz a pleading, woolly look. 'Of course I've only been able to spend a short time with him. But someone to care about them's what they're all looking for.'

'Yes, I suppose it is.' She wanted to say, please don't have expectations of me, I'm opting out.

'Trouble is the people they turn to — if they manage to find someone, that is — have a way of pulling out when the going gets rough. And it can get pretty rough.'

'Yes,' she said. How much did he know?

'You know Thomas is a State Ward of course? Or was.'

She shook her head. 'I don't even know what a State Ward is.'

'It means the state has officially taken over the role of parent or guardian, because of unsatisfactory home life, or a complete lack of home life.'

'Then it's a pity the state didn't do a bit more about providing him with a home life.'

'I agree. But there's not a lot they can do in fact; there aren't the facilities. It's all political, basically, of course. I can tell you this job's opened my eyes. Anyway, what I was going to say is that having been a State Ward, and also through the probation office a few times, means that there are extensive files on Thomas so that rather compensates for the limited time I've spent with him. And in this report for the court I plan to stress the fact that he's retarded.'

Liz sat absolutely still. 'He's what?' she said at last. It was little more than a whisper.

Daniels raised his eyebrows. 'But you knew that, surely?'

She shook her head, feeling a kind of revulsion. Something hollow and dark. Horror but also pity.

'They've done tests,' the probation officer was explaining gently. 'IQ tests. And then there are his school records....'

She thought of a wall bricked into Tug's head, limiting him. She remembered the mongoloid face he sometimes pulled.

174

'No,' she said sharply. 'I don't believe it. He's not....' Her voice faded. Did the compilers of files and social scientists, in passing sentence on Tug's mind, see something that she had refused to acknowledge?

'They're scientific tests,' Daniels pointed out, almost apologetically. 'They cover areas a layman mightn't observe. But if you think they're wrong...?'

'I don't know.' She felt confused, and she didn't want Daniels to realise the extent of her distress and make deductions.

'There's no suggestion that he's severely... disabled.'

Liz thought of something. 'He can almost always beat me at chess,' she said. 'And I'm not retarded. Doesn't that prove something?'

'It might,' Daniels conceded. 'But then he can barely read, even at the most elementary level.'

Liz wanted to laugh in her relief. 'He can now. He's been reading *The Ginger Man*. Have you read *The Ginger Man*?'

Daniels shook his head. Liz leapt away to fetch the book and pushed it triumphantly into his hands. Daniels flicked through the pages and looked up with a grin.

'And how does he like it?'

'He thinks,' said Liz, forgetting discretion, 'that it's a bit short on the sexy bits.'

Daniels laughed. 'Well you've just demolished my strongest argument for leniency. Though I suppose we could always pretend you hadn't told me and I believe what the files say.'

'That means he stands up in court and has it announced that he's retarded?'

'My report goes to the magistrate. It's not intended to be read out.'

'What do you think he'll get?'

'Impossible to guess. Magistrates are notoriously inconsistent. He may get borstal since he's got quite a record.'

'But he didn't do what he's charged with.'

'So he assured me. But if I'm to believe what my clients tell me half of them don't do what they're charged with.'

'And do you believe them?'

He gestured vaguely. 'I try to keep an open mind. To get

175

back to Thomas, what happens to him rather depends on you.'

She'd feared as much. 'I'm leaving,' she said. 'The day after the court case.'

'Regardless of the outcome?'

She hesitated, then said, 'Regardless.' But her voice lacked conviction.

'That's unfortunate for Thomas. Unless you're thinking of taking him with you?'

'I wasn't. Well I haven't really decided.' His look made her defensive. 'I'm tired,' she said, trying to explain. 'I think I have to look after my own interests first.'

'Of course,' he said. 'I understand.'

No you don't, she thought self-pityingly. No one does.

Daniels sighed to himself a little ostentatiously. 'It had occurred to me that, *had* you been prepared to take Thomas, I could have included a strong recommendation that he should remain in your care. That way he might have got off with a fine and probation. As it is... well, the law takes a very dim view of assault on members of the constabulary.'

'That's not fair,' she objected. 'That's no more than blackmail.'

He raised his hands. 'Sure it's blackmail, but it's also the truth.'

She felt cornered. 'What if I told you I'd take him and then happened to change my mind?'

He considered this. 'Well, I suppose then I would have acted to the best of my knowledge and Thomas may be spared borstal which, short of providing food and shelter, never achieved anything much for anybody.'

'He might not even want to come.'

'I think you under-rate his affection for you.'

How much *did* Daniels know? 'Did he tell you that? That he wanted to come?'

Daniels smiled. 'Our talk was confidential. Maybe you should ask him?'

'All right,' she said, feeling battered. 'I'm telling you I'll take him. You haven't left me much choice.' The gap at the end of her tunnel was narrowing.

'There's one other thing. Would it be possible to delay

your departure date for another couple of weeks? It's always on the cards that the case may be remanded.'

'I can't really afford to. Well, I suppose I could try.'

'Thank you.' He shambled to his feet. 'You'll get your reward in heaven.' He took out a notebook and tore out a page with an address written on it. 'Thomas can get work there if he turns up tomorrow. Magistrates think much more kindly of those who have jobs.'

'You're sure they'll take him?'

'Yes. I play squash with the foreman.'

'We could have done with that kind of help months ago.'

'I know.' He stood, filling up her doorway, his head on one side. 'At least I think I know, but I'm always aware that I'm on the other side looking in. After work I go home to my wife and son. I switch off — shut it all out. The hypocrisy of that bothers me, so I'm looking for another job. I don't have your kind of courage.'

'I'm not brave,' she said wryly. 'I'm punch-drunk. For six months I've been in this ring with Tug, getting knocked down and trying to get up and getting knocked down again. Now I don't even have enough sense left to get out of the ring.'

'You'll be all right,' he said.

Going home to his wife and son.

The job was as a builder's labourer on a construction site in the city. Tug endured the first three days and then, almost despite himself, began to enjoy himself. Although he once or twice stayed in town with the boys until late, he began, generally to come home as soon as he had finished work and made his obligatory appearance at the police station.

There was still an evasiveness between them but Tug's anger seemed to be giving way to a gentler anxiety. 'Are you pleased that I'm working?' he would ask repeatedly.

She had quizzed him about Harry Daniels. 'How much did you tell him?'

'Nothing.'

'Nothing about us?'

'Just that you were good to me.'

Ailleen came to visit one afternoon and they sat drinking

177

coffee until she left to pick her youngest up from playcentre. Relaxed by the other woman's air of confident and hard-won wisdom Liz told her about Tug. I have a young lover; she was astonished to find how emancipated and mature this sounded. She was aware that the version she told to Ailleen was only one perspective on the truth. She could say to this apparently understanding woman 'He's very sexy', but she could not say 'I love him'. She didn't want to strain her credibility in the eyes of her new-found friend.

Ailleen acknowledged no dilemma and pointed the way briskly through Liz's confusion of conflicting loyalties.

'You want to go on your own, go on your own. There's no question of obligation. Look, you're like a computer that's had generations of shit and humble-pie fed into you. All along the line women have been conditioned to consider everybody *but* themselves. Don't let any guy manipulate. Only do what *you* want.'

Liz wondered if she had explained it so badly.

The people versus Thomas Morton on charges of assault on a police officer and resisting arrest.

It took a long time coming. All morning and then through part of the afternoon Liz and Tug sat anxiously on the public benches not breathing as each new case was called.

Just before the lunch adjournment Lua was escorted from the side door to the dock. Although his eyes swept over the spectators he gave no sign of recognition. Liz noticed a blankness about his eyes as if he had vacated them. His jeans were stained and grimy, his jacket torn at the shoulder. The vain and graceful Lua brought down. Ringless, beadless.

He was charged with burglary of a warehouse. In a soft flat voice he pleaded guilty. The magistrate remanded him for sentence and refused a solicitor's request for bail. Liz noted that with a guilty relief. If he had been granted bail would she have gone surety? And would he have dutifully turned up in court again to face certain imprisonment or would he have shot through? What was a fair price for friendship? Ailleen would have an answer for that.

Escorted back to the holding cell, Lua was bent forward, walking with an old man's shuffle. Liz looked at the magistrate, ugly as a Toby jug, florid squat face tufted with grey hair. The revenge of age and decay on youth and beauty. Was that, in the end, what it was really about?

Calling Thomas Morton.

Tug sauntered to the dock, his watched walk. Liz's stomach contracted in dismay — to the magistrate that walk would proclaim insolence.

Once he had climbed the steps into the wooden box Tug's back was to her, but from its uncompromising slouch she knew the sullen line of his mouth and the narrowed eyes. *Tug, my love, grovel a little for your future's sake.*

The lawyer grovelled for him. His client (he whimpered) pleaded guilty but wished to explain that the injuries he had inflicted on the officer in question had occurred without intent. The officer had in the course of his duty — and naturally, sir, unwittingly — exerted considerable force on the defendant. It was, sir, early in the morning and my client wasn't yet fully awake so he acted impulsively, being understandably upset at awaking to find police officers in his room.

You will note, sir, that the probation officer in a very conscientious report has outlined the difficult and unfortunate background of Mr Morton's upbringing, and you will observe his recommendation that the defendant should be allowed to continue to live with a Mrs Harvey who, according to the report, has been able to provide my client with a stable and steadying environment. Mrs Harvey is shortly moving to the North Island, sir, and is prepared to take my client with her. The report is of the opinion that if my client is removed from her care at this point, sir, it could prove detrimental to his chances of rehabilitation. You will further note, sir, that my client suffers the disability of mental retardation. Despite which he is currently working as a builder's labourer in the city.

The magistrate, having listened without expression, bent his head to study the much aforementioned report. Having done this he shuffled through some other papers, exchanged a few muttered comments with the clerk of the court on his left and returned to his reading. On the public benches people around Liz resumed sporadic and whispered conversations.

At her desk in the limelight the solitary news reporter searched through her handbag and surreptitiously fed herself a mintie. Tug looked behind him, agonisedly, at Liz.

The magistrate took up his pen and made notes. Or perhaps just doodles. He looked with weary unblinking eyes. Then he began a speech about the courage and diligence of the police and the contempt in which society held those who made their unenviable task more difficult. It was intolerable, he said, that the police should run the risk of assault from people whom they sought to assist. He noted grimly that Tug had a substantial list of juvenile convictions.

I'll stay and visit him, thought Liz. Of course I'll stay.

'However,' continued the magistrate, glaring to still a voice in the back row. 'However, I have decided to allow you one final chance to make something of yourself. You are to be fined one hundred and fifty dollars and to serve a year's probation and you are to live, as directed, with this Mrs Harvey.'

'Thanks, mate. You was really good,' Tug solemnly shook the plump lawyer's hand.

The lawyer looked across at Liz. 'Mrs Harvey doesn't think so.'

'He wasn't sent away,' Liz conceded.

'There's not much room for ideals in there, I'm afraid,' he said, almost smugly.

'I'm learning,' she told him.

Driving home she complained, 'I still think it's a lot of money for something you didn't do.'

'You're never satisfied,' said Tug. He thought for a time. 'Am I gonna *have* to live with you now?'

'Not necessarily. You can tell Mr Daniels you'd rather not. Or I can tell him I've changed my mind. Maybe you could tell him I'm corrupting you into untold depravity.'

'I jus' might.' He grabbed the steering wheel without warning and wrenched it so that they almost hit the curb, then twisted it back, laughing humourlessly at her look of panic.

'Don' wanna go up there, anyway,' he said. 'Bet it's a stink place.'

The kindergarten mothers were never like this, with their matt-finish faces and demure skirts and neat little smiles. These ladies were punchy, with a profusion of hair and determined voices. They frightened Liz as the kindergarten mothers before them had frightened her. She sat on a cushion in the corner and listened. And the longer she listened the more she felt that she was, just as in the kindy days, out of step with her peers. A year ago — two, three years ago, *then* she would have been of them. She would have laughed with them in the relief of recognition, she would have offered up anecdotes as evidence, she would have been nourished by this proof that the nameless misery wasn't *her fault*.

For they were talking about Ken. They were Johns and Nigels and Davids and Rogers and Peters but they were also Ken. They made their wives feel dull and dumb and negligible, they were secretive, they were hardly ever home, they turned over in bed and pleaded headaches, they left socks in the bathroom, they were mean about money, they were emotionally repressed, they were arrogant, they wouldn't lift a finger. All they cared about was status and promotion and their chosen sports.

'You weren't impressed?' Ailleen probed as she drove Liz home.

'I'm sure it's all worthwhile. It just didn't seem very relevant to me anymore.'

'I thought it'd give you a perspective on your own situation. No? I thought at least it'd convince you of the importance of considering yourself a valuable person. Which means doing what's best for you.' Liz made no reply. 'Or don't you know what's best for you?'

'I know what'd be best for me — at least I know what'd be easiest.'

'Well there you are! He'll have to manage without you sometime. It may as well be now?'

'He *is* a burden. It's not really his fault but that's how it is.'

'You see,' said Ailleen, 'you're facing up to things. It's not so hard really.'

Liz watched the shining street and the drizzling rain that seemed to be not falling but suspended in their car lights. How lucky to be leaving this place! And how lucky to have a nest egg in the bank (even one that was being nibbled away at a rather alarming rate).

'The thing is,' she said, more to herself than her companion, 'I think I'd probably survive either way, but I'm not sure that Tug would.'

'Of course he would.'

'Perhaps. Perhaps not.'

'Everyone likes to imagine their man couldn't survive without them. It's part of the brain-wash. No one dies of a broken heart.'

What about a broken spirit? Liz wanted to ask. But she said nothing. Ailleen, it had just occurred to her, was like Irwin, who was like her mother, who was like Ken, who was like a whole lot of people. The world was not divided into a brotherhood and a sisterhood, as Ailleen supposed; the division was between the people who were sure they knew and the ones who thought they felt.

Tug was waiting up for her, aggressive with anxiety. She never went out at night without telling him.

'Where the fuck you been?'

She was off-hand. 'To a women's liberation meeting.'

'What for?'

''Cos I felt like it.'

He looked at her with curiosity. 'What was it like then?'

'Oh. A lot of talking.' She grinned at him. 'About how oppressive men are.'

'Am I whatever it is?'

'You try to be.' She collapsed into a chair and held out her arms to him. 'No, my love, you're not an oppressor. You're one of the oppressed. You and me both.'

He sat warily, making no move to come to her. 'You been drinking?'

'Only coffee.'

He went to her. 'I don' like you going out with other people. I think they try and turn you away from me.'

'Like the boys do with you?'

'Something like that.'

'Then the sooner we get away from them all the better. Have you told them at work you're leaving?' She was watching his face, seeing in it a kind of release and then a

182

rush of pleasure. And she thought, if nothing else goes right for us — even if I'm making the wrong decision, just seeing his face opening like this must make it all worthwhile.

Still, he said, 'I'm not sure that I wanna come. I mean you haven't even asked me like you mean it.'

She knelt at his knees. 'Tug, my darling, let me take you away from all this!'

'Okay,' he said magnanimously.

As they closed the car boot and debated where it would be possible to cram in the last container — the box containing Mitzi, drugged for the journey and now reduced to weak and pitiful mewing — a big old green Mercedes came cruising up the street towards them. Heads protruded out of the windows like wayward broccoli. The car drew up on the other side of the street and they poured out of it. Tony, Bones, Billy, Max, Sherl, Louanne and Brent.

'Nearly missed yous.... We come to see you off.... So you fullas really are going....'

'Bloody car wouldn't start,' said Max, clutching three bottles of beer to his chest.

'Billy said he knew how to cross wires. Couldn't cross a fuckin' street.'

Brent wiped the rim of an open beer bottle on his shirt and passed it to Liz. 'All this time I never really believed you was Tug's missus,' he told her, gawping.

'I really am Tug's missus,' she said.

Tug beamed across at her.

Bones opened another bottle on the fender of the car.

'Max,' said Liz, 'what's happened to Lua? We saw him in court. I ought to have gone and seen him, I know, but....'

Max shook his head. 'He's still in remand cells. This time he'll go down the line for years and years. I dunno, almost seemed like that's what he wants. But I'm doin' good Liz, keeping right outa trouble.'

'Who's car is it?' asked Tug with an air of innocence.

Max turned to Liz. 'Lizzie, we wouldn't want to lie to you, so tell him not to ask.'

'It was just sitting around,' said Sherl, 'looking lonesome, ay, Max?'

183

'Right.' Max tucked an arm around Liz's shoulder and the other around Tug. Liz looked around at their faces and felt sentimental, a stab of regret at leaving them.

'We're gonna miss yous two,' said Max.

'Fuckin' arse you will,' said Tug. 'We sure as hell won't miss you lot.'

TWELVE

'WHADDA Y' RECKON they make of me?' Tug was probing beneath a rock with a sharpened stick.

'Who?'

'Them. You know.'

'I don't know. Who?' It's outright laziness, she thought. Thinking's too much effort for him. What if I refused to indulge in these silly quizzes? Would we live, after a time, in complete silence? Sign language maybe?

'Course you know. Them. Your friends.'

She could see a spiky leg with cruel pincers. Two more and they'd have enough for dinner. All the same she hoped the crab would find a safe hole to back into.

'I can't remember what you were saying about them.' She could, but he made her perverse.

'Whadda they think of me?'

'Oh, they approve of you. I mean they're bound to, no matter what they really think of you.'

'How's that then?' He sighted the leg and stabbed inwards. 'Missed the bastard. I'll get him though.'

''Cos Maoris are fashionable in these kind of circles, maybe because there aren't many of them *in* these kind of circles. It makes you something of a treasure.'

'Why are we fashionable?'

'You're s'posed to have an inborn instinct for nature and the land and all those things they're into.'

He put his weight against the rock and tried to shift it.

185

'D'you think I have?'

'Dunno,' she said. 'Maybe I get in the way of your instinct. Maybe I block it off. I mean you're not exactly the mighty crab hunter!'

The rock turned and two crabs scuttled for safety. Tug kicked at them, landing one up on the stones. He grabbed his spear and impaled it with a gutteral shriek then waved it still flailing in front of Liz's face. 'What was it you said?'

'There were two. Where's the other one?'

He went back to his prodding, leaving the crab in Liz's upturned sunhat with its dead companions. Liz sat on her rock and thought about true words spoken in jest.

Was she estranging Tug from his heritage? Heritage had recently become a word of substance. Maoritanga, which she understood to mean Maori culture, or Maoriness, was a word that was cropping up all the time in newspapers and magazines. Her friends used it respectfully as if it had magical qualities; spokesmen and women for groups of radical young Maoris in the cities used it passionately and demanded its revival. She saw justice in their demands and sometimes she could even imagine a future New Zealand with fewer rules and sharp edges, mellowed by Maoritanga.

But on a subjective level the word seemed a rebuke. Implicit within it was the conviction that, severed from his own community and culture, a Maori was but a shell of a person. Should she then, as senior partner, send Tug off to discover a true and cultural identity? Was she robbing him of his birth-right? Were the two of them condemned by racial origin to be divided by differences that reached like a chasm into history?

He'd located the other crab. Watching him blocking off its water exit with stones she was reminded of Michael dispatching his troops. The crab edged sideways, his back end exposed and Tug had him, the shell grasped between finger and thumb. A big one.

Was Liz to believe that the satisfied grunt Tug emitted as he killed the creature was a reflex of generations? Was her involuntary shudder a product of her Anglo-Saxon heritage?

'Poor little buggers,' said Tug stirring the contents of her hat.

Maoris were different. Ever since she could remember, that point had been conveyed to her explicity or implicity by the people she knew. (*Her own people*?) Only in the last few months, feeling that for all his unpredictability Tug was closer to her — more like her — than any person had ever been, had she decided that difference was a fallacy. Yet now Maoris were saying it too, in the newspapers. We're different. You're different. And how could she, being different, have the presumption to dispute what they, being different, told her was true.

Yes she *was* different to Tug. She was different to Ken. And to Ailleen. And to her mother. Everybody different in ways, alike in ways. How could you measure and conclude about difference?

Tug had grown bored with crabs and climbed out to the end of the rocks. She could see him perched there looking out to sea, his legs dangling in the water. His hair reached halfway down his back.

And yes, a difference. He belonged in this bay — he *fitted* — in a way she did not. He was the beach, the rocks and the bush. She was the houses, transported and conspicuous. Take her apart and she was full of joints and angles and little dark corners.

They were living in a small bach with corrugated iron walls and no roof lining. When it rained — which had so far only happened once — the sound was deafening. The place had become available after they had been with Martyn and Pete for little more than a week. It was almost on the water's edge and because that seemed such a bonus, and because Wai Bay was so altogether lovely, to find fault would have been churlish. True, some of the windows could only be opened by pushing the frames out of their surroundings and stacking them against the wall. And the toilet, up a track behind the house, was no more than a bottomless bucket over an almost full hole in the ground and the shed which housed it was doorless and rotting. But these were small matters, part of the adventure.

Enthroned on the bucket and its precarious wooden seat you looked out at the crumbling remains of a toolshed overgrown with jasmine and behind it two banana trees with the beginnings of fruit emerging in fat green fingers.

When Liz was a child their toilet had opened off the bathroom. It had shiny pale blue walls and the roll of paper was demure in frilly blue tulle. The seat was covered — for comfort or hygiene, she had never worked out which — with dark blue towelling gathered with elastic.

At Maling Drive the toilet had been across the hall from the bathroom. It had been papered by Liz, red and black flowers on a white background. On the back of the door was pinned a large diagram of a human body. Minus genitals, but the shape and face was male, Caucasian, and within the body's outline, muscle and fibre in red and blue waved and swerved like anticyclones on a weather chart.

Considering the toilets of her life, Liz pondered their direction. Were they leading upwards to enlightenment or downwards to the bottom of the social heap? Wai Bay suggested the former, but Wai Bay might be only a passing hallucination.

In their first few weeks, the bay had exceeded even her glowing expectations. Tug, too, had been enthralled by it from the time of his first glimpse from the top of the hill. So Liz knew in her Calvinist heart there must be a catch somewhere. The place was too good to be true.

If Tug belonged to the place itself Liz belonged to the community. She had never found friendship so easy and abundant. She had never before felt so appropriate. Looking at these people she saw herself — not the way she was but the way she could be.

They were so confident. Continually they confirmed and reaffirmed among themselves the virtues of community, creativity and simplicity. They invest their poverty — for most of them seemed to be poor — with an air of achievement. Their homes smelt of incense, camomile and baking bread, and featured unlined walls and worn wooden floors with pride. The structural beams and mantelpieces and brick-and-plant bookshelves were cluttered with incense holders, tiny china bottles with stoppers, children's creations, drift-wood, growing things and crumpled packets of tobacco. Their walls were pinned with lengths of batik fabric and

Indian cottons and sketches (many with Martyn's signature).

An eager novice, Liz pummelled at bread dough, nurtured cuttings from other people's herb gardens, tied her clothes in scientific designs and boiled them in dyes made from onion peelings. She read books by Christian Humphreys.

'The uncle I lived with once was always on about hippies,' said Tug. 'Smart-arsed layabouts he called them, reckoned they were the worst kind.'

'Are you trying to make a point?'

'Not really. There weren't many people he did like.'

Tug was fond of Pete and Martyn. The rest of their acquaintances he regarded without hostility but with a measure of suspicion. 'They're just playing at being poor. When they get sick of it they can run home to their rich daddies or go back to being teachers or whatever they were.'

'You don't know that. You're just guessing.'

'I can tell. Anyone can tell. And another thing, they all screw around, they're all into each other.'

'Well that's their business, I guess.' She *had* noticed. 'Maybe it happens no more than anywhere else but they're more open about it.'

Tug, sitting quietly in a corner when visitors called, would absorb details of gossip and extract undercurrents and innuendo real or imagined. These he would later fashion for his own entertainment.

'What do you feel about thingee?'

'Who?'

'Sarah?'

'I like her. Why?'

'You see the way she looks at you?'

'You imagine it.'

'What if she does fancy you? Just imagine these are her fingers.'

'No, Tug.'

'Please?'

'No. It's an invasion of people's privacy.'

'Pretend. Doesn't harm anyone. I'll pretend you're someone else.'

'No!'

'Then you pretend. Would you like me to be Hugh?'

'No thanks.'

'Why not?'

'I don't fancy him. I only fancy you.'

'Sarah's got lovely big tits. You could hold them in your hands. You could do that for me?'

She closed her eyes and nibbled at Tug's hard little nipples wanting to please him. 'Sarah,' she murmured up at him, holding back a giggle with difficulty. His fingers trailed across her thighs, shy like a stranger's and his hair spread over her face, long like Sarah's. In her mind she made Tug's nipples large and soft and could feel a fullness growing around them. Tug's exploring fingers took on an unfamiliar delicacy. 'Sarah,' she whispered effusively.

There was no clap of thunder, the mirror did not topple from the wall and Sarah, next time they met gave her no knowing glance of reproach. A whole new avenue of entertainment had opened up for them. Tug was so good at inventing games. Sometimes, though, Liz would look at her friends and wonder how they would feel if they knew all the uses they served.

'How high d'you reckon Porter's hill is?'

'I don't know.'

'Guess. Just guess.'

'I don't wanta guess. I don't care how high it is.'

'D'you reckon it's over a thousand feet?'

'I've no idea.'

'But what would you say it is? Over a thousand?'

'All right. Yes. I'll say that.'

'It's not.' A triumphant grin. 'If I shout, how long would it take for my voice to reach Pete's place?'

'It wouldn't.'

'Yeah, I know. But if it did? How long does it take noise to travel, say a mile?'

'*I* don't know.'

'Wouldn't you like to know?'

'No, love, I wouldn't.' How wearying facts became as you got older and information more and more irrelevant. Ideas, too? Why was he so young? *That* was the unbridgeable gap. The radio always played tormentingly loud — she did not object to the music, but ears grow fragile and the brain forms little nervous knots like barbed wire. Things he could not understand. You grow out of the desire to live large.

Just as Liz was beginning to despair over the way they were eating into her precious capital, Luke told them of a farmer needing scrub-cutters.

'Would he take me?'

Luke looked doubtful. 'Give it a try.'

The farmer had no doubts. 'You couldn't hack it, lady. I'll take the young feller, though. Seven-thirty Monday. On the dot.'

Tug drove off Monday morning like a condemned man. The early stillness of the morning promised a day of stifling heat. 'Luke'll be there,' she consoled him, 'so you'll know someone.' She half expected him to be home by mid-morning. *Stuff that for a joke! You go and do it if you think it's so okay.*

But he stuck it. By the end of the first week the blisters on his palms had turned to callouses but his body still protested. He would come home sullen with resentment at the old woman who condemned him to the unnatural agonies of slashing gorse and manuka in blistering heat on a disguised cliff-face. He would come home, eat and go to bed to sleep until she woke him next morning. That seemed in itself a rebuke.

'He'll get used to it,' said Luke calling around one night after tea, looking in at Tug's sleeping head. Luke was a man of optimism and enthusiasms. 'He told them at work he's twenty-three. How old is he?'

'Seventeen.'

'When I was seventeen,' Luke eased himself astride a kitchen chair, tipping it forward till it rested against the table, 'I was in my second-year sixth. I wanted to get a job, bum around a bit, my father wanted me to go to university. He's a magistrate. Was — he's retired now. He and my mother bickered all the time, I wanted to get away, go flatting. But he vetoed that too and I never had the guts to disobey him. He insisted I was too young to get a job, too young to leave home.

'One afternoon I bunked school and went along to court to see him in action. No, I can't have bunked school, it must've been holidays. Anyway there was a guy my age — Maori or Samoan maybe — up for breaking and entering. He'd gone into a house and eaten a loaf of bread and some cold sausages. He spoke for himself, didn't have a lawyer. He said he couldn't get a job and he was hungry.

'My father went into this great tirade about how this kid was a burden on the community and how he should be responsible for his own support and not a burden and all that tra la. Fined him a hundred dollars.

'I brought it up at dinner that night. Said it seemed a little inconsistent, considering.'

'What'd he say?'

Half of Luke's mouth smiled. 'Said it was remarks like that proved my immaturity.'

Luke and Jenny, Sarah, Hugh and John. They were the core of Liz's new friends. Luke had dropped out of university towards the end of a science degree. He was a gardener and handyman and casual labourer. His wife, Jenny, screen-printed T-shirts with stylised nursery rhyme characters. They had two young children.

Sarah made macrame plant hangers and macrame screens and crocheted bags. Hugh worked on a fishing boat and had poems published in literary magazines. They had five children but the oldest two had been fathered by John.

John was a potter. He lived and worked in a small bach behind Sarah and Hugh's large old house, having moved there several months before when he returned from travels. The arrangement impressed Liz who saw in it possible alternatives for herself and Tug. She was also impressed by the creativity of her friends and determined that she too would learn to make things as soon as she managed to sort out just where her talents lay.

But before she had decided on her special aptitude she was offered a job. The crafts men and women of Wai Bay had formed themselves into an association and arranged to lease a small shop in Titoki for the display and sale of their wares. Jenny was to man the shop two days a week, Liz for three days. It would scarcely provide her with a living, but it would help. Things were falling into place just as they all had promised her.

The Magic Mushroom (Wai Bay Crafts Inc) didn't attract an immediate onslaught of custom. Jenny's carefully understated window display and Martyn's elves and mannikins capering around the margin of the window were a three-day wonder for Titoki residents as they passed from the garage on one side of the Mushroom to the hardware store on the other side.

But Christmas was close and city people with more adventurous tastes and holiday pay-cheques would soon be swarming up the coast. Crafts Inc was unreservedly optimistic.

In the meantime Liz sat proudly among the evidence of her friends' versatility and initiative. She watched the population of Titoki pass by, made coffee for members of Crafts Inc who called in to pass the time, and wrote letters.

Dear Ailleen, I still can't really believe this place, it's so good. I'm sure you'd love it here. I can't believe how things seem to just work out with no effort. I've no regrets about bringing Tug, though of course as you said there's got to be an ending sometime, and that will be the big hurdle. Still, in the meantime everything seems hopeful and possible....

Dear Lua, Don't know if this will ever find you. Billy wrote to Tug that you were in Rolleston but may be shifted somewhere else. He didn't say how long you got? Is it very awful? I guess they read your letters first. (Hello, warden, how's things?) You maybe know Tug and I came up North, we live at a place called Wai Bay. Tug's working as a scrubcutter, doesn't like it much, you can imagine. Are you okay? Is there anything we can send you? Write and let me know, okay?

Dear Mother, I'm afraid this letter may come as a shock to you. You see your letters are still being forwarded to me by the Post Office but actually I left Maling Drive months and months ago. Ken and I aren't together any more and Michael's with Ken.

She screwed that one up and burned it slowly in the ashtray. Why go over all that now? Besides her mother owed her a letter; just before they shifted Liz had mailed off an aerogramme fiction of continuing domestic tranquillity, almost expecting the Post Office to indignantly return it, so blatant was the deception.

Dear Michael, Please reply, love. This is the third letter, and I do love to hear from you. Since I missed seeing you in Wellington I've been worried that something's happened. I'm putting in a note for your Dad. Just send me a couple of lines so I know you're okay, then I'll write a big long letter.

Dear Ken, What's happening down there? Your mother seemed evasive, and I haven't heard from Michael. I think I'm entitled to know. Of course I may be worrying about nothing, but I'd appreciate some communication.

On the long drive up (the magnificently long drive up — for Liz and Tug, enclosed in that motorised bubble between past and future, away from responsibilities, comparisons and obligations, had been childishly, wildly happy) they had called at Ken's address. It had taken them an hour of wrong turnings and street-map consultations to find the place and then, at six on a Thursday evening, there was no one home. She had peered into the nearest window and recognised the bedroom suite. So he hadn't sold it!

Tug had been keen to head north at once but at her insistence they'd booked into a shabby-looking motel a few blocks down the street. Motels were to become a source of entertainment. 'Mr and Mrs Morton' they would say and watch the motelier's face. Then in the privacy of their unit they would giggle together. Being travellers made them inviolable.

That evening they drove back to Ken's house and found it still empty. And the following morning, the same. Reluctantly Liz rang her in-laws from a phone box. She had called them Mum and Dad, what to call them now?

Mrs Harvey answered. He would be off to work already, driving sedately in the big car with its official monogram.

She pressed the A button. 'It's Liz.'

'Oh.' Not a word but a small popping sound. The elegant

194

manicured nails would have been tossed dramatically against the long silver hair. At eight o'clock the hair would be already brushed and folded beneath a tortoiseshell comb.

'I'm in Wellington. Passing through. I wanted to see Michael but the house is empty.'

'Yes Elizabeth. Well you see....' She was flustered. The hands would now have fluttered down to comfort the vast compressed bosom. 'Ken's... well he's just out of town for a few days. Nothing important.' It wasn't in her nature to be deceptive, the discomfort showed.

'Is Michael with you then?'

'No, dear, he's not.'

'Is he all right?'

'Yes, yes. He's fine. But he's staying with some friend and I don't know how to contact them. Ken didn't say. How long will you be here?'

'I can't really wait.'

'Then I'll tell them to get in touch with you. I know Ken was intending to. And Michael is well.' She was herself again now. Her voice had the sweet, bright lilt of one who cultivates small talk as an art form. 'Would you like to come round for coffee?'

'I would, but I really must get on the road.' She wanted to say sorry, I liked you, we shouldn't be like this, but wasn't able to. When she had hung up she consoled herself that Amy Harvey would be adept at understanding what wasn't said for she had to do it every day.

Working in the shop consolidated Liz's position as a member of Wai Bay's alternative society. She tried hard to be worthy of their acceptance and to embrace their attitudes and ideals.

On Tuesday nights she went with Jenny to yoga classes run by a sleek woman whose embroidered peasant blouses hung in The Magic Mushroom awaiting wealthy peasants. Liz's body was willing, even eager, to contort but her spirit remained non-committal. She suffered from a recurring urge to laugh. Later she would describe and demonstrate the evening's activities for Tug's entertainment, enlarging its potential for ridicule and obscenity, but ashamed of herself for so lightly obscuring this road to possible enlightenment.

She also attended, with John and Jenny, a course of Buddhist instruction held at the home of Titoki's progressive vet. For six Thursday nights she sat on the vet's Indian carpet listening to tape-recordings of an Oriental Zen Master and thinking about Tug. Considering the seven hairs on his chest, the line she loved at the top of each leg, his perfect pink fingernails. What would he be doing at this moment? In bed, wanking? Thinking about what?

But maybe he wasn't in bed. He had adjusted to work, no longer came home exhausted and he was increasingly resentful of the nights she went out. Maybe he had taken a late swim and maybe that moon creature — that delicate blonde waft of a solo mother who had just moved into the brown cottage up the hill — had chosen that night to take a stroll, and maybe they had met and....

Or maybe the bold Margaret, the one who stared at Tug so openly when they met her at the shop, the seaman's woman with a reputation for bizarre tastes — maybe she would call round to return the garden fork she had borrowed when the seaman was last home?

In the face of such possibilities it was difficult to concentrate on the paths to wisdom.

'It's just the same as it used to be, only this time they're *your* mates.'

'It's not at all the same. Really it's not.' She ran her hands down his chest, wanting to placate him. 'I mean you can't compare Jenny and Luke to the boys, can you? Besides you said yourself *you're* easily led.'

'All the same they come between us.'

'We need other people. We can't cut ourselves off from everybody.'

'We should get married.'

'We can't.'

'Why can't we?'

'Because legally I'm still married.'

'You wouldn't marry me anyway? Would you?'

'I don't know.'

The thought of such permanency chilled her. He would not make such a suggestion if he were older. He hadn't lived long enough to appreciate impossibility. If she were the man and he the woman it could all have been different. Then she could have used her advantage — her sense of knowing how the game was played — to sustain them both. But Tug was the male and a married woman was but an extension of her husband. *If I was a carpenter, and you were a lady / Would you marry me anyway / Would you have my baby?* Even in the song the lady did not answer.

'They're not that special. I don't see what you find so great about them?'

'About who?'

'Your hippy friends.'

'They're like me, really. I suppose that's it.'

'I bet you talk to them about me.'

'Sometimes. Sometimes I do.'

'And they tell you what to do?'

'What to do about what?'

'About me?'

'No.'

'What'd they say then? About us?'

'Nothing really. Nothing that I remember. It's not important.'

It's the Lolita syndrome really. (Annie, the bee-keeper.) *You're trying to live out a fantasy, Liz. Well I know I get terrific yens for young guys, specially since I passed thirty. Last year when I was relief teacher at the high school I had erotic dreams about one of the sixth-formers, for God's sake!* (Sarah). *Young guys are so boring. They want to screw all the time. I mean it's just a boring scene.* (Angela, the doll-maker). *You're the one with the sexy young man, aren't you.* (Mitti, solo mother). *He's dependent on you. What'll happen when you split up? But I guess you've thought about that one?* (Jenny). *What's an intelligent woman like you doing with a guy like that?* (Lou, the Titoki vet.) *I like Tug but I do wonder... sort of, what d'you find to talk about.* (John). *I fancy your young man, let me know when you've finished with him.* (Marti, potter).

'The women say you're sexy. Some of them.'

'I know *that*. The way they look at me.'

'Who?'

'I'm not telling you,' he teased.

The anxiety had been growing for weeks. Wai Bay women were emancipated. Ownership rights had been abolished. A screw was a screw was a screw and they didn't wait to be asked. Fear and jealousy were doing terrible things to Liz's insides.

'They're only after one thing,' she said sharply. 'It's not for yourself they want you.'

'I know.' He closed his eyes and jerked his pelvis eagerly. 'They just wanta use me.'

There were times when she hated him.

'... So I wondered,' Liz finished uncomfortably, 'if maybe he could stay here for a while till he got something organised?'

Martyn was painting wide, cruel lips on a fat woman. The woman was seated on a crooked kitchen chair, knees spread apart. Her vast yellow balloons of legs showed beneath the floral dress that spread like an awning over her knees. He worked carefully at the awful brown mouth and took a long time to reply.

'Why are you so sure you need to be apart?'

'I need to be on my own. I want to sort of sort myself out. It's hard to explain.' He went on working. 'There are too many difficulties....'

He looked at her, eyebrows slightly raised.

'All we've really had going for us was sex.' It came out bitter.

Still he painted. 'Of course. That was obvious. But if it was *good* sex, and we speculated that it was....'

Her mouth opened in disbelief. 'Who speculated?' she asked weakly.

He shrugged. 'Everyone. Of course we're all curious. We look at you two and our minds flash SEX in big red, yellow and blue lights. Like the POW in Superman. We can't help it.'

Was he joking? She couldn't see his face.

'I never felt that of *you*,' she told him.

'But of others?' He put down his brush and turned towards her. She nodded. 'After a while,' he said gently, 'you really don't notice. After a while you stop feeling it's something you have to make jokes about or draw attention to so that

198

they know that you know. Then you can get on with just being people. But at the beginning you can't seem to get beyond the SEX sign in the eyes of all those nice normal people. And you get so you're not sure if it is there or if you just imagine it, and either way you get convinced that that's how it is — that's *all* it is.'

'I never thought of that — you being in the same boat.'

He stood up. 'I don't want Tug to come here because I like him, he's a friend. I don't want to watch him being hurt and I don't want to be in the middle of that kind of situation. Besides I think you're acting hastily and because of outside influences. If you really need to get out of it Liz, you will, and you won't need my help.'

She sat before him looking at her feet in their blue jandals, feeling rebuked. 'I get frightened,' she said helplessly.

'So do I,' Martyn said. He took up his brush. 'You're still coming for Christmas?'

Tug wore the red satin trousers with elastic round the ankles, her present to him.

'A fuschia,' said Pete.

Tug gave a shy smile.

'What's a fuschia?' he asked Liz a few minutes later.

She led him around the side of the house and pointed to the large bush dripping crimson bells.

'Let's go back,' he said, 'so I can show myself off to the bees.'

She wanted to have him all to herself. She wanted to pounce on him and drag him into the bushes and fight off predatory poachers with snarl and claw. But Tug was enjoying himself at this Christmas gathering.

She hadn't expected a crowd but people kept arriving up the path, locals and strangers carrying bottles and bowls. Children and dogs everywhere. Tug went off to play cricket with a pack of children and a few energetic males. Liz wandered into the kitchen and was handed a bowl and an eggbeater and two half-pints of cream.

'I've been admiring your young man,' said Mitti, scrubbing at potatoes.

Liz's beater whirled furiously. She thought of her shop

customers; the way they touched and stroked, turned over, murmured, deliberated and replaced. The power of the purchaser.

'He's not for sale,' she shouted above the clatter of the eggbeater. Mitti gave her a strange little smile.

Liz whipped the cream until it was able to stand up for itself, then went looking for Tug. Sarah's son Damien was batting. Tug was sitting on the grass with the moon woman whose name was Della. She was leaning towards him, saying something and he was looking at her in a sidelong, embarrassed way. He saw Liz watching. She looked past him, through him, pretending she was looking for someone, ashamed at being seen. She went up the track that led into the bushes walking purposefully nowhere.

The track led to the top of the hill, coming out on the road between Wai Bay and Titoki. She walked only part of the way, remembering from an eternity ago a school dance and a dark-eyed boy called Alex who only danced with her once, then always with other girls and how she blamed her dress for being wrong and ugly and her shoes and her legs. She calculated — twenty years ago, at least. And she was no further ahead. She remembered that then too she had felt the hurt right through to the end of her fingers.

He followed her. Padding up the track on his broad bare feet, peering ahead. Then coming right up to her.

'Liz? What are you doing?'

'Nothing.'

'You're sulking.' She shook her head. He put his hands on her shoulders. 'Yes you are. You're jealous. Just because I's talking to someone. You're really jealous.'

'It's a sickness,' said Ken. 'You've got to get on top of it. It's a sickness of the mind.'

'I'm sorry,' she said. 'It's stupid, I know. Horrible.'

Tug wrapped her in his arms and squeezed the breath out of her. 'You're jealous! My darling you're jealous.'

'Only a bit,' she said pushing back for breath. 'I try not to be.'

'Why?'

'It's such a horrible thing.'

Tug looked at her with fatherly tenderness. 'It's natural.

200

Everyone's jealous. It's part of loving. If you're not jealous means you don't love them. I want you to always be jealous for me.'

'I think I'm quite good at it,' she said, and suddenly felt like laughing.

It was Jenny who took her to the house. It was not in Wai Bay proper but perched above a smaller bay to the north. Bush surrounded it. At the back of the property there were apple, fig and feijoa trees. The building sagged with neglect and the door was open. Inside was a kitchen and four small bare rooms. A balcony, tilting ominously, led off one of the rooms. Beneath the house was a bleak concrete bathroom.

It looked neglected and Liz yearned to take care of it. She saw it with a fire sparkling in the grate, the walls stripped of their shabby paper, the floor comforted with rugs. She could imagine living there happily ever after.

Liz didn't tell Tug she had seen the house. Maybe she wanted to surprise him. Several times that night she had been going to tell him but then she didn't.

John knew someone who flatted with the owner of the house in Auckland. The owner had bought it for next-to-nothing five years before but only used it occasionally as a holiday bach. He had talked about selling. Jenny arranged for John to go with Liz to see the owner.

They went on a Tuesday after Luke had picked Tug up for work. They saw the owner and then John's solicitor. John was no older than Liz and yet he seemed to know his way around in such matters. She felt frail and childish in her ignorance.

It was nearly seven before they got home. There had been no obstacles, the house was hers, virtually. Only formalities, the transfer of the money. She was a tycoon, drunk on achievement; a bottle of good wine and three red fillet steaks in her shopping basket.

Tug's work boots (an old pair donated by Pete) were at the door but the house was empty. She fried the steaks while John made salad — his capability made her wistful. How nice it was not to be the responsible one. They ate without Tug, Liz chattering to cover her increasing anxiety. She always told

201

him where she was going. Always except this time. She'd expected to be home before him.

John left straight after the meal, being household baby-sitter for the night and already a little late. He declined a ride home and waved aside her thanks for the day's successes. She watched him walking along the darkening beach in his worn brown leather jacket and felt her uneasiness grow. Behind the constant pounding of surf the house had an unnerving silence. She stacked the dishes, put a record on the stereo — *Dark Side of the Moon,* her Christmas present from Tug — and tried to return to her earlier delight about the house-that-was-almost-hers.

'Where were you?' It was eleven o'clock and he was mean drunk, leaning against the door post.

'I went to buy a house.' But he wasn't listening. The question had been in his head for so many hours the answer was irrelevent. She was sitting on the floor holding a pencil and sheets of writing paper were scattered around her. She'd been making sketches of how her house would look someday, where the furniture would stand and plants be hung, where she could build a workshop if she became a potter. Tug walk-ed unsteadily across the floor and stood among the paper. He reached to gather up some of the sheets and ripped them into pieces.

She stifled nervous laughter at the impotence of the gesture; the sketches were nothing to her. Then he grabbed her by the wrist and yanked her up and towards him and she tripped against him and fell half onto the folded mattress that served them as a chair. She saw his arm drawn back and she protected her head, an instinct, tucking it down and shielding it with her arms.

He had slapped her before, but never this. His fists were hard and heavy as a sledge-hammer and they came and came pounding at her shoulders, her back, her upper arms. Her thoughts seemed very clear. *He could kill me. He is capable of killing me. I must remember this moment of clearly know-ing that — must not let it melt away in forgiveness. If I live.* And if I don't live, she thought absurdly, imagine the satisfaction the manner of my dying would give Irwin!

When the blows stopped she lay very still waiting for him

to move away. He grasped a handful of her hair and wrenched her head up and back until he could see her face then he
shoved the head down again contemptuously and walked to
the window. She waited for what seemed a long time, afraid
of the pain of moving, afraid of worse to come, and when she
did move she was surprised to find that her body still obeyed
her head in the usual way. She got up quietly and without
looking at Tug made for the door. He got there before her.
He no longer looked drunk, Liz thought with an extra lurch
of fear, just crazy.

She reached towards the door knob but he chopped her
hand away with the side of his. Trapped, she thought of a
weapon. She went into the tiny kitchen, becoming more
aware of her body's hurting, and he followed her. She made
vague gestures of clearing the bench, but there was little to
clear. She was looking for something heavy and solid — a
rolling pin preferably but she'd never owned one. The heavy
frying pan. She lifted it tentatively, testing its weight, and
glanced at Tug. He knew. He reached above him and his
fingers closed on the handle of the serrated bread-knife. She
put the frying pan down. He raised his hand from the knife
handle. She went out of the kitchen and he glided past her to
take up guard at the door. She was crying now, wishing that
John would come back or Martyn would call — someone to
save her and say silly girl, never mind, it's all over now. Her
left shoulder shot pain when she moved it and her teeth chattered. She went into their bedroom and crawled beneath the
top blanket.

After a time he came and sat on the bed. She cowed away
from him.

'I'm sorry.' His voice was hoarse.

She felt the melting; relief that it was over, the urge to
comfort. She said nothing. He fumbled for her hand beneath
the covers. 'Forgive me?'

'*Why*? Why Tug?'

'You've been with John.'

'Yes. We went to Auckland to see this guy he knows who's
gonna sell us this house. But how did you know?'

'Mark saw yous. He slept in, saw you on the way to work.'

'That's still not a reason.'

'What sort of reason do I need?'

'There can't be a reason for... that.'

'I didn't mean to hurt you. I's jealous. You can't blame me for that, it's only natural.'

'You could have killed me.' She said each word very clearly, wanting to get it through to him.

'But I didn't.'

For a second she thought he expected to be praised for his restraint. 'You killed something else,' she told him allowing herself a little melodrama and feeling genuinely bereft of some small nurtured thing.

'You pregnant?'

She shook her head and was reminded of her bruises and the aching shoulder. He leaned towards her and his face looked young and gentle and tender.

'Did you know we've been together seven months and five days?'

THIRTEEN

'WHY,' HE ASKED. 'Why now?'
'Because,' she said, keeping a distance between them,
'things have changed. You've made me afraid of you, Tug.
How can you live with someone you're afraid of? That's
crazy.'

She could see him struggling to get together a reply, to find
the right words to convey a feeling he'd never bothered to
distil.

'Nobody's not afraid of someone if they love them,' he
said finally. 'They're always gonna hurt you sometimes, one
way or another.'

'That's different,' she said easily, not sure that it was. For
a whole week she had been nurturing a sense of outrage over
the tender purple bruises across her back and upper arms,
beating down a recurring inclination to shrug them away as
an episode past and of no great consequence. She would
unveil her shoulders in private, like Exhibit A, and examine
them, craning over her shoulder at the mirror. And she would
summon up feelings of shame and incredulity.

All week she had been, with Tug, polite and punishingly
remote. In his absence she had checked and found that,
although the house was not yet strictly hers, there was no
objection to her moving in there, and now she had informed
Tug of her plan — she would move, alone, to the house and
he could stay in their rented bach. 'We'll still be friends,'
she'd said, 'but I really need to be on my own for a bit.'

She'd steeled herself for a scene; entreaties and threats, yet he seemed remarkably calm.

'So when are you going?'

'I thought I could move in the weekend. I'll leave you the stereo if you like.'

'I s'pose you expect me to help you shift?'

'Only if you felt like it.'

He shrugged. 'I'll see.' He pulled on a jersey and went towards the door. On the doorstep he turned and said, 'You know, you shoulda stayed with your husband. He'd never'a tried to kill you, just had to wait for you to do it yourself.'

He slammed the door behind him.

The telegram was delivered to their letterbox the next day, along with a corso envelope. PLEASE RING 875219 WELLINGTON THURSDAY 8PM STOP KEN.

Tug had not come home after work, which was both a relief and a worry for he could be somewhere drinking, fuelling his resentment. At seven-thirty Liz walked along the beach and round the rocks to use Sarah's phone.

The line was bad. Ken's voice crackled distantly from another planet, saying sorry that he hadn't contacted her before this. He'd been giving things a lot of thought and perhaps the custody situation was unfair on her. A mother had special needs, he understood that now.

Liz might have laughed if there hadn't been so much at stake. She wondered how she could have ever considered Ken to be formidably convincing.

'What are you saying?' she shouted through the static.

'I'm saying, do you want custody?'

'For the holidays, do you mean?'

'No. Custody. I'd have access of course. Maybe holidays sometimes.'

What was behind it? 'What if you change your mind?'

'Look, I've this idea of travelling a bit so I might not even be around for the next few years. I'll get him on a plane and let you know when to meet him. Okay? This line's terrible.'

'Okay,' she shouted back.

She replaced the receiver feeling stunned; leaning against the wall until her jubilation became tempered with little worries. Would Michael like Wai Bay after being all his life a city child? Could she support the two of them on her three-day income? (Not a chance. It barely met her own needs, and now her nest egg was all taken for her little house.) How could she earn more? And how would Michael feel about life on the poverty margin?

But at least, providentially, she would not have to face the added complication that Tug's presence would have provided.

When he withdrew himself from her he turned away and she longed to reach out and say, 'I didn't mean it. Stay with me. I was only pretending.' But she thought of Michael and how much better it might be for him if there were only the two of them, then she too turned to face the empty dark.

Tug not only helped her shift, he enlisted Pete and Martyn to assist. They were relentlessly efficient, overruling her suggestions about where things should be placed and making her feel dull and superfluous. On Michael's behalf she had bought an old TV set from the Titoki auction room, and as a final effort they banged and clattered above her head arguing cheerfully about the manner and position of the aerial's installation.

She suspected the sense of exclusion she felt was being deliberately inflicted. A who-needs-you game organised by Tug. When the TV reception was established to their satisfaction they declined her offer to lunch and went off together to play pool at the Titoki pub. She was not invited and she was surprised at how much that hurt.

The back of her mind expected to see Tug later that day, or at least the next day. Consequently she spent a lot of time looking out the kitchen window with its view of the track which led down to her house. And on the Sunday morning she was almost certain that she saw someone dark lurking in the manuka beside the track, so she made a pot of tea, smiling to herself about his games. But no one came to the door so eventually she drank the tea alone.

On the Tuesday there was a letter from Ken telling her that Michael would arrive on the following Monday.

On the Wednesday she saw Tug outside the Wai Bay store,

207

but though she drove by very slowly he didn't see her, or pretended not to see her.

On the Thursday Angela, who made dolls, called into The Magic Mushroom with a banana-legged doll almost as tall as Liz and said, 'So I hear you're on your own now? How does it feel.'

'Good,' said Liz. 'I've been very busy.'

She had been making, in all her spare moments, bright cotton crocheted booties. Already several pairs hung in the Mushroom's window awaiting babies with progressive parents. She had calculated that if she could make and sell twenty pairs a week she and Michael would have sufficient means of support. But in the whole of Titoki there were probably only about sixteen babies.

Angela moved a coffee set out of the window area and placed her doll in the most prominent and central position. 'I saw your ex-young man earlier,' she said, 'with that astrologer woman.'

'Oh?' said Liz, stage-managing her voice. 'Who's she?'

'Myra someone. She hasn't been here long.'

'Jenny?'

'Mmm?' Jenny, tongue protruding and upturned, was tracing a night-gowned figure onto cardboard.

'D'you know someone called Myra?'

'That new one? She lives in old Mrs Bagnold's place down by the creek? Luke's met her.'

'What's she like?'

'He seemed to think she was okay. She does horoscopes I gather, if you want yours done. She's been to playcentre once or twice. That's where Luke met her.'

'She's got kids then?'

Jenny grinned up at her. 'Unless she's a play-dough freak. Why?'

'Oh, just that someone mentioned her. Who's that?'

'Wee Willie Winkie. It's supposed to be obvious.'

'Sorry.' Pause. 'Hey, you know that action group Hugh keeps telling me I should join? Do you know when they meet?'

'Thursday night. That's tomorrow. You thinking of

going?'

'I just thought I might.'

'It sounds pretty boring, Liz.'

She yawned, then looked guiltily around the group to see if anyone had noticed. But, apart from the bald and argumentative orchardist from Porter's Hill who now sat with his eyes closed, they were all watching Murray the wood-turner. Murray was talking in his slow and ponderous way about storm drainage and erosion. Liz wished she had brought her crochet.

Hugh, as if he'd sensed her glance, looked up and proffered tobacco and papers. She reached for them apologetically; she'd left her own at home and this was her fourth bludge since the meeting began. Still, perhaps Hugh owed it to her. If it hadn't been for him she'd never have come. 'You're like me,' he'd told her. 'We're basically political animals. All this crap about sunflower seeds and Eastern religions, well it might be all right for some but what does it achieve? Now I'll admit that the Wai Bay Action Group is soft politics, but you've got to start somewhere. You should come along some time, you might have some new ideas for us, a different perspective.' He'd meant, because of Tug.

And she'd thought she had. In her pocket was a letter that had arrived that morning, from Max. *Tony's been put away again Long stretch this time armed robbrey it was Two grand well they wont do him much good now ay Remember young Tana well hes into hard gear Steff too Well thats the way it goes No news on Lua dont now were they took him.*

Poke a finger into the soft centres of our cities, she wanted to say, and how many Tonys were there? How many Luas and young Tanas and Billys and Stephs and Tugs?

But the Action Group had an agenda. Tonight they had already covered the playcentre's need for a permanent building, the County Building Inspector's harassment of certain members of Wai Bay's alternative community and the Council's acceptance of a Road Board's grant towards the sealing of a no-exit road to a councillor's property.

As for me well Im won of them cool street cats again Did a

few days in the coola for fines I didnt now about so had not
payed so lost my job but still have the same house seven of us
hear now.

But why should the Wai Bay Action Group care? What
had it to do with them? What had it to do with Liz? It was
another island, a time past.

Still the letter lay in her pocket like an accusation. Was it
being apart from Tug that made her suddenly burdened with
abstract concern? Or was the letter just a tawdry excuse? Was
she really here because there might be, among these play-
school activists some available, presentable male Myra? Just
to show him.

She took Max's letter round on Friday night, because of
course Tug would want to read it.

There was no one home.

She propped the letter on the bench. He would see it and
know she had called.

He seemed to be managing quite well without her.

The reason why she was sleeping so badly could be lack of
exercise and fresh air. On the Saturday morning, after a
wakeful night, Liz decided to go looking for mushrooms on
the farmland above the bush fringes of the bay.

She set off with an orange plastic bucket, wishing she had a
dog to walk with. Thinking, a dog would be nice for Michael,
a small dog with a small appetite.

She walked through three paddocks and found three
toadstools, four puffballs, and a fungus fashioned like a
plastic shopping bag. Not one solitary mushroom. How
embarrassing, she thought, to be so ignorant of nature and
seasonal things in a community that was so eagerly in tune
with such phenomena.

Perhaps there would be blackberries? She remembered
having seen clumps of blackberry bushes down in the valley,
and she headed down the hill. It wasn't a promising day for
walking. Heavy clouds hung above the sea like the sky in a
child's drawing. She crossed the road, climbed down a steep
slope and there indeed were the blackberries. Young green
berries and, well out of reach, some lush black ones. Others
had been there before her.

She skirted around behind the bushes, aware now, unavoidably aware, that the house up on her right, the little house that was patchily visible behind two Norfolk pines, was old Mrs Bagnold's place. Aware of that coincidence, and walking innocently in its direction with her orange bucket and her eyes on the blackberries she had no hope of reaching.

There was music coming from the house, familiar music that Liz struggled to identify. Jefferson Airplane? Tug liked Jefferson Airplane. Lots of people liked Jefferson Airplane and anyway perhaps it wasn't.

From the bare earth between the Norfolk pines she could see into two windows. In one there was a blue teddy bear with his nose towards the pane and beyond him a bright alphabet poster pinned to the wall. Through the other window she could see a solid Scotch dresser spread with a delicate lacy blue shawl and the corner of a bed with a rumpled Indian bedspread. Liz stood staring and staring at that lived-in looking corner of bedding. And she wished that the heart might be like an abscess: a moment of acute enforced agony and then it would heal as if it had never been.

It began to rain. A few fat, sulky drops clattered into her bucket and then it began in earnest. Liz began to run, stumbling across the sandhills towards the beach, though the rain wasn't cold, and it had brought her a certain sense of release.

The beach was deserted. She removed her jandals and ran in the shallow water.

The door to Tug's bach was ajar. She would go in and borrow some dry clothes, why not?

She didn't bother to knock. He wouldn't mind. She still had a few rights. She took the towel from behind the kitchen door and, still rubbing her hair, let herself into the bedroom.

Tug was in bed, alone, awake, looking at her.

'Hi,' she said. Transformed, restored. 'I thought you were out.'

'Well I'm not, I'm asleep.' He pulled the bedclothes over his head.

'You don't mind if I borrow some dry clothes?' She considered the grimy pile of them that lay at the foot of his bed. 'Haven't you done any washing?' She yearned to take them home and wash and iron and mend.

He peered out. 'I dunno how to.'

'You spit on them and rub.'

'There's a clean shirt in the cupboard but there's only them dirty jeans.'

'They'll do I guess.' She found the shirt alone in the cupboard. It was an old one of hers, with bust darts, but he wore it anyway.

'How come you're so wet?'

'I got caught in the rain.' She had forgotten, already, the problems of being heard above rain on an unlined roof.

She took the dry clothes through to the other room.

'Where you going?'

'Nowhere just yet. Shall I make a pot of tea?'

'You going out there to change? Whassa matter? You forget I've seen wrinkled old flesh before?'

She grinned to herself, thinking it was the first time she'd been insulted in a whole week.

Did he insult Myra, or was it all sweetness and devotion?

She rolled her wet clothes into a ball and filled a saucepan from the tap. 'You got milk, Tug?'

'In the safe.'

She found the bottle, half full, and sniffed it doubtfully, but it smelt all right.

When he sat up in bed to take the cup the blankets wafted a warm body smell so familiar it hurt. Globules of buttery cream floated on top of the tea.

'I don't know about that milk. It smells okay.'

'It's only yesterday's.'

She thought, he's matured when I wasn't looking; Myra no doubt considers him an adult.

'Are you still working?'

'Nah. I chucked it.'

'Why?'

'Was gonna finish in a week anyway.'

'So what'll you do?'

'Don't worry about me. I got something worked out.'

'So I hear.'

He grinned. 'Can't keep a secret round here.'

'So you're quite happy?'

'I'm doing okay. When's Michael coming?'

This Monday. Who told you that?'

'So you'll have someone else to look after.'

Liz walked to the window, cradling her cup. She needed the space. 'And does this Myra look after you okay?'

'Whassat supposed to mean?'

She thought of Ken, but said it all the same. 'Is she a good screw?'

'Not bad.'

She went to the foot of his bed, demolished beyond further pretence. 'Tug....'

He tossed back the bedclothes and swung his legs to the floor. Even in winter he slept naked, yet never felt cold to the touch. He stood for a minute, firm and smooth like a bronze statue. 'I gotta go out,' he said. 'Better wait till the rain stops or you'll get soaked.'

She watched him zip himself away.

'So will you.'

He gave her a quick sidelong glance. 'S'okay. I haven't got far to go.'

As he let himself out the door he said very casually, 'I might come round tonight, if that's okay. There's a Bruce Lee movie on TV.'

'Sure,' she said. 'If I'm out I'll leave the door open.'

He didn't come. Having cancelled her arrangement to go to a film in Titoki with Jenny and Luke, Liz stayed home and watched a Bruce Lee movie. She thought it very bad indeed.

She watched Michael walk down off the plane in his tailored grey trousers and contrasting sports jacket and was glad Tug wasn't there to comment.

'Gosh, but you've grown,' she told him predictably. 'Is this all your luggage?'

'There's a suitcase. And grandma's sending the rest of my stuff up later, by train.'

'What stuff's that?'

'My bike. And my skateboard. And my train set.'

'You still got those old soldiers?'

'Them too.'

In the car, on the way home, she explained anxiously,

'There won't be a lot of places you can ride a bike, love. The roads are mostly metal and rough. But I suppose on the beach.'

'What about where the supermarket is?'

'Well I'm afraid there isn't one. Only a store.'

'Least you've got a car now,' he said.

And he really tried to be polite about the house. 'Maybe some day we could get carpets. And put paper on those walls?'

'Yes, someday. When I get rich.'

'At least you've got TV.'

'I got it for you. But I'm afraid we can only get one channel here.'

He switched it on and she saw his face droop with disappointment when the black and white images appeared.

'Tomorrow,' she said, 'I'll show you the beach.'

He knocked on their door, and she was afraid for she could tell he'd been drinking.

'I came to see you,' he said.

'That's nice,' she said cautiously, stepping aside. 'Michael, do you remember Tug?'

The two of them sat side by side, watching the cartoons.

'I like the Roadrunner better.'

'Me too,' said Michael.

Liz stood at the kitchen bench slicing beans. 'Have you eaten, Tug? Will you stay for tea?'

'Yes please. If that's all right.' Polite as a vicar.

At the tea table they discussed the relative merits of The Marvel, Batman and Superman. Liz hadn't seen Michael as animated as this in the three days he'd been with her.

'There's a coupla Mickey Mouses and a Spiderman down at my place. If you wanta come and get them some time. If you like we could go fishing some time when your mother's at work.'

Michael nodded with enthusiasm.

'I been having my horoscope done and it says I'm gonna be lucky this week.' He looked at Liz but she gave no response. 'Maybe it's wrong, perhaps I should go and have it done again.' She saw his smirk but looked stonily past it.

214

'Michael,' said Tug, leaning towards the boy in a clumsily confidential way, 'd'you understand about love?'

'I think so,' he said uncertainly.

'Your mother doesn't. She hasn't got a clue. She thinks you buy it in Woolworths and you take it back if it doesn't quite fit.'

When did he grow so old, she thought.

'Oh boy,' she said, 'you're sly.' Shaking her head at him, unable to hold back the grin that had begun inside her.

'Did she really do your horoscope?' She reached for his hand, interlocking their fingers brown white brown white like flecked wool. Her head was tucked beneath his armpit and she breathed in the gloriously rank smell of his sweat.

'She read my hand.'

'And what did your hand say?'

'It said I had a lotta... potential. Potential?'

'That'd be it. Did she tell you this before or after you went to bed with her?'

'Before.'

'That figures.'

'It wasn't my idea. Guess she was lonely.'

'And what did she tell you afterwards?'

'She said it'd been exciting.'

Liz giggled. 'Like the Big Dipper? Roll up, roll up, get your new thrill here, ladies. A genuine native youth.'

He tweaked her hair. 'You can't talk. You know, maybe I shouldn'ta come tonight. I shoulda held on till you really grovelled. You would've. You nearly did that day you was wet. But I thought this time you could really sweat. I was gonna really show you.'

'You know you have a terrible conceit?'

'Lotta women like it.'

She rolled away from him then held out her arms. 'Come here,' she ordered, grinning. 'Excite me.'

FOURTEEN

'IF YOU LET me take the car....'
'Drive fifty miles there and back each day?'
'Well, what else?'
'You don't even have a licence. I mean if someone was hurt.... It's a helluva risk.'
'I can't help that.'
'If I helped you....'
'You gonna go in there and answer all the questions for me?'
'I think you could do it.'
'Maybe on my sixth try!'
'Oh God,' she said. 'Why is it always the fucking same for us? Why can't something just for once be easy.'
'It's not my fault.'
'I *know* it's not your fault. Anyway the car's just about stuffed. That knocking's worse. Did you tell them you had transport?'
'No. I knew you'd say no.'
'There must be some jobs out this way?'
'They said there was none. Only in the city.'
'And there's no chance of the dole?'
'Not so long as there's jobs in the city. That's what they said.'
'You told them there's no regular buses out this way?'
'Yeah.'
'And what'd they say?'

'Said I should get board in Auckland.'

'Well maybe....' She saw his expression. 'But if it was just four nights a week?'

'You know I couldn't. You know what I'm like. You gotta know that by now.'

'I know, love, but....'

'I told you you shoulda come with me.'

'I couldn't. I was working.'

'Maybe we should shift to the city?'

'No,' she said. 'This is my house and I'm not going to leave it. Anyway do you really think we'd survive in the city?'

'No. But can we survive out here?'

I could, she thought with dull familiarity.

They were all leaving the bay. Jenny and Luke, Hugh, Sarah and John. It felt to Liz like desertion.

'But you knew we were planning it,' Jenny reminded her. 'We've been talking about it for ages.'

This was true, but Liz had supposed that such talk was, like so much of their talking, just dreams and diversion. She couldn't comprehend why anyone would wish to leave Wai Bay and she couldn't envisage their shared life together on some remote acreage in that mythical region they referred to as 'up north'.

'We'll be able to grow things,' Jenny explained rather vaguely.

'You grow things here.'

'Not properly. It's what we intended to do all along. Wai Bay was just sort of compromise and now that the right place's come up....'

Reason didn't soothe Liz's sense of personal rejection.

'What about the shop... with you and John and Sarah all going...?'

'I know. We think it'll have to close up. But that won't be for a month or so and something else'll come up for you. The shop's never been a great success anyway.'

'I can't imagine the bay with all of you gone.'

'We'll soon be replaced.'

'Not for me you won't.'

Jenny gave her a small hug. 'You could come too. Why not? Really. There's the big house plus the barn, oodles of room. Everyone'd be happy for you to come. Two more won't make much difference.'

'There's three of us.'

'Three then.'

Liz shook her head, imagining herself and Tug throwing jealous scenes in communal corridors. 'It wouldn't work.'

Wai Bay's only public phone featured a specialised line in graffitti. *A weed a day keeps the asthma away,* Liz read. *Work is the curse of the smoking man. Group gropes at Greta's are grouse.*

'Hello,' said the fruity voice of the probation officer. 'Are you still there? Sorry about that, Mrs....'

'Harvey.'

'Excuse me Wai Bay caller,' cut in the operator, 'but your three minutes is up. Do you wish to continue.'

'Yes, please.' She hadn't even started yet.

'Then you'll need another fifteen cents.'

Liz jingled through the small change in her pocket. 'Yes. I've got it. I'm putting it in now.' The coins clattered in her ear. 'Hello. Are you still there?'

'Yes. What I was going to say before all that was that you can't pick up jobs the way you used to. Jobs are getting scarcer all the time. It's happening everywhere.' He said it with satisfaction.

'That's why I hoped you might be able to help.'

'I doubt it.' He sounded pleased about that too. 'There is one possibility, though. They're starting up these relief schemes for the unemployed. I think there's actually one planned for up your way. Ask the Labour Department, they'll know.'

'But he's tried there.'

'Well they tend not to tell you about these things unless you ask.'

'You couldn't put in a word for him?'

'Wouldn't make any difference really.'

'They think he should move to Auckland, you see.'

'That wouldn't do him any harm either.'

Liz wanted to shout, how the hell would *you* know? The man at the end of the phone had met Tug for approximately ten minutes when they had dutifully called at his office on the way up. To date his care and supervision had been limited to the few rather disparaging remarks he had made to Tug on that occasion. Liz sadly remembered Harry Daniels.

'How's he been behaving himself anyway?'

'Just fine,' she said crisply, hoping it might spoil his day.

Although Liz had never been inside this building before the place had an unmistakeable familiarity. As soon as they step inside the door and look around at the silent waiting faces she feels cornered and defensive. They sit on benches and wait.

'Hope I get a woman,' Tug says in a low voice. 'They never seem to hate me as much.'

'A relief job will be fine.' Liz is hopeful despite the surroundings. She took history and social studies for U.E. and knows her country has a proud record of social reform and opportunity for all. 'I wonder what you'll be doing. At least it'll be outdoors.'

They get a woman.

'You talk to her,' says Tug and edges behind Liz when they reach the counter.

'We're enquiring about relief work,' Liz says. 'We understand that they're going to be starting relief work in our area and Thomas would like to be included.'

Tug nods his endorsement and Liz has a brief silly thought that the two of them are a ventriloquist act.

'Yes,' the woman says. 'They are starting up relief gangs. What's your area?' She's tall and looks down at them through spectacles that cling to her nose.

'Wai Bay. Well, Titoki area.'

'There will be one around there, but you realise only people who receive unemployment benefit will be eligible for relief work?' She looks at Tug. 'If you're receiving a benefit...?'

He shakes his head.

'He was told,' says Liz, 'that he can't get a benefit because there's jobs in the city and he should move here.'

'That's correct.'

'But,' Liz stands very straight in an attempt to look her in the eyes, woman to woman, 'Thomas has been placed under

219

my care by a court order and is required to live with me, and
I'm not in a position to move from my home in Wai Bay.'

'Well I'm afraid that those are the regulations.'

'But he needs the job.' Liz hears the note of desperation in
her voice and knows she's losing. Still she feels obliged to let
this woman know that not everyone who can speak nicely has
cushy jobs in government departments. 'I have only a part-
time job and there's Thomas, myself and my son. I can't support us all on my income.'

'Then I suggest this young man should move to where the
work is.'

'Then he'd need rent in advance and probably a bond and
we don't have that kind of money. He's spent all his savings.
All we're asking for is a job.'

'And I'm telling you we can't help you.'

'We could sell the car.'

'How'd you get to work?'

'When the shop closed we could sell it.'

'Get fuck all for it. And then if we get work how're we
gonna get to it?'

'Yeah. There's that.'

'Sell the TV.'

'Michael would hate me.'

'All the same....'

'I only paid thirty dollars for it. What about the stereo?'

'No. Anyway it's old. Everyone's into fancy hi-fi stuff
now. You'd get more for the TV.'

'There's my books, but they wouldn't be.... If we had
fancy clothes we could sell them.'

'If we had a Mercedes we could sell it.'

'And if we had a castle....'

'And after we've sold everything, what then?'

She got fifteen dollars for her camera and ten for her transistor radio. They offered two dollars for her rings, twelve for
the TV and four for her Chinese ivory pelican. She took them
home again.

'Mike's got that bike,' said Tug. 'And his skateboard.'

On the days she didn't work she applied for jobs, even

some right in the city, without success.

'If something turns up,' she told Sarah, 'I'll take it right away. I can't afford to wait till the shop closes.'

'If you're really scratching why don't you ask John for a loan?'

'I couldn't do that.'

'He wouldn't mind. He's loaded. You knew that's how we got our land? He got all this money from his father's estate. He's still got more than he needs. Ask him, why don't you?'

'Maybe.'

The next day when John came into the shop with the bowls from his latest firing he tossed a slip of paper onto the desk that served as a counter. 'That enough?'

She turned it over. Pay to Elizabeth Harvey the sum of two hundred dollars. 'I can't take that, really. It's very kind of you John, but....'

'But?'

'Well, I don't want to get into debt.'

'Then you'll have to pay me back some time.'

'And I'm scared of strings.'

'There aren't any. Truly. I promise you.'

'Okay.' She picked up the cheque. 'I don't know what to say except that we need it desperately and I'll pay you back as soon as I can.'

'There's no hurry at all.'

Liz ran the fine, hot sand through her fingers watching the changing silhouette of that which remained on her palm. Tug lay on his belly beside her with his chin cupped in his hands and a leg between hers.

'Mike's a country boy now,' he said, nodding towards the rocks where Michael was fishing along with Sarah's son Damien.

'I thought you'd be awfully jealous of Michael,' she said. 'I was sure you'd give him a hard time.'

'Sometimes I am jealous of him, but I'm not really a monster. Don' you know by now that half the problems we have are there 'cos you get them in your head and decide they're gonna be problems?'

'And the other half?'

'They're 'cos of the shits that run the world.'

'If we just stayed on the beach the worries might just go away. It's hard, down here, to believe in jobs and money and all that.'

'We could just live off the sea, and outa the garden you know.'

'Maybe *we* could, but it wouldn't be fair to Michael.'

'There were times when *I* ate outa rubbish tins.'

The Magic Mushroom was dismantled and packed into boxes. The fairy folk around the window now framed a view of bare boards and a disconnected telephone. There was a closing-down and farewell party that night at Luke and Jenny's.

Liz found the party depressing. Next week, she kept thinking, there will be strangers in this house. No Jenny. No Luke. Other people, other parties. Her best friends leaving, and how many people do you meet in this world that you really like? Of course there was still Martyn and Pete, but they were more Tug's friends now. Despite that middle ground of sexual preference they were in the end men, and mates of men.

She was sitting with Jenny in the kitchen when Annie the bee-keeper came in with wood-turner Murray. 'Picking winkles,' Annie was saying. 'He's a winkle-picker, just like those shoes, remember? They're those little wiggly shells and they pick them off the rocks and kill them to save the oysters. Starting next week, with our Billy. Relief work, they call it. He does the work and I get the relief.'

'Why Billy?' asked Liz. 'They wouldn't put Tug on?'

'I can't think why, dear. In Billy's case they suggested it. Thank God, I was going nuts with him home all day.'

'They told Tug he should move to Auckland.'

'That's a bit strange. Perhaps it's because he's not your family. They're getting very tough about these things. You could say he was your son? Say you had an affair with a magnificent coal-black man from Nigeria and out popped Tug.'

'Annie, you're coarse,' said Jenny.

'She's lovely,' said Liz. 'You say the job starts next week?'

222

It was a kind of a game, she'd learned that much. They gave you the forms and you filled them in hopefully and conscientiously. Then you handed the forms back and they smirked and said 'Fooled you.'

Tug, ballpoint poised for action, says 'What if we get the same old bat I got last time?'

'We just hope we don't.

'But what if they tell my pro and he decides you're corrupting me?'

'Just fill in the form, my love. We don't have a lot of alternatives.'

Repetition and familiarity don't make the forms easier for Tug, nevertheless he insists on filling them in himself. Liz stands beside him trying to be helpful without being obtrusive, aware of his mounting frustration over his ineptness at setting down words.

'Has moved got two 'o's?'

'Just one.'

'Why shall I say I left that scrub-cutting job?'

'Why did you?'

'You know why. You left me. So whadda I say here?'

'I don't know. Domestic problems. No. Did you have transport? Was Luke still picking you up?'

'He finished up before me. Then I walked to the main road and Mark'd give me a lift.'

'But Mark left when you did.'

'Yeah.'

'Then put *no transport*.'

'How'd you spell transport?'

Tug takes the completed form up to the counter. Liz is reminded of school and the handing in of exam papers. Except in those days she was confident of passing. The man at the counter takes the form away and then returns.

'Mr White will see you in a few minutes for an interview.'

Mr White is younger than Liz, which she hopes is an advantage. He wears walk-shorts, and socks to below his knees which are firm and tanned. He has a trim brown moustache and hair in a boyish Kennedy cut, and he courteously waits for Liz and Tug to sit down before he

223

resumes his seat.

'Just a few queries....' He gestures at the form which lies before him and they all look at the sad evidence of Tug's misshapen printing. 'You only mention your last two jobs. What came before that?'

Tug looks out the window at a girl typing in the next building.

'Valleyview,' Liz prompts him.

'I was in hospital,' Tug says, still looking at the girl through the window.

'You don't mention any illness here.'

'They cured me,' Tug says very seriously and Liz suppresses a nervous grin.

'You say here you're married?'

'I am.' Tug sounds astonishingly sure on this point. 'I'm de facto married.'

Mr White looks across at Liz. 'And are you his guardian... or...?'

'I'm his de facto wife.' Afterwards Liz is able to recall this moment with considerable pleasure. The young man's head jerks up and his eyes widen; he looks rather like a jack-in-the-box released. Then he struggles to compose his face into a mask of professional indifference.

'You have a child?'

'By my previous marriage.'

'Um. The periods when Mr Morton was without employment — am I right in supposing you were supporting him?'

'Sometimes, when he had no savings left. But while he was working he was contributing to my support. And my job has now folded so we have no income at all.'

White rests his chin on a cupped hand and dandles his ball-point pen. 'Your child? Would you say he looks upon Mr Morton here as a father figure?'

'Well he's only been back with me about five weeks — my son I mean. I suppose he sees him as — well, a brother or something.'

He leans forward. 'And do you think that's a suitable relationship to include a child into?'

'I don't think it's unsuitable.' But she has not expected this and her voice lacks conviction. They both know it. She would like to suggest that it's none of his business but as long as there's still a chance she must not risk offending him.

White swings back in his chair, tilting it, stretching. 'So,' he says, 'since you have lost your job you would like the taxpayers to shoulder the expense of your gigolo?'

'I beg your pardon?' Liz's voice is faint and incredulous.

The young man realises he has gone too far. 'Perhaps I put that a bit crudely....'

'You put it okay,' says Tug, suddenly with them. 'For someone who needs his face smashed in.' He begins to stand up, but Liz mouths a frantic NO and he sinks back into his chair. White is visibly shaken. He keeps the corner of his eye on Tug.

'We're not asking for the dole,' Liz says. 'He just wants a relief job. There is no other work where we are.'

Recovered now, White waves his upper hand. 'With his work record I doubt if we could find him a job anywhere. However,' he gets to his feet, looking magnanimous, 'I'll give you a form to take to the Social Welfare office and you can try your luck. I'll ring them and say you're coming.'

In the Social Welfare office they are required to complete another form detailing Liz's financial assets, hopes and failures and swearing their conjugal status. They hand the form to the tidy little Indian behind the counter. He studies it carefully with no apparent surprise. Liz wonders if he has a wife at home who was designated his from the age of seven and finds all Western marriages bizarre.

'What happens now?' she asks him.

The Indian looks uncertain and goes off to consult with a woman. The woman looks over at Liz and Tug, then approaches the counter. She has large saggy forearms that bulge around the sleeves of her cotton dress.

'It will be sent to head office,' she tells them. 'They will decide whether you qualify as a married couple.' Her tone implies they will certainly decide otherwise.

'What do you mean, qualify?'

'They'll decide whether you are or you aren't.'

'How will they decide?' Liz genuinely wants to know.

'That's nothing to do with me,' the woman says.

'So when will we know if we're a married couple or not?'

The sarcasm is wasted. 'Three weeks, I'd say. At least three weeks.'

'Three weeks!'

'At the very least. It has to go all the way to Wellington.'

Tug drove deliberately past the red light and took the corner too fast and too late. Liz braced herself against the dashboard but still fell against him. The driver of the yellow utility heading towards them veered towards the gutter and the two vehicles passed with half an inch between them. The driver of the ute swore out his window as Tug accelerated up the suburban street.

Liz had known this would happen when he'd wrenched the keys from her and hurled himself into the driver's seat. And knowing, she should have stayed on the pavement outside the Social Welfare offices. Let him die alone.

'Please,' she begged, 'please Tug.'

'No more stealing,' he said in a silly high voice. 'Watch out you silly old bitch.' An old woman with a large shopping bag and a look of terror stepped back onto the footpath just in time to be missed. Tug waved his left hand above his head crazily. 'Oh no Tug my way's better.' The silly voice again. 'Just be nice and ask the good people to help us. You'll see.' He drove with two wheels over the white line. Oncoming drivers braked and veered and cursed. Liz thought of Michael: a policeman at the headmaster's office door breaking the news. Was Ken still in the country? Did the senior Harveys know his address?

'I was wrong,' she wailed against her knees. 'Please, Tug! PLEASE!' Where were the traffic cops when you needed them? The Vauxhall had an expired warrant, two bald tyres, no horn and a broken rear-vision mirror. In other circumstances she saw traffic cops' cars everywhere she looked.

She felt him brake. The car slowed to a sane speed then came to a halt. She raised her head cautiously. They were parked outside a dairy in some unknown suburban shopping centre. She felt relief — more than relief, a kind of miraculous good fortune. In the big things like death and pregnancy someone was on her side despite the formidable odds.

They sat in silence for what seemed a long time. She gave

226

him a couple of glances but he was looking stonily out through the windscreen. She tried to think of something reassuring to say.

'At least we've still got fifteen dollars of John's money left. And I'm bound to find a job soon.'

'Even if I got the relief job I wouldn't get paid till the end of a fortnight. That'd be five weeks away, at least.' His voice sounded normal, the anger had passed.

'But if *I* found something...'

He drummed on the steering wheel with his fingers. 'I's better off the way I used to be. On the streets. On my own.'

She retaliated. ' I was better off too.' She hated the way it always came to this. She wanted to take Tug's hand and establish some unity but sensed her gesture would be rejected. He was looking towards the dairy, watching a man coming out of the store and pushing a wad of green notes into his pocket.

'Go in there and have a look around,' he said.

She looked at him sharply. 'What for?'

'Just have a look. See how many people're in there. See where the till is.'

'Like hell I will.'

'We need money.'

She thought about it. Tug running up the street, people shouting, chasing him, her round the corner with the get-away motor running. She realised with shock that the scene in her mind seemed credible and even exciting. 'Go and look for yourself then.' And if he did?

But Tug didn't move. He looked away from the dairy and then sighed. 'So what're we gonna do then?'

She shrugged. 'We oughta keep the money we've got for petrol so we can look for jobs.' Her vision of the crime was fading only slowly. She remembered Tug telling her once at Valleyview with a cynicism she'd taken to be a pose that it was very easy to be honest when you had money in your pocket.

'What about food?'

'Max told me once that the Salvation Army give you food vouchers. It's worth a try.'

Tug pulled a face. 'I'm not gonna ask. That's for alkies

227

and dead-beats.'

'I'll ask,' she said.

A woman walking along the footpath looked into the car with passing interest. She carried plastic-lined library books under one arm and held a shopping basket in the other. Her face seemed vaguely familiar. Liz wondered if they had once met, and then realised that the woman resembled her. Similar age, similar build, similar features. She could have been Liz — as she once was or as she might have been.

'I'll ask,' Liz repeated. The prospect gave her no qualms. This was just an aberration. She was actually out there, disappearing up the street with her library books. When she got home she'd pour herself a gin and tonic and get into those books. There were a couple of quality novels and a sociological thesis, for she was an intelligent woman and interested in knowing how the other half lived.

FIFTEEN

'IF YOU WERE younger,' they said. 'If you'd come a bit earlier.' 'If you had references.' 'If you had experience.'

'We don't want someone with education,' he said. 'They never stick at work like this.'

'I would,' she said. 'Truly I would.'

He shook his head. 'Perhaps if you were younger.'

Or if she had longer legs, or bigger boobs or a prettier nose. She hadn't known she was old. Employers had a special gauge. She was old and inexperienced, Tug was young and inexperienced, and between them there was a whole population that was just right.

Tug borrowed sixty dollars from Pete 'until the relief job came through'. It kept them in gas and essential foods.

And towards the end of the third week Liz landed a job as a dinner waitress in a North Shore hotel. Part time, five o'clock to eight six days a week. It couldn't have been less satisfactory. With driving time she would scarcely see Michael except on Sundays and part of Saturday. She found it hard to accept that an available parent was a luxury her child would have to forego.

'Once I'm working you'll be able to look around for a better job,' said Tug. He was pleased with his new status as a married man, more or less.

When the three weeks was up she rang the Welfare office. Head office, she was told, had not yet replied — she could give it another week.

229

At work the waitress who did breakfast and lunch was to go into hospital for a long-awaited varicose veins operation. Liz was offered her job until her return. She couldn't afford to refuse.

After another week she again rang Welfare. 'We would prefer it if Mr Morton rang us,' said the voice on the phone.

I'll bet you would, thought Liz grimly. 'I *am* his wife.'

'That may be, but the application's in his name. Anyway we still have no information for you. As soon as we have we'll inform Mr Morton by post so there's no point in continuing to ring.'

For the first few days of Liz's extended work-hours Tug played housewife with some enthusiasm. He swept, laundered, cooked and cleaned. But the novelty slowly wore thin and the time came when Liz, arriving home exhausted would find the beds unmade, the floors littered and the dinner dishes left uncleared on the table while the occupants of the house sat watching TV.

'I'll sell it,' she threatened. 'I'm gonna sell that bloody thing.'

'Then we'll go up the hill and watch theirs,' said Tug.

Michael giggled his support.

They were like a couple of dead albatrosses round her neck.

Tug used to talk about television with contempt, but now he watched it avidly. He preferred documentaries, especially those that dealt with racial oppression, past and present, and pin-pointed the common enemy.

Liz, unarmed and unprepared, would arrive home at night with her blatantly pale face. Tug would be at first conversational.

'You heard of Martin Luther King?'

'Of course.'

'You reckon he was one of the greatest men that ever lived?'

'One of them, I suppose.'

'Greater than Shakespeare?'

'I dunno. You can't compare them.'

'If he'd been white you'd say he was greater than Shakespeare.'

230

'I doubt it. They did different things. There's no way you can compare them.'

'They shot him.'

'Yes, I know. Hadn't you heard of him — at school or something?'

'Nah. School they only told us about the white heroes. Your lot.'

'I thought that'd changed.'

'They probably say it has. Usual white bullshit. You reckon you're civilised? Hah. In the end you're gonna have to answer for it. You know that?'

'*I* am? Me?'

'You're one of them, aren't you?'

'I'm not to blame for what my ancestors did.'

But she's not sure about that. Somewhere inside her there's this residue of shame. When the taxi-driver looked at Tug and drove off, when the employer lied that he had no vacancy it was guilt she felt, more than anger.

'I don't even talk like a Maori anymore. D'you realise that?'

'Is that my fault?'

'I'm just a brown Pakeha.'

'Maybe I'm just a white Maori.'

'Don't talk stupid. *You* couldn't be a Maori.'

'Oh Jesus, give over will you? We don't really belong anywhere, either of us. We're just US.'

But she thought, he's lucky to have an identifiable enemy that he can think of in terms of *them* against *us*. For her it seemed to be *us* against *us* which was so much more confusing.

In her wheezing asthmatic Vauxhall, grey smoke billowing ominously from the exhaust, Liz would leave Wai Bay at daybreak and return after dark. Her day was devoted to expense account executives, tourists and the occasional small hushed family group. The executives would sometimes have a try at chatting her up, pleading loneliness and implying personal favour. She found them singularly unattractive; indeed comparing their brief-cased and blow-waved maturity to Tug's smooth, rude and no doubt shallow youth she felt

231

inclined to laugh at the absurdity of their propositions. The hotel guests lived in a different world from hers; one world was real, one was an aberration. She could never decide which was the real world.

Wai Bay was no longer a place of joy and comfort, but the end point of a long and arduous drive. The motorway remained, despite growing familiarity, a daily and nightly ordeal.

Denny belonged to a new breed of tramps and Wai Bay was one of their favourite spots for winter hibernation. With that season approaching Denny arrived and set himself up in an old abandoned shack in the bush above Liz's house. The shack had no power or cooking facilities or running water but Denny called it home. He did so, usually, in absentia, for having made Tug's acquaintance the day after he arrived in the Bay, Denny spent almost all his waking hours in the comparative comfort of Liz's house.

Denny was in his mid twenties, a veteran of the Asiatic drug trails and the psychedelic sixties. LSD, methadrine, peyote, amanita muscaria, datura and alcohol in various combinations had effectively anaesthetised or eroded some fifty percent of his wits. Those that remained were sharp and extravagantly original.

Liz found him, at first, entertaining. She thought him a poet if not a prince. He seemed like an antidote to executives, and after a long day in the service industry her judgement was not at its most acute.

With familiarity Denny's entertainment value wore increasingly thin. At his best his stories were repetitive, his charm manipulative. And he was rarely at his best. On his bad days his talk was incoherent or incomprehensible, he fell against the furniture, he spilt coffee down the front of his greasy jersey and his small black eyes glistened with crazy intensity. Nights when she came home and found Denny in this state Liz could believe in demonic possession.

'He can't keep coming here, Tug. I don't want him around Mike.'

After years of being Michael Wai Bay had made him a Mike.

'But we're going into business, Denny and me.'

'What business?' Appalled by the possibilities.

'We're gonna make posters and sell them. He's got all these contacts.'

'I bet he has.'

'It's better than sitting round doing nothing.'

'Look love, Denny couldn't even organise himself into a clean shirt.'

'He used to be in business. He was a company director.'

'I'll bet.'

'I believe him.'

'Maybe he was. Any little con man can start a business and appoint himself company director. It doesn't mean anything.'

'You just don't want me to make something of myself.'

'He's evil, Tug. That's what I think.' She half expected Tug to laugh, forgetting how thoroughly he believed in such elemental states.

'A lot of me is too,' he said. 'You oughta know that by now.'

'That's too easy,' she said after some thought. 'I don't really believe in evil. It's just an excuse for people who don't want to change the way they are.'

'I'da thought you'd feel sorry for Denny.'

'I s'pose I do.'

'You don't.'

That was true, and she wondered why. 'Well,' she protested, 'he chose to be the way he is. He went to a posh school. His father owns a chain of hardware stores — unless he makes all that up and I don't think so. So he's had lots of chances.'

'He can't want to be the way he is now. Can't even take care of himself. *I* feel sorry for him.'

'Well I just can't. Sometimes when his eyes go funny it makes the hair prickle on the back of my neck.'

'That's because you're old,' said Tug, not unkindly. 'Old people are really weird about druggies. They can't understand so they get really uptight.'

Dear Mr Morton, This is to inform you that after due con-

sideration it has been decided that Elizabeth Jane Harvey cannot be deemed to qualify as your de facto wife. Your application has therefore been declined. You are advised that should you consider this decision to have been reached without due regard for all relevant facts you have the right to lodge an appeal. Appeal forms can be obtained from your nearest Social Welfare office.

Tug looked up at her. 'Does it mean what I think it means?'

She nodded, feeling numb with responsibility. Would it have been a different decision if Tug was a white boy? Racial origin, the form had asked.

'So? No job. What'll we do now?'

'I guess we could appeal,' she said without hope. 'And I'm earning enough to keep us and even pay a little back to Pete.'

'I don't wanta be kept,' he shouted at her. 'And anyway what happens when that other woman gets out of hospital? What then?'

'All right, we'll appeal then. It's worth a try.'

He rolled his eyes to the ceiling. 'Jesus,' he said. 'You never learn do you?' He looked away from her. 'There's another letter. From Max.'

The envelope was open, addressed to them both. An airmail letter with Australian stamps. *Dear Liz and Tug, havent herd from me in a long time ay hope you are well and happy. As youl see from this letter Ive shot thru to big oz things was geting a bit hot for me — bit of busnes went wrong you now how it goes Mostly Im writing to tell yous about Lua in case you dont know and I rekon youd want to Just before I left NZ he hung hiself in a cell A sheet or sumthing poor Lua poor bastad but thats the way it goes ay*

'Did you read it?' she asked Tug.

'Yeah.'

'Lua....'

'Reckon he's better off out of it,' said Tug. He was watching the television screen. It was *The Sweeney*.

It's the same everywhere, she thought.

Between lunch and dinner servings Liz drove to the Social Welfare office and when her turn in the queue came she ask-

234

ed for an appeal form. The woman took a long time to find one. When she was finally handed the form Liz asked, 'How long does it take for an appeal to be considered?'

The woman shrugged. 'Can't say. It would depend.'

'Just approximately how long?' Liz persisted.

'Four months. Maybe six. Maybe more.'

Liz began to laugh. 'It's a joke, isn't it?' she said to the woman. Her laugh kept coming though she gave it no encouragement. She held the form up and ripped it lengthwise then dropped the pieces onto the floor. The people in the room were all watching her and the ones behind her in the queue moved back to give her space. She felt dizzy with attention, a solo act with nothing to lose. She pointed to the woman behind the counter. 'She's only doing her job,' she told her audience. 'You can't blame her.'

It was a joke, but none of them laughed. Liz's light head began to settle, she thought for some reason of Denny, wondering if this was the way it was for him inhabiting some loose and incautious region of the mind with everyone an audience.

They continued to watch as she walked across the room and out the door. She took the stairs in preference to the lift. Her steps felt light and she wondered if she was cracking up. There were people who could sense out your weak spots and worm away at them. With her it was the mind — her Achilles head. First Ken and now the Social Welfare people. Was that why Denny with his loose screws frightened her so? Did she see in him her own reflection?

They were playing Steppenwolf. She could hear it as soon as she switched off the engine, before she had even found her torch and started down the track. They were playing it that loud. *He said he wanted heaven but praying was too slow.* It was Denny's record. He owned three, but no record-player. He took his records visiting, and sometimes a flagon of cheap wine. *In some unholy bathroom in some unGodly hole.* An old record, Ken had it on cassette. She had liked it then, she remembered, had listened with respect and a sense of vicarious degradation. Now she thought it menacing. It made her feel repelled and rigidly middle-aged.

Tug, Denny and Mark, Tug's ex-workmate, were spread out on the floor around an almost empty flagon of sherry and a pack of cards. The room was littered with clothes, spilt cigarette butts, unwashed cups and spoons and crumbs. Liz stood just inside the door looking at the debris. The others looked at her and saw that she was repelled and rigidly middle-aged. Crew-cut Mark got hastily and unsteadily to his feet and turned the stereo volume to a whisper. He threw Liz a tentative smile.

'The lady of the house.' Denny attempted a flourishing gesture which failed badly and left him lying on his side looking up at Liz with a foolish warped smile.

Tug didn't move. His eyes glanced at Liz then away.

'She's mad at us.' Denny shielded his face with an arm and peered out from beneath it. His legs were curled up and his feet were bare, dirty and pink with cold. 'Oh moon mad lady,' he crooned in a lilting voice, 'get down from your silver high horse. All will be forgiven in the sweet spring when they detonate Fifth Avenue.'

She turned away and opened the door to Mike's room. He was asleep with the light on, a miracle of sleep despite the earschplittenloudenboomer through the thin wall. She pulled the bedclothes around his shoulders. Asleep he frowned in worry or disapproval. And justifiably, she thought, switching off the light.

The tableau of dissolution in her living room hadn't moved. She went without comment through to the kitchen and plugged in the electric jug. The dinner dishes had been washed and set in the rack to dry. That at least. Tug came into the kitchen and stood behind her. She sensed it was him without looking. She stiffened involuntarily.

'Whassa matter with you?' His voice was thick and furry.

'Nothing,' she said carefully, watching the jug.

'You thought I was gonna hit you.' She said nothing. 'Jus' 'cos I'm drunk you're scared I'm gonna hit you, right?'

Attempting to change the subject she grabbed at another incautiously. 'I went to the Welfare office today to ask about an appeal.'

'You fuckin' what? Haven't we had enough of their shit? How can you go crawling back to them?'

She measured coffee into a cup. 'It was no use anyway. They said it'd take months.'

'How many months?'

'Four. Six. More.'

Tug turned away from her and leant his forehead against the wall. She thought, he did want me to try — he had hopes of an appeal no matter what he says. Just as she reached out towards him Tug drew back a bunched fist and smashed it into the wall. The lining board caved and crumbled. Tug punched again leaving the hole bigger and blood-smeared, the four-by-twos revealed like exposed bone.

His knuckles were dripping blood onto the floor.

'You better go and put something on that.'

'S'all right.' He wiped the blood off on his jeans. Activity had sobered him slightly. 'I suppose you want them to piss off.'

She nodded. She had forgotten they were there.

'Mark's got no way of getting home. Less I drive him.'

She shook her head. 'You're much too drunk. He can walk. Sober him up before his parents see him.' It was about five miles.

'Guess he could stay here?'

'No.'

'He's not up to walking all that way.'

'Then he can crash in a ditch.' She had a kinder thought. 'He can sleep at Denny's.'

'I better go with them. I'm soberest.' He glanced at the gaping wall, then at Liz. 'Where's the torch?'

She pointed to it.

He bent forward and kissed her lightly. 'Won't be long.'

She patted her pocket to make sure the car keys were still there. Then she switched off the jug, which was boiling. Strange, she thought, how much could happen in the time it took to boil a jug.

She heard them leaving, guiding each other out the door with bleary politeness. Like three old men leaving a senior citizen's meeting.

When she was sure they had gone she put her hand into the hole, wondering at the astonishing frailness of something like a wall, that sounded so substantial.

237

How long can you keep going round and round in the same hopeless circle, she thought as she yanked the suitcase from under their bed. You could only keep trying for so long before you gave up. *It wasn't his fault*. No, but if two people were drowning wasn't it right that the one who could swim tried to make it.

She was crying and dragging clothes from their shared drawers. Hers. Hers. Hers. But of course, most of them were, even now.

Mike, still more asleep than awake, made no protest. She wrapped him in blankets and hustled him up the path to the car. Already she'd packed two suitcases into the boot, with enough of their clothes. (Enough for what?) Her selection had been dictated only by a blind sense of urgency. Tug was likely to return soon — they had taken the remains of the sherry but that wouldn't occupy them long. There was also the matter of Liz's resolve which, given its track record, could be expected to melt with regrettable haste.

She dithered over Mike's gleaming bicycle. If they left it he may never see it again. But they could not take it. And she had lesser qualms over some of her own abandoned possessions. Would losing them matter. (Yes, it would.) But in the long view? Re-assess your priorities.

Tug, from Denny's hut, would be able to hear the car. There was no music up there to drown out the night sounds. She thought painfully of his return to the empty house, and at the last minute found a ballpoint and wrote, on the back of the letter from Social Welfare. *Darling*. She changed to print which he found easier to read. *I've given up. It's not you, just everything else. I want something better for Mike. I think we'll be better off apart*. (I think *I* will, she corrected herself, but let the sentence stand. *Look after yourself*. (How?) *I'm sorry, Love. Liz*. She propped the letter on the turntable, turned off the lights and closed the door behind her.

When she reached the main highway she turned north. Mike slept, frowning, in the back seat. Liz thought, suddenly, of Mitzi. Should she have brought her? Would Tug look after her? Would Tug stay around even? But Mitzi had adapted happily to rural living and would survive on her bush trophies. Liz rejected the thought of going back for the cat.

Her priorities were so wobbly; that she could think of abandoning Tug but taking the cat!

She was driving in unknown country. The empty dark on either side of the road was broken only occasionally by the lights of farmhouses. She had only a general idea of where she was heading. She remembered Jenny bent over a map pinpointing the spot. 'Our property runs from here to here,' pencilling in a tiny square. To Liz it had seemed like the other end of the earth.

She knew the name of their nearest township and the postal delivery zone — R.D. 3. She would ask someone how to get there — in the country everybody knew everybody else. The petrol gauge said quarter full. She would drive till it was almost empty then park and wait for daylight. Perhaps by then she would feel like sleeping.

This, she thought, is the furthest north I have ever been in my whole life. Up there — up, up, over and up — her mother would be tidying her home. (Or did she have a 'treasure' to come in and do that for her? Had she ever mentioned her 'daily'?) She might be drinking tea from a silver teapot and eating cucumber sandwiches. How had the bitter, cold woman Liz remembered turned into that sleek and mindlessly frivolous social climber? Was that what happiness did to you? Or did Liz misinterpret those repetitive letters?

If she sold the house she could take Mike to Britain to visit her mother and the estimable Roy. Not an altogether enticing thought, but people needed mothers didn't they? Warm, wise and available mothers. Was she still trying to find such a creature — Tug as substitute mum? Hard to imagine. Tug as fellow-traveller, then, in the great mother quest? Tug seeing in Liz the mother he scarcely remembered?

But she didn't want to think of Tug — better to dwell on the future. It wasn't yet too late to provide Mike with a warm wise and available mother. It was just a matter of getting started.

SIXTEEN

*N*O WORRY ABOUT *your house. Pete and I went over and everything seemed in order as far as we could tell. We brought most of the obviously movable stuff back here and stored it — but the books we're reading and the records we're playing. So you see all is under control. There was no sign of habitation. Tug and the Denny creature are apparently in Auckland. Someone saw them in K Road — at least their physical selves were in K Road but who's guessing where their heads were. Seem to remember browbeating you with my own views. Sorry, Liz. Whatever you have to do has to be the right thing. If that makes sense? Almost forgot the bad news — local Council conducting a stomp-on-hippies campaign and doing a big house inspection. Your house and ours on their repair-or-demolish list due to quaint and original drains, outhouses, plumbing or what have you. But understand that long as it's not being lived in they can't enforce anything. So what the hell! Love, Martyn.*

'So what'll you do?' asked Sarah. 'About the house?'

'Nothing I can do.' It seemed for the time irrelevant. Liz was thinking of Tug on K Road, stumbling.

It was almost four weeks since she'd left Wai Bay — since she and Mike had arrived as refugees and been welcomed into this big old house which despite people, noise and possessions still had an air of being empty. As if, deserted for so many years, the emptiness had grown into the walls and seeped from the high ceilings.

It had taken only a few days for Liz to feel she and Mike were residents and no longer guests. Although she hadn't taken the official step of enrolling Mike at the local school he went off in the mornings with Solly and Ester and Alice and Luther and Damien along the rough and mud-slushed track that served as a driveway, then up the metal road as far as the corner where the school bus picked them up. Mike was in the same class as Solly and was accepted as Solly's visitor and although at home the two boys merely tolerated each other at school Mike was bathed in the overflow of Solly's great popularity. Mike had no time to mourn his bike, it was never mentioned.

'I like it here, Mum,' he said at regular intervals. 'Can we stay?'

'I don't know, love. We'll see.' Wishing that meeting his needs was sufficient to meet hers. For in the midst of kindness and companionship she continued to feel unsettled.

Having arrived with very little money and no useful skills she did more than her share of the housework, despite their protests, and put in long hours in the vast garden under Luke's direction. She worked not just from a sense of being indebted — activity was diversion; she felt a need to be constantly occupied. She even volunteered to help Hugh hack down the gorse that encroached down the ridge, and came to a belated appreciation of the endurance Tug had shown in sticking it out as a scrub-cutter as long as he had.

The big house and behind it John's barn, partitioned into a studio and sleeping quarters for himself, Damien and Solly, lay in a valley. The company land — for they had taken the step of forming themselves into a company — stretched above and behind the house. It was mostly steep and ragged with gorse and blackberry. Curious volcanic boulders were dotted about, round and white like bloated sheep. A creek at the valley bottom disappeared, up behind the house, into a thick little forest of native bush. Resting her slasher and her blistering hands Liz could look down at it all from her workplace on the hill. Then she would see herself as a tiny creature doing a dilapidary job on the voluminous thighs of a slumbering earth woman.

In the garden area Luke, between dissertations about

drainage, kikuyu and mineral contents, would wave his arm
to encompass the hills and eulogise about space, the openness
of this new life they were building. But privately Liz felt their
life here to be enclosed, womblike. She admired the way they
were attempting a shared life yet it was impossible not to be
aware of certain tensions and discords which were neither
aired nor eased at their weekly and semi-official meetings. As
the non-member of the company she became, unwillingly,
confidante. Sarah was unhappy about the meagre male contribution to the household chores. Luke was unhappy about
the way John arranged weekend outings with only his own
children. John, Luke said, should take them all or none at all.
Jenny was unhappy about the way Sarah strode about the
house with no clothes on. Sarah, Jenny said, had a history of
getting bored with her partner and replacing him. Hugh was
unhappy about John building a kiln alongside the barn when
clearing the land was a more urgent priority. John was
unhappy about the adherence to majority decisions when
they wouldn't even have the place if it hadn't been for his
money.

Liz listened and nodded and murmured. She was deeply
grateful for their acceptance and support, yet in her efforts to
be cooperative to all but aligned with none she felt less than
herself. Sometimes she got an uneasy feeling that she was but
a reflection of these five people — that beyond them she had
no substance.

Each day she spent a little more time looking along the
rough driveway in the direction of the road. And she waited
very anxiously for the mail although Martyn was the only
person to whom she'd written — apart from the hotel. After
putting that off for a week she'd written to the manager there
explaining that she'd suffered an urgent domestic crisis and
would not be returning. She gave no address so that he would
feel no obligation to forward the pay owing to her and
therefore would be in some way compensated for
inconvenience.

'You're bloody crazy,' Hugh had told her. 'Waitresses
shoot through every day. Look what he was paying you, for
God's sake. He should be the one apologising.'

Hugh spent a couple of days working on her car. 'It's shot

really,' he explained. 'The best I could do was a patch-up. It should chug around for a while but you'd be wise to get rid of it before it craps out completely.'

Another factor to be considered in the suspended decision of where she should go, what she should do.

'Stay here,' urged Jenny. 'You could sell the house and buy a share in the company.'

'Take your time,' Hugh advised. 'When the right move presents itself you'll know sure enough.'

She slept with John twice because he asked and because she owed him, still, and because he too was on his own. But only twice because she was not *so* indebted.

Two days after Martyn's letter had arrived Liz and Jenny drove to the township for supplies.

'That chap find you?' asked the woman at the store as Jenny wrote out the cheque.

'I don't think so,' said Jenny. 'What chap?'

'Tuesday he came in. Youngish chap. Looked a bit... unsavoury I'd say to be honest.' She leant on the counter thrusting forward her broad shoulders in their grey cardigan and giving a look that encompassed the nod and the wink. I didn't let on I knew where you lived. There's some people'd rather not have the whole world knowing where they are, if you get my meaning. Reckoned if he was keen enough he'd track you down anyways. Plenty folks round here got tongues like dog tails, but me I like to see you young folk giving it a go up here. I stick up for your sort, always have.'

She paused long enough for Liz to ask, 'What'd he look like — the man who came?'

The woman got a far-away, recollecting look that would have done credit to any police witness in *Kojak*. 'Youngish, like I said. Dark hair, small eyes, skinny, about average height though I wouldn't know what that was in the decimal business. I'd say seedy-looking though really I didn't take that much notice.'

Jenny looked at Liz and shrugged. 'Doesn't sound like we missed much.' Liz grinned and edged their last box of groceries off the counter.

'There was a friend with him. Another chap. Waited for

him outside. Maori he was. 'Bout average height and a great lot of hair.'

'Did you see if they had a car?' Liz had stopped very still.

'Didn't see one. Might have been walking. It's amazing how many hitch-hikers pass through here.'

'I bet she thought one of us owed him money,' said Jenny waving a bag of marshmallows in front of Liz.

'No thanks.' Liz made a U-turn. There was only one parked truck in sight.

Jenny examined the bitten half of her marshmallow then said gently, 'It could've been anyone. John and Sarah know people from all over. You sure you don't want one of these?'

Liz shook her head.

'If they'd really looked they could have found us. If it'd been that important.' Jenny's voice bulged with marshmallow. Liz slowed and swerved past a horse and rider. The rider, a woman, waved. They waved back.

'Hugh says I ought to sell the car while it's still going.'

'He'd know,' said Jenny.

'I was thinking maybe I should try and sell it in Auckland. Might get a bit more.'

'Mmm. You might.' Liz thought she heard a smile.

'It might take me a couple of days or more. D'you think it'd be all right if Mike stayed here?'

'Of course it would.'

'Then I might go tomorrow.'

'May as well. If you really think it's necessary?'

'It seems to be,' Liz said with a certain regret.

Jenny reached over and patted the hand on the steering wheel. Her hand left a moist stickiness on the back of Liz's.

The motorway seemed almost a sentimental journey and the harbour bridge made her stomach rise in a lurch of urgency and expectation. She took the Ponsonby turn-off. Jenny, in her neat and careful hand, had copied out two addresses of people who would be happy (Jenny said) to provide Liz with a bed, or a mattress, or at least a stretch of floor. She chose the Ponsonby address for its accessibility.

Jenny had also provided her with a sleeping-bag and eighteen dollars from the company petty cash box. 'It's for members,' she'd said, 'and you've done so much here. Don't mention it to the others; I'll tell them when you've gone. But it won't go far, what'll you do then?'

God knows.

Rose — the name Jenny had listed above the Ponsonby address — stood at least six-foot-six in black-stockinged feet. Liz stood on the bottom step, craning up like a lost child. Rose beamed down and reassured.

So *how was* Jenny? And Luke? How were the kids? Really? And when would they next be down? Maybe Rose'd go up some time; was it really at the arse end of nowhere?

Liz could use Lyn's room. No problem. Lyn was on one of those visits to China that everyone was going on now. The room was there, and Lyn wouldn't mind a bit. And living room and dining room through there, if she felt like food or company. Usually someone around.

Lyn's room was crammed with possessions; books, ornaments, typewriter, saddle — even a bicycle. Everything jammed in any old where. But for the double bed, carelessly made, and the stray piles of clothes it could have been an auction room. On a dresser was a bowl with three goldfish. Liz wondered if someone was feeding them in Lyn's absence and if they were hungry now. This reminded her that Martyn hadn't mentioned Mitzi in his letter. She pictured Mitzi in the empty house, pining. Can a cat comprehend the enormity of having been abandoned?

She began with the pubs, wishing she had thought to ask Rose or even Jenny which ones catered for which kind of clientele. But then, if they *were* at a pub, they may have just chosen the nearest. Nearest to where? Only now did she realise the odds against finding him. How could she know, having looked somewhere, that he wouldn't walk in ten minutes after she left?

A likely bar, with a live DJ playing requests; a disco with no place to dance. Young women with scarlet lipstick and tight unfaded denims, trendy young men and shaggy ones left over from the previous generation — a few animated faces here and there, but most of them blandly watchful. Tug was not among them but she felt encouraged. You're getting warmer, she told herself.

She bought a beer and took it to a table occupied by two girls who sat with their eyes fixed on the DJ.

'Excuse me,' she said to the one closest, 'but I'm looking for someone.'

They both looked at her in a distantly curious way.

'Young guy. Maori. He's got long, very thick hair. Well, longish.'

The nearest girl shrugged.

'I just wondered if you'd seen him in here? If he comes here at all?'

They just looked at her.

'He gets round with a guy called Denny.'

'Denny who?' the nearest girl asked. She moved her glass in little circles on the table.

'I don't know his other name.'

The other girl thrust her face towards Liz, chin first.

'You undercover or something?'

It took Liz some moments to comprehend. She gave a dry laugh and shook her head.

'Don't know him anyway,' said the first girl.

'What are the other places like this? Pubs or whatever where younger people go?' They still distrusted her. 'He's my boyfriend,' she said. 'We had a row... you know... and I left and I've heard he's been looking for me and I want to find him. It's nothing sinister.'

They weren't convinced.

'You said a young guy?'

'A lot younger than me, yes.' She said it defiantly to show she'd got the implication.

It was the second girl who softened. 'There's a few places,' she said. 'D'you know the city?'

'Not really.'

The girl dipped a finger in her glass and drew a damp line on the table. 'Well, this is Queen Street for starters. Right? And this one off here....'

Although she had half-suspected that the girl had been presenting her with an elaborate wild-goose chase Liz found the information was correct. They were likely places but neither Tug nor Denny was among their customers. Nor did she find them among the crowds drifting out of the movie houses. She walked home to the goldfish.

The next day she wandered the busiest streets. From a phone box she put a call through to Mr and Mrs Greig of Wai Bay and asked to speak to their son Mark. Mark said he hadn't seen Tug for about three weeks, had no idea where he might be. Last Mark knew Tug was hanging round with Denny.

She tried, again, the more likely pubs. In public bars of a certain breed there was always the wit who offered good humouredly, 'Looking for me?' Sometimes she would ask, 'Excuse me, but I'm looking for someone.'

Easier to ask the men. They would listen and joke, or advise or propose alternatives. From women she got looks she interpreted as pity or contempt.

She watched the people come blinking out after matinee movies. She was tempted to try the police station. It was perhaps the most likely place of all. Certainly it seemed probable that Denny — if not his precise whereabouts — would be known to them. Yes, that's him officer. You have a list of dens he frequents? Once she used to believe that the police were there for her assistance and protection. That was a lifetime ago. She did not try the police station.

She bought a cup of wax-smelling coffee and fish and chips at a takeaway. It was the nearest thing to a meal she'd had since leaving on her journey south the previous morning. Then she looked in at a few more public and private bars with a mounting sense of embarrassment, not to mention futility, and very slowly walked back towards Rose's place.

The next morning she drove past innumerable second-hand car dealers' yards and selected the one whose vehicles looked most aged and down-at-heel.

'To tell you the truth lady,' said the dealer after having studied her car in the manner of someone examining a handkerchief which has been freshly used by someone other than himself, 'it's not worth a bag of marbles.'

'There must be somewhere that would take it?'

'We-ell. You might make a private sale. Wreckers might take it. But see, even the tyres are shot.'

But it still goes, she thought. How dare he dismiss it as

junk when it still goes.

She drove back to Rose's house and took a final walk along K Road and into the city and a final look into the record shops and amusement arcades and fast food emporiums and likely pubs. *I'm looking for someone.* And she thought — an expert now on city drinkers — *so are they all.*

She counted her remaining money and deducted sufficient for gas to get her back up north. It left seventy-two cents.

She could try and sell the car to a wrecking yard. She would get, surely, enough to repay the company's petty cash box and she could hitch back. Or she could drive back and try and sell the car there. Or she could keep the car and try and borrow more money to find a home for herself and Michael and a job for her. Or she could go to the Welfare and see if she qualified for the solo mothers' benefit. *Dear Mrs Harvey, after due consideration it has been decided that you are not a mother.*

So what the fuck?

She wandered into a department store, delaying a decision. She had forgotten, or never before noticed, how department stores were, their greedy splendour. Now she was dazzled by over-abundance. She saw chairs far too elegant to accommodate bottoms. She saw a dining-room suite that cost more than her poor condemned house. She tried on a coat priced at six months of waitressing wages. And all around her people were striding past these amazements without so much as a sidelong glance.

Fuck them. Fuck the lot of them.

She began, almost idly, to look among the profusion of goodies for something that would please Jenny. Practical or frivolous? Pocket-sized. But it was all so glossy and impersonal.

She lingered over a pocket calculator and then saw the blank-faced watches beside it. She picked one up and pushed the winder. 3.27. Hugh had a watch like that, Mike was entranced by it. She pushed the silver button again. 3.28. An absurd little miracle.

The counter assistant was chatting to a customer, her back half-turned. Liz closed her fingers over the watch and slipped it easily into the pocket of her black coat. She waited for a tap on her shoulder, but none came.

She picked up a second watch and pressed the knob. 3.29. Tug would be rapt. The assistant was still chatting. Liz put her hand and the second watch into the pocket and slowly wandered off towards BOYSWEAR and then the safe street outside.

She felt terrific. She wanted to jump and skip and laugh out loud. A block up the street she turned into Woolworths, just to kill time.

The Ponsonby house was deserted when Liz got back so she chalked her thanks to Rose on the blackboard propped against the kitchen wall, gathered up Jenny's sleeping-bag and said goodbye to the goldfish.

It was already dusk when she reached the Wai Bay turn-off. She would call at her house and look for Mitzi then spend the night at Pete and Martyn's. She must reassure Pete that the rest of his loan hadn't been forgotten. He wouldn't mind but still she must remember.

She didn't think ahead, beyond Wai Bay. Tomorrow was a blank space over the edge of the world. Tug had been tomorrow; she realised now how confident she had been of finding him. Perhaps Martyn would have heard something? Perhaps in the morning they'd lend her some gas so she could go back to the city and try again?

Though it was not really dark there was a light on in the house. She saw the glow of the bulb as she came down the track. How stupid, she thought; I should have had the power cut off. I'll be billed for this. Yet the glow of light made her hurry down the track with her stomach knotted in hope.

She could hear voices before she pushed open the door. Voices, then a desultory collective laugh. And then silence. They all turned to look as she walked in. Their faces showed no concern, nothing more than mild curiosity. Tug sat in the corner.

There were only six of them, yet the room seemed crammed with bodies. Tug sat at one end of a mattress. Next to him sat someone with a shaven head. Male, Liz presumed, since he wore a bush shirt and heavy boots, but the bald head gave him a sexless, ageless look.

Above the stale smell of tobacco and the peppery smell of dope, Liz could smell bodies.

Tug gave her a blank-faced glance of non-recognition.

Denny was lying on the floor, his shoulders propped against the wall. A girl lay with her head on his lap. Denny raised a languid wrist and said, 'Hi there.'

'Liz? Remember me?'

Liz looked at her. She sat on the mattress on the near side of the skinhead. Long dark hair and a sallow, strong face; sores with white pus around her mouth, pitted skin. Liz struggled with elusive recognition; a name, a time, a place.

'Audrey. Remember? Your room-mate?'

'Of course,' she said. Then automatically, 'How are you?'

But Audrey had turned already to the shaven boy and was telling him something amusing.

Tug sat with his knees drawn up and his hands clasped in front of them. Even clasped, his hands shook as if he was holding an invisible road drill.

Liz was an interruption. The assembled company was beginning to exchange glances, scratch legs, scuff feet. Why didn't she shove off?

'Like a cup of coffee?' offered Denny. He shifted his thighs to indicate to the girl lying on them that some action was required of her.

Liz was about to say yes for lack of knowing what else she could do. She glanced at Tug, wanting even recognition, but Tug was examining space. Just below his cheekbone a muscle twitched and pulled at the corner of his eye. Liz watched and the twitch came again, involuntary and sad.

Liz, standing there unhappily centre stage, thrust her hands in the pockets of her old coat, and came up against her forgotten treasures and remembered that she had new abilities.

'No thanks,' she told Denny. And she went on standing there above them all, pleased to observe their growing discomfort.

'Get out,' she said, finally. Not loud, but very clear. 'Get out of my house. Just fuck off.'

They were very quiet. A bearded man in the corner was the first to move, and then all the others began to get to their feet. They seemed to take a long time. Only Tug spoke.

'My God,' he said, 'you're a bitch. These are my friends.'

'It's my house,' she said. 'If you wanta be with them you go with them.'

'Don' have much choice, do I.'

She stood against the wall and they began to file out.

'You've got a choice. It's up to you,' she told him.

He laughed. 'I've heard that one before.' He said it wearily and without apparent anger.

'Goodbye, Liz. Nice meeting you again.' Audrey left grinning.

'I'm sorry,' mumbled the bearded man as he passed her.

Denny lowered his eyelids to contemptuous slits and slid past her pulling his girl behind him.

And they were gone.

Someone had left behind a cigarette packet with three cigarettes in it. Liz lit one and sat down on the stained and lumpy mattress. She thought it was almost funny. Her baby had shuffled out with the bath-water.

She wondered where they would go. Would they feel vindictive? Push her car over the cliff or slash it's threadbare tyres. It didn't seem to matter much.

What the fuck, she thought, dragging on her cigarette. It was the first she'd had in three days. She would have to ration the other two; save them for special treats.

When it had burned right down to the filter she began automatically to tidy up. Handle-less cups, tin lids full of cigarette butts (sort out those that may be reuseable), two torn comics — *Archie* and *Horror* — an old copy of *Mad* magazine, a battered *Penthouse*.

He crept in on bare feet and she heard nothing. Only when he touched her from behind did she feel a cold jolt of terror. Then he slid his arms around her and she knew it was him and it was all right. She pressed herself back against him and his arms tightened around her until she could no longer breathe. Then he let her go and she turned towards him.

She thought fleetingly, as his tongue pressed blindly against hers, of the absent diaphragm. And she thought a little longer about disease and the sores around Audrey's mouth.

What the fuck, she told her new self.

She sat on the lumpy mattress with her coat pulled around her naked shoulders. Tug's head pressed against her belly. She cradled his head with one arm and the other rubbed helplessly at his bare brown shoulder. He was crying and it was terrible to hear. His face was red and wet and clenched up like the face of a newborn baby giving its first scream. The noise of his weeping was something between the cry of a gin-trapped animal and a rusted machine grinding into action after years of disuse.

Awed by such weeping Liz rocked his head, patted, made small ineffectual noises of comfort. She pulled at her coat trying to include some of him beneath it. His skin was goose-fleshed. The rest of their clothes were beyond her reach so she began to rub at his shoulder in brisk little circles trying to warm him. He raised his arm and obligingly she began to rub along its length. In the soft skin of the elbow bend there were small red marks like insect bites without the swelling.

Liz shivered. Her mind drew her a picture of herself standing in a soft white dress on the sands of Wai Bay looking out to sea. Watching Tug walk across the water to some psychedelic island.

Liz knew about gravity and the fate of those who'd walked on water.

The noise of his crying subsided into muffled gulps. He turned on her lap and reached out an arm to their discarded clothes retrieving a shirt. Hers. He blew his nose on it.

'Yyyuck!'

He grinned up at her.

She needed to talk. 'You came up there looking for me?'

'How'd you know?'

She smiled mysteriously.

'You knew I would,' he said. 'And I knew you'd come looking for me. Sooner or later.'

She wrinkled her nose, unable to believe in such confidence.

'Why did you come?' Touching her face as if it was new or beautiful.

We're the same, she thought. All the time wanting declarations, testimonies, reassurance.

'I missed you,' she said. 'I couldn't stop missing you.'

'Why? Why did you miss me?'

'Oh Tug love,' she protested, 'how could anyone answer that?' She saw a kind of caution come into his face. 'I won't leave you again, truly. Or chase you away.'

'And how d'you reckon we're going to manage? What'll we do?'

'We'll stay together.' She squeezed her arms about him.

'Don't be thick, love. What're we going to do for money?'

She waved her hands breezily. 'Anything.'

He was becoming exasperated. 'Like what? Come on, what d'you suggest?'

She was smirking at him, delving into the pockets of her coat. She dropped a watch on his belly.

'For me?'

'If you want.'

He picked it up. 'Where'd you get it?'

'From a shop.' She was pleased with herself. 'Go on, push that little knob.'

He tossed the watch aside. 'I've seen them before.' He was watching her closely. 'You didn't nick it?'

She nodded, grinning.

'Oh Christ,' he said. 'I didn't think you could be so stupid.'

'It was easy.' She grabbed the coat and shook it so the pockets emptied onto the floor. The second watch tumbled out, along with her Woolworths selection — a pen, a lipstick, a pack of cards, a blank cassette.

Tug looked at them. 'What a load of cheap junk. What good d'you think that's gonna do?'

She was offended. 'I only had my pockets. And we can sell the watches.'

'Who to?'

'I thought you'd know?'

'Well, I don't, do I? Anyway there's too much risk. It's just stupid.'

She gave a little laugh of hurt disbelief. 'Well what d'you suggest we do, if you're so smart?'

Mitzi came bounding in with a mew of recognition. She went straight to Tug. Liz reached out to stroke her but he pushed her arm away.

'D'you mind? You pissed off and left her. She'd be dead by now if it wasn't for me.'

'You're wonderful,' she said, and he looked for signs of sarcasm but found none and puckered his lips to blow a forgiving kiss.

'Maybe I'd get work up there,' he said.

'There isn't any.'

'I could try for the dole then. Maybe,' he said with a faint smile, 'they'll bring in a benefit for gigolos. Do you think,' with nonchalant pomposity, 'that might be a foreseeable eventual plausibility?'

'Gee but you talk nice,' she said. 'It's neat the way you use all them big words.'

'Really, love, what *are* we going to do?' He was so concerned and grown up and serious.

She reached among her Woolworths pile.

'I'll give y'a game of something. Poker? Come on,' she coaxed. 'I haven't played poker for ages.'

For a complete list of books available from Penguin in the United States, write to Dept. DG, Penguin Books, 299 Murray Hill Parkway, East Rutherford, New Jersey 07073.